D0070340

Kissing in Manhattan

DAVID SCHICKLER

KISSING IN MANHATTAN

THE DIAL PRESS

Published by
The Dial Press
Random House, Inc.
1540 Broadway
New York, New York 10036

The author gratefully acknowledges *The New Yorker,* where "The Smoker" first appeared, and *Tin House,* where "Jacob's Bath" first appeared in the spring 2000 issue. Excerpt from "Disillusionment of Ten O'clock" from COLLECTED POEMS by Wallace Stevens. Copyright 1923 and renewed 1951 by Wallace Stevens. Reprinted by permission of Alfred A. Knopf, a division of Random House, Inc.

LIBRARY OF CONGRESS CATALOGING-IN-PUBLICATION DATA

Schickler, David.
Kissing in Manhattan / David Schickler.
p. cm.
ISBN 0-385-33566-0
1. Manhattan (New York, N.Y.)—Social life and customs—Fiction. I. Title.
PS3569.C4848 K5 2001
813'.6—dc21 00-052286

Book design by Kathryn Parise

Manufactured in the United States of America
Published simultaneously in Canada

June 2001

10 9 8 7 6 5 4 3 2 1
BVG

with thanks and love
to my parents
Jack and Peggy Schickler
and to my three sisters
Anne Marie, Pamela, and Jeanne

When two kisses kiss, it's like two tigers
talking about infinity with their teeth.

Tess Gallagher

CONTENTS

Kissing in Manhattan

Checkers and Donna

Donna didn't want to meet Checkers. It didn't seem right.

"Checkers?" said Donna. "What kind of a name for a man is Checkers?"

"He's strange," admitted Lee.

Lee and Donna sold Manhattan real estate. They were in their early thirties. They shared an office on Bleecker Street.

"Checkers." Donna tried it on her tongue. "Checkers, Checkers."

"He's attractive," said Lee.

"Checkers is a name for a dog. Or a henchman." Donna stared at her computer screen. Listed on it were SoHo prices.

"He's strange but attractive," said Lee.

"A henchman in a movie." Donna wore a suit and important shoes. "Not a *nemesis*. Not suave like that. Just a henchman."

"This isn't a movie," said Lee. "This is real life."

"How do you know this Checkers?" asked Donna.

It was ten minutes till five on a Thursday. Donna and Lee's office was on the twenty-first floor. It had a bay window facing south, and just before five every evening, Donna and Lee stood at this window and looked at the sunlight on the rivers. Lee, who was a lesbian, loved the East River best. Donna loved the Hudson.

"I don't remember." Lee shrugged. "He's just one of those men you meet."

They looked at New York, which they routinely broke into pieces and shuffled around and sold.

"Checkers what?" said Donna.

"What?" said Lee.

"Checkers what. What comes after Checkers? I mean, Checkers is his first name, right?"

Lee was frustrated. She had long, graceful fingers, but beady eyes. "Look, I don't know him. All I know is, his name has nothing to do with the game of checkers. He was very clear about that."

"Hmm."

"He's attractive," insisted Lee. "He's in need of a woman."

Donna laughed. "I'll bet he is."

Lee frowned. She was single, just like Donna. "That's how he said it. He used those exact words. Checkers said, 'Lee, I'm in need of a woman.' That's how Checkers talks."

Donna's hair was cut short. It tapered to a point at the nape of her neck, and there was a fine scoop of air between her shoulder blades that had been there since she was sixteen.

"When did he say this? That he needed a woman, I mean."

Lee sighed. "Last night. At a bar. Checkers said what he said, and I told him about you."

Donna and Lee, combined, were worth three and a half million dollars.

"What bar?" asked Donna.

"Flat Michael's," said Lee.

Flat Michael's was a restaurant bar in the East Village where poetry wasn't allowed.

"Why me?" asked Donna. "Why tell this Checkers about me?"

Lee sighed again. Donna was one of those women you told men about. Her hair was the color of a medieval peasant girl's. She was not in the habit of licking her lips, but her chest was full and her waist was slender.

"This Checkers," said Donna. "Why's he so attractive?"

"He just is," said Lee.

Donna closed her eyes. She imagined a man who was a spy, or an idiot. She pondered the potential hairiness of the knuckles of a man named Checkers.

"All right," she said. "I'll meet him."

"Great," said Lee. "He'll be at Flat Michael's at eight tomorrow night. He'll be waiting at a table for you."

"It's all set up? He's not going to call me or anything?"

Lee smirked, shook her head. "Checkers said he knew you'd say yes."

Donna snorted. "He's awfully presumptuous."

"He's Checkers," shrugged Lee.

"I don't know if I'd like such a presumptuous man."

"Try," said Lee.

Donna had grown up in Manhattan. As a girl she took ballet classes at Ms. Vivian's, on the Upper East Side. Ms. Vivian watched Donna's body carefully, to see whether Donna had a vocation for ballet. Ms. Vivian was an expert on the matter of young women's arches, calves, breasts, and demeanors. Fable had it that Ms. Vivian possessed gypsy blood, that she could read in a girl's limbs and attitudes that girl's destiny. Jezebel Hutch, for instance, grew up with Donna and took ballet at Ms. Vivian's for seven years, until the day Ms. Vivian tapped Jezebel's shoulder and said: "You are an astronaut."

Jezebel giggled. She was twelve. "What?"

Ms. Vivian was stone faced. "You are an astronaut. You will fly to the moon in the machines that men make. You will be noble, but you will not dance."

Jezebel's face collapsed. "But—"

Ms. Vivian pointed to the door. "Farewell," she said.

Jezebel left, weeping, in the arms of her mother, Jennifer Hutch. Jennifer called Ms. Vivian a freakish bitch. The next day, though, she started Jezebel on Einstein and calculus.

As for Donna, she lasted at Ms. Vivian's till she was sixteen. In fact, it was just two days after her sixteenth birthday that Ms. Vivian summoned Donna to the office.

"You belong to a man," said Ms. Vivian.

Donna held her breath. She'd kissed an ugly boy named Harold three months earlier. Harold was from Queens.

"Your body is destined to belong to a man. That is your vocation."

Donna's eyes teared up. "Harold's just a friend, Ms. Vivian."

Ms. Vivian gazed at the wall. "You will not dance."

"He—he didn't even get up my shirt," blubbered Donna.

"Farewell," said Ms. Vivian.

Donna believed that she'd proved her teacher wrong. As an NYU undergraduate she'd slept with two men—one was timid, the other Libyan—but neither of them had ever come close to owning Donna's soul. In her twenty-sixth and twenty-seventh years, when she was founding her business with Lee, Donna lived with a man named Charles, who smoked pipes and worked at the Strand. Charles was sweet, but he had chronic dandruff and a tendency to handcuff Donna to major kitchen appliances during sexual intercourse. Bored with these conditions, Donna left Charles. She'd been single since, except for the occasional stray dog that never lasted.

By thirty Donna felt mostly pity for men. Their eyes always seemed starved or dead. They earned money, yet felt it necessary to bungee-jump or climb Tibetan mountains. Their biceps and laughter were ungodly strong, but, as far as Donna could see, men never used the full force of these strengths against women. This was cowardice, Donna felt. She wanted a man who would crush himself into her—psychically, sexually, utterly, daily—and never apologize.

By thirty Donna was convinced no man could impress her. She tried a fling with a woman named Maxine. The experience was disastrous, in part because Maxine owned thirteen cats and treated Donna as a fourteenth. Maxine wanted Donna to cuddle against her, or to lash out at her and move off indifferently into the night. Donna broke Maxine off in two weeks.

No one, it seemed, man or woman, could muster the power it would take to claim Donna. Frustrated by this, Donna would strip naked sometimes, late at night, and stand on her bed and dance. But her dancing wasn't ballet anymore. It wasn't about grace and structure. It was like this: Donna would let her hair, arms, and breasts sway and flail. She'd kick, stamp, and groan, and her thighs would sweat. Sometimes, she would grab whatever smart outfit she'd worn that day and rend the silk or cotton to shreds. At the peak of these tantrums, as she shrieked and thrashed, Donna expected Ms. Vivian's words to come true. She expected a man—a cloven-footed man, perhaps with the head of a goat—to throw open her bedroom door and roar and mount her. She'd fight this man with her claws, her intelligence, her body. She would beg freedom, demand independence, but the man would work himself into her without mercy, and Donna would gasp and gasp, and, finally, smile.

On Friday night Donna took the F train to Flat Michael's. Lee always took cabs, but Donna feared automobiles. Having grown up in the city, she'd never gotten her driver's license. This was a source of embarrassment for Donna, but even deeper was her suspicion that cars were chariots of doom. In the movies they housed corpses in their trunks or blew up at a bullet. All over the island, doormen were always packing women into taxis and grinning like conspirators. Where were these women going? Donna wondered.

The subway was safer. It was like a good dance floor, crowded but anonymous. If you were on your way to meet a man named Checkers, it gave you time to consider your perfume and your mood. Donna was wearing a black shift and black pumps.

"You look sexy," an old man told Donna. The old man was sitting with an old woman, probably his wife. The wife read a newspaper and ignored the old man.

"Oh my God," said Donna.

"You resemble, in my opinion, a girl from a blue-jeans advertisement." The old man smiled meekly.

Donna pointed at the newspaper the wife held. "Oh my God, I know that woman."

The wife glanced at Donna, glanced at the paper. On the front page was a picture taken at Cape Canaveral. The picture showed four men and one woman, all in puffy space gear.

The old man cleared his throat. "Not a cigarette advertisement, you understand. *Blue jeans.*"

"That's Jezebel Hutch," declared Donna. "She's from Germantown. I grew up with her."

The wife stared at the picture.

"Jezebel's an astronaut," whispered Donna. "She did it."

The old man cleared his throat again, louder. "Goddammit," he declared, "there's nothing sexy about cigarettes."

When Donna arrived at Flat Michael's, there was only one man sitting alone, at a window table. The window looked out over East Fourth Street. The table had a candle on it.

"Are you Checkers?" Donna held out her hand. "I'm Donna."

Checkers stood. He smiled, shook Donna's hand, took her coat, sat her down.

"I thought you'd be black," he said, sitting himself down again.

Checkers was thirty-three. He had blue eyes and brown hair that came down, thin and casual, to his shoulders. He was six feet tall. He wore a black Irish fisherman's sweater, white painter pants, and sandals. He held a glass of dark draft beer.

"Excuse me?" said Donna.

"I thought you'd be black," said Checkers. "Donna. *Donna.* It sounds African-American." Checkers shrugged. "I just thought you'd be a Negress."

Donna stared at the man.

"Don't worry about it," said Checkers. "You look great."

Donna took a breath. "Didn't Lee tell you anything about me?"

"She told me your name would be Donna and that you'd look great. She's right."

Donna looked Checkers over. He was holding his beer and

watching Donna like a man who was content to hold a beer and watch a woman. Not depraved, Donna thought, just content.

"You're in need of a drink," said Checkers.

"Sure," said Donna. "Sure, all right."

"Our waiter's from Ecuador." Checkers flagged the bar. "His name's Juan."

A short, stout man came out from behind the bar and trundled over. He had light brown skin and eyes and a beaming smile.

"Yes, ma'am," said Juan. He touched Donna's shoulder. "For you, a drink, exactly." Juan had a thick accent. "A drink, for pleasure. Right?"

Donna ordered vodka with ice and lemon. Juan brought it, set it down before Donna.

"Pleasure," said Juan. "Right?" He vanished.

"It's busy in here," said Donna, looking around.

Donna had never eaten at Flat Michael's. She'd had a drink once in the lounge, where there were no televisions, a wooden bar, and chairs. Everything about Flat Michael's was simple. The owners brewed their own beer, and the taps on the draft handles read simply: Lager, Pilsner, Stout. The owners also fetched their wines from a vineyard of undisclosed origin, and their liquors from unknown stills. The racks behind the bar held unadorned bottles labeled Vodka, Gin, Rye, or Chardonnay, Chianti, Port. As a rule customers never quibbled over these libations. If you demanded a brand-name sherry or a particular year of a champagne, you were asked to leave.

The dining room was no different. The tables were wooden, with one white, lighted candle on each. The chairs were wooden, too, and the menu had just ten items each night. These items were listed on a giant chalkboard, with no prices or side dishes assigned. On this particular night the menu was: Trout, Tongue, Eel, Veal, Moussaka, Shoots, Lamb, Brains, Noodles, and Snake.

"It is busy," confirmed Checkers.

Checkers and Donna were right. Flat Michael's was busy. The dining room was filled with patrons, who, unlike the restaurant itself, were a menagerie of details. There was a couple seated two tables from Checkers and Donna, a man and woman, the man in a fedora, the woman in silk. This man and woman—one ate Lamb, one ate Snake—were discussing their marriage in audible tones, arguing fine points of sympathy and sexuality. Meanwhile, four skinheads with razored hair were hunched over another table, feasting on Brains and Schnapps.

There was a regular customer, a young accountant named James Branch, dining alone at a table far from the bar. He had sleepy blue eyes and straight teeth, and, as was his habit, he was talking to himself quietly, whispering the name of his entrée as he waited for it to arrive.

"Moussaka," whispered James. "Moussaka." As he sat and whispered, James Branch was also admiring a pair of opal earrings that lay in his palm.

Finally, at a corner table, sat a woman in a purple, wispy dress. She ate only Noodles and drank only water, but she possessed a terrible beauty. Her face was pale and sorrowful, and her throat looked as if it ached. Her ankles, naked and fragile, seemed about to crumble into dust.

Among all these were Checkers and Donna, meeting for the first time.

"Trout," said Checkers, when Juan came for their order.

"Veal," said Donna.

"Pleasure," said Juan, and off he went.

Checkers took a draught of beer. "I've never had the veal here," he said. "I hope you like it."

Donna smiled, her first of the night. Try, she thought to herself.

"I hope so too," she said.

"I wouldn't want you to be bereaved," said Checkers.

"Excuse me?"

Checkers jutted his chin toward the strangers, the other patrons.

"Manhattan's full of people," said Checkers. "People who have one meal they don't like and become immediately bereaved."

"Bereaved," said Donna.

"Never mind Manhattan. People all over the world." Checkers licked his lips. "The world is full of people who have one meal they don't like and become immediately bereaved."

Donna thought about this. She was smart.

"Disappointed, maybe," she said.

"Oh, no," said Checkers quickly. "They're bereaved. Absolutely."

"Hmm," said Donna.

Checkers searched Donna's face. "People take food very seriously. It's amazing. You have clever-looking ears."

Donna had been sipping her vodka. She sputtered. "Excuse me?"

Checkers frowned. "Stop saying, 'Excuse me,' whenever I bring up something new. It's just that your ears are clever-looking, is all. Like an elf's, or an otter's."

Donna digested this information. Her date felt she looked like an otter.

"Oh, you know what I mean, for Christ's sake. Don't you?"

"Well." Donna forced a smile. After all, Checkers looked good in his sweater. Also, his legs were long. "Well, do you *like* elves and otters?"

Checkers stared at her. "You're going the traditional flirting route."

"Excuse me?"

"Excuse you?" said Checkers. "Excuse you? Excuse you?"

"Sorry," said Donna. Then she wished she hadn't said it.

"The traditional flirting route," said Checkers. "You know, I say you have clever-looking ears like an elf's or an otter's, and you feel compelled to ask whether I like elves and otters. As if elves and otters were necessarily cute, implying that you're cute too. Well, otters I'll give you, but there've been some nasty elves in stories I've read, you know? Freaky elves, with fucked-up-looking feet. Never mind all that, though. I mean, I already told you you look great. What more can I say?"

Donna's eyebrows were officially raised. "I have a feeling you're going to say a lot more."

Checkers laughed. "I knew you were clever."

Donna learned some things. Checkers had been born in Germany to military American parents. He'd grown up in Washington, D.C., Minneapolis, San Diego, and Wheeling, West Virginia. He was double jointed, he worked as a headhunter, he drove a souped-up Plymouth Duster.

"In Manhattan?" asked Donna.

Checkers blinked. His eyes had spent time on Donna's neck and breasts, which Donna felt was a good sign. On the other hand, he had a vicious scar down his left jawline that looked like it had been carved by a knife.

"You assume," said Checkers, "that a souped-up Plymouth

Duster would be more at home in the yard of some West Virginia hick?"

Donna cleared her throat. "I don't know."

"What you also don't know," said Checkers, "is that my souped-up Plymouth Duster purrs like a kitten. It's got eight cylinders, comfortable upholstery, and just last week, a very mature female client of mine said what a refreshment my souped-up Plymouth Duster was among the cabs and limos of this metropolis. That's the word my client used. Refreshment."

"I don't like cars," said Donna.

"I don't drive a car. I drive a mature, souped-up refreshment."

Donna wondered who this female client was. Checkers leaned back in his chair. His Trout and Donna's Veal hadn't materialized.

"I'll bet you're a certain kind of girl," said Checkers.

"We all are," said Donna.

"I'll bet you're the kind of girl who, if you were walking down a street and a guy pulled up in some macho car and said, 'Hey, sexy mama,' you wouldn't even smile."

"I probably wouldn't," she said.

"I'll bet if the guy got crude and said maybe you and him could get some together, you *still* wouldn't smile at him. You'd be too sophisticated for him."

"Right again."

Checkers slapped the table. He looked angry. "Goddammit," he said loudly.

Donna was surprised. She thought they'd been talking.

"Goddammit," said Checkers. "Who the hell do you women think you are?"

Donna frowned.

"You think men are subtle? You think we're all just happy as clams to go the traditional flirting route? Take a girl out to dinner and make conversation? Jesus!"

The diva and the skinheads turned toward Checkers.

"Don't you understand?" Checkers's eyes were locked on Donna's. "Don't you understand how perfect it is when a guy says, 'Hey, sexy mama,' to a girl because that's all he can say?"

Donna stared at Checkers. His face, which had been so easy with smiles, was grave. Donna didn't know what to say. She considered leaving, but Juan appeared, bearing a tray.

"Pleasure," he explained. "Dinner."

"How'd you get that scar on your jaw?"

Checkers ate his Trout quickly, efficiently. He worked his utensils like a surgeon.

"In a knife fight," he said, "with a West Virginia hick."

Knife fight, thought Donna. I am absolutely not going home with this guy.

"And your name?" she asked. "How'd you get that?"

Checkers looked at his watch. "Not bad. You went sixty-seven minutes without asking."

"I'm sorry," said Donna. "It's an unusual name, though."

There was music in Flat Michael's dining room. It was a bass guitar track, with no other instrumentation.

"My name is Checkers," said Checkers. "It has nothing to do with the game of checkers. It's the name my parents put on my birth certificate."

"Did they ever explain why?" said Donna.

"It's what they wanted to call me. It's something I can't control."

Donna ate her Veal.

"There are other things I *can* control, though," said Checkers.

"Like what?"

"Like I want to be happy. I don't want to be bereaved. I want a woman."

Unbelievable, thought Donna.

"That's why I wanted to meet you," explained Checkers. "Lee said you were a beautiful woman. 'Great,' I told Lee. 'A beautiful woman is what I'm looking for.' You know?"

"Is this how you talk to everybody?" asked Donna.

"Oh, come on. I could go the traditional flirting route, but for Christ's sake, look at yourself. Look at your lips and your cheekbones."

"Checkers," said Donna. "Please."

"Look at the tiny down whiskers around the edges of your mouth."

Donna blushed. Women weren't supposed to have whiskers.

"They're almost invisible," said Checkers. "They look very . . . I don't know. Gentle."

"They do," said one of the skinheads.

Donna ducked her head. She put down her utensils.

"Please stop," she whispered. "Stop talking about . . . my face."

Checkers lowered his head so his eyes met Donna's. "Say something, then. With a mouth like yours you could say all sorts of beautiful things."

Donna kept her head lowered. "I have to go to the rest room," she said.

In the rest room Donna imagined the kind of women that Checkers had had. She imagined waitresses, mermaids, philosophy majors. She wondered if his mouth tasted like smoke.

"Try," she told herself in the mirror. "You're thirty-two years old. Come on."

When she was nineteen, Donna had dated a man in his late twenties, a man with a passion for skydiving. Donna had loved him deeply. She hadn't understood his battles with gravity or his country music. Still, she devoted herself to him, and he gave her irises on the first of each month. Donna thought he was the man of Ms. Vivian's prophecy, the man to whom she would belong. But that man died on her—died horribly, in a skydiving accident. He crushed himself into the ground instead of Donna.

"Come on," Donna told the mirror.

"He likes your lips," she whispered. "Come on, girl."

When Donna got back to the table, she'd missed something. Checkers was laughing. He was talking with the waiter, Juan, and laughing like an animal.

"What?" said Donna.

"Listen," panted Checkers. He was out of breath from laughing. "Say it, Juan."

"Knock on boot," said Juan.

Checkers erupted again.

"Exactly," said Juan. "Knock on boot."

Checkers wiped a tear from his eye. "Knock on wood. He's trying to say, 'Knock on wood,' Donna."

"Yes," said Juan. "Knock on boot."

"He can't pronounce wood," tittered Checkers. "He keeps saying boot. It's his accent."

Donna took her seat. She tried to focus on Checkers, her date, tried to smile at him. But Checkers was focusing on Juan.

"Try it slow, Juan," said Checkers. "Concentrate."

"Yes," agreed Juan.

"Wwwood." Checkers looked gleefully at Juan. "Wwwood. Wwwwoood."

"Boot," said Juan.

"All right, Checkers," said Donna. She meant, That's enough.

"Wwwwood," said Checkers.

"Boot," said Juan.

Checkers lost it. He slapped at the table. His laughter came in yelps. Donna could see his diaphragm working. People were watching.

"Stop it," pleaded Donna. She was frightened. Laughter, like cars, could frighten her.

"Oh my God," howled Checkers.

"Stop." Donna's voice rose. You're ruining it, she thought. Stop.

Juan grinned at the two of them, oblivious, ready for more.

"Oh my God," begged Checkers, waving Juan off. "Oh God."

Juan left.

"He didn't know." Checkers exhaled, got control. "Wood and boot. He couldn't hear the difference."

"That was cruel of you," said Donna. "Laughing at him."

Checkers collected himself. He drained his beer, his second. The plates were gone.

"You had to be there when it started," said Checkers.

Donna hadn't been there. She looked on him with wrath.

Checkers tried to explain. "It was just one of those things," he said.

There was no dessert. The candle burned at half mast.

"What are you thinking?" asked Checkers.

"Nothing."

Donna finished her vodka. She thought about what it was like to lie beneath a man, his weight on her weight. She thought about Charles, with his books and handcuffs. She thought of her sky diver, the way he'd tugged on his shirts.

"You're thinking I do strange things," said Checkers. "You're thinking I'm strange."

Donna nodded.

"You aren't planning on seeing me again."

Donna shook her head.

"Why? Because I laughed at Juan?"

The married couple, the skinheads, and the diva were gone. The bass music was fading. Only the young accountant remained, still staring at the opal earrings in his palm. Outside, on East Fourth Street, it was close to November.

"It's not just that," said Donna.

"Well, why, then? Do you want me to be bereaved? Do *you* want to be bereaved?"

Donna sighed with an ancient despair.

Men are doors, she thought. They close in my face.

"I just . . . don't think I'm good at talking to you."

"So what?" Checkers seemed astounded. "I'm good at talking to you. I can do the talking."

"I'm sorry," said Donna. "I just want to go home."

Checkers gazed at Donna. Flat Michael's was emptying out.

"I'm a headhunter," said Checkers quietly. "I spend all day matching people up with their lives. Don't you think—"

"I can't explain it," said Donna. She almost shuddered. "I want to go home."

Out on the street it was cold. Leaves and trash blew around. Checkers and Donna walked together, not speaking.

"You don't have to walk with me," said Donna.

Checkers looked at the sky. He was thinking about what happened when he was alone in his apartment at night, sleeping. He knew he curled around himself at some point, because that's how he woke every morning: curled up tight, hibernating.

"There's a subway stop." Donna pointed.

"My car's near the next one," said Checkers. "Broadway-Lafayette. Come on. Just five more blocks of your life. Then I'm vamoose."

They kept walking. A ragged white cat watched them from an eave. Something smelled like rubber. Slouched in a doorway was a lanky, black-eyed street vagrant tuning a guitar.

"The holidays are coming," said Checkers.

"I guess so."

Donna watched her pumps clopping the sidewalk. The subway station loomed.

"Well," said Donna. "Thanks for dinner."

Checkers nodded east. "I'm parked around the corner."

They could see their breath.

Donna stuck out her hand. "Nice meeting you."

"Sixty seconds," said Checkers. "Just stand where you're standing for sixty seconds."

Donna detested how she felt.

"Checkers," she said. "The night is over."

Checkers was already trotting away.

"Sixty seconds," he shouted back. He disappeared around the corner.

Forget it, thought Donna.

She moved toward the subway. Then she stopped.

There's nothing to try, she told herself. She didn't move, though. She stayed standing still and looked up at the stars, which were dull blobs of gas.

Jezebel's up there, thought Donna. Jezebel, with her perfect calves, is floating around like an imbecile.

I'm an imbecile, too, thought Donna, shivering. An imbecile with no coat.

"Screw it," said Donna.

She walked to the top of the subway stairs. A car braked. A horn honked.

"Whoa, baby," shouted a voice.

Donna turned. A midnight-blue Plymouth Duster was pulled up to the curb twenty feet from her. The passenger window was rolled down, and through it Donna could see Checkers behind the steering wheel, staring out at her.

"Hey, sexy mama," shouted Checkers.

"I'm not coming with you," said Donna.

Checkers rolled down the driver-side window. He leaned out, waved at some pedestrians.

"Hey." Checkers jabbed a thumb toward Donna. "Anyone else see this package over here? She spoken for, or what?"

"Cut it out, Checkers." Donna's arms were folded on her chest. "I know it's you. I get it."

"Is she the bomb?" hollered Checkers. "Is she the word? Is she the motion?"

Two cars were stuck behind the Duster, unable to pass. One was a cab, the other a Honda.

"Move that thing," yelled the cabbie.

"Checkers," said Donna.

Checkers turned his attention back to Donna. He widened his eyes at her, raised his eyebrows, honked his horn. He revved his engine, whooped like a schoolboy. He slid himself over to the passenger window.

"Say there, fine thing." Checkers hung his tongue like a dog. "You got the eyes and you got the thighs. Know what I'm sayin', love chicken?"

Donna scowled. She gave Checkers the finger.

"Move that fucking thing," yelled the cabbie. He laid on his horn.

Checkers licked his pinky, made a summoning motion.

"Come over here, woman," he growled. "Come over here and get nasty with old Checkers."

Donna rolled her eyes. She tossed her hair. There were goose bumps on her neck.

"Come on now," said Checkers.

"You've got cars behind you," warned Donna.

There was a rush and rumbling in the earth. A train was pulling in.

Checkers thumped his chest. "Come get in the love machine," he told Donna. "Papa Checkers'll make you a woman."

"You're sick in the head," said Donna.

The driver of the Honda was out of his car. He was an angry man in a bow tie.

"What's the story?" he demanded.

"Papa Checkers will screw you cross-eyed," yelled Checkers.

Donna gasped. She was thirty-two, in a tight dress, with goose bumps and good lipstick. She sold real estate, loved children, voted.

"Come on, now," said Checkers quietly, holding his hand out to Donna. "You're all about obeying Papa, aren't you? Get on over here right now, little girl."

The man in the bow tie stuck his face in the Duster's driver-side window.

"What's the story?" he bellowed at Checkers.

Checkers didn't flinch. His hand was still out, reaching toward the woman.

"Now," he whispered, and Donna smiled.

Jacob's Bath

The legend of Jacob's bath began on May 1, 1948, the day Jacob Wolf married Rachel Cohen.

The wedding took place in the West Eighty-ninth Street synagogue and the reception was at the Plaza Hotel. Jacob and Rachel's mothers—both named Amy—coordinated these events. Both families had histories of propriety in Manhattan. Centuries back the Wolfs had been Romanian tailors. They now owned Wolf's Big and Tall on West Seventy-second, where they trimmed the prominent and took in the monstrous. It was rumored that Sherman Wolf, Jacob's father, had been personal tailor to both the mayor and the Scapalletti crime bosses. The exact clientele of Wolf's Big and Tall was never known publicly. What was known publicly was that the Wolfs were in league with giant men, men whose paws you were afraid to shake. That's what made it such a disgrace when, in the summer of 1943, twenty-four-year-old Jacob Wolf, Sherman's only son, took work as a jingle writer.

"A what?" Sherman Wolf stared at his boy. "What're you handing me, here?"

"I'll write jingles," said Jacob. "Songs for products."

"Songs for products?" Sherman Wolf was six foot seven. His son was five eleven.

"What songs?" demanded Sherman. "What products? What're you handing me?"

"It's for the radio, Dad." Jacob sighed. "It's for a conglomerate."

"What now? What're you handing me? A condiment?"

Jacob sighed again. The conglomerate was a team of businesses whose common association mystified Jacob. All he knew was that a man had offered him a paying job writing jingles. If the man called and said, we need a poodle-collar song, that's what Jacob wrote. If a thirty-second-long ode to mouthwash was required, Jacob would create a thirty-second-long ode to mouthwash.

"A conglomerate is a team of businesses, Dad."

Sherman looked down on his son. They stood facing each other in the drawing room of Sherman and Amy's penthouse on West Seventy-fourth Street. The penthouse contained two original paintings by August Macke. It also contained a black grand piano that Sherman had bought when Jacob was a boy. At an early age Jacob had shown musical talent and a chronic deficiency in athletics, and Sherman hoped to promote the former. True, his son was short and a disgrace at stickball. But, with arduous training, perhaps Jacob could become a musical genius of stormy temperament, a kind of Jewish Mozart who would bang out his tragedies at Carnegie Hall or the Met. Sherman wasn't averse to culture. But he presupposed that his only male offspring would crave power, notoriety of some respectable cast. A war was on, and anything that smacked of the trivial was disgraceful to Sherman Wolf.

"Amy," barked Sherman, "get in here. The boy wants to join a condiment."

So Sherman and Jacob never agreed about Jacob's profession. In 1944, when Jacob netted a fat paycheck for his Grearson's Soap Flakes jingle, Sherman held his tongue. He did the same during his son's 1946 Bear Belly Cupcakes phase. But, in the fall of 1947, Sherman's patience died when he heard the following ditty on the radio:

It's time to be kind
to your child's behind.
Switch to Kyper's . . .
the dapper diapers!

"Diapers can't be dapper," fumed Sherman. "Men's clothes are dapper. Suits and vests, dammit."

"It sounded good," said Jacob.

"Besides," said Sherman, "I know Mitch Kyper. He dresses like shit."

"Dapper diapers," explained Jacob. "Alliteration, Dad."

Sherman threw up his hands. His exasperation and embarrassment over Jacob seemed like divine decrees, permanent curses on his life. All he wanted was for his son to be a man. A man worked hard, played cards, drank whiskey, thought about women's tits. A man paid for things, and then, if he wasn't sick or dead, he laughed. But a man did not write songs about toothpaste and hair cream.

"He just needs a wife," Amy Wolf told her husband.

In January 1948 Jacob Wolf found his wife. To Sherman and Amy's undying relief the girl was Rachel Cohen, daughter of Alex and Amy Cohen of West Seventy-ninth Street. Alex Cohen was the sports editor of *The New York Times*. His family hadn't been in news for as many generations as Wolfs had been cutting cloth, but Alex's published opinions about the Yankees and the Giants were sober and correct. Alex Cohen, Sherman Wolf felt, was not a man of levity. Alex understood the honor a man bore when he crushed an opponent, whether that opponent was Adolf Hitler or the Boston Red Sox. Sherman hoped that some of Alex's nobility had come down to his daughter Rachel—as much nobility, anyway, as a woman could carry—and he hoped in turn that Rachel's nobility might rub off on Jacob.

As for Rachel, she loved Jacob. She was twenty-two when they met, and she worked as a fact checker in the *Times*'s features department. Rachel was responsible for discovering and accurately reporting to her superiors the exact height of Benito Mussolini, or the wing speed of the hummingbird, or the precise ingredients in the vichyssoise at Duranigan's of Madison Avenue. In fact, Rachel was at Duranigan's, arguing with the chef—who had agreed over the phone to publish some recipes, but was now being tight-lipped and haughty—when she noticed Jacob Wolf eating lunch alone at a corner table. She'd seen Jacob while growing up, at temple on Eighty-ninth, but she'd never *noticed* him. She'd never noticed the particularly strong cut of his jaw, or the frailty of his fingers. She'd never been privy to the sadness, the unselfconscious melancholy with which Jacob ate a Reuben sandwich when he figured no one was looking.

"My God," whispered Rachel. "Jacob Wolf?"

"I say nothing." The chef shook his head in triumph. "The vichyssoise, it is private."

Rachel floated out of the kitchen, toward her lone and future lover, who glanced up to meet her gaze.

"Private," the chef hollered after Rachel. "You hear?"

Four months later Jacob and Rachel married. It was a regal wedding. Cousins poured in from Long Island and Washington, D.C. Pure-white long-stem roses were strewn on the synagogue floor. Susan March, Rachel's close friend and fellow fact checker, was the maid of honor. Susan wore a dress that revealed her excellent calves, and many guests felt privately that Susan was more beautiful than Rachel.

At the Plaza reception, under Amy and Amy's discerning command, steak tartare was served, and champagne, and then lemon sorbet and then dinner. All the best people in Manhattan attended, including June Madagascar, the Broadway soprano, and Jacqueline Hive, who ran an orphanage, and ominously tall men in waistcoats. During a lull in the gaiety Robby Jax, the famous comedian, grinned and called for a toast.

"Ladies and gentlemen," said Robby, his glass of Scotch raised, "for the love of summer, for the love of husbands and wives, for the love of Cutty Sark and dancing, for the love of Jacqueline Hive's stupendous bosom, for the love of your mothers and fathers, for the love of Jews and starlight and well-crafted wool suits, but mostly, God bless them, for the love of Jacob and Rachel Wolf . . . cheers."

A hurrah went up. Glasses clinked. Dancing was permitted, children smiled, and a cavalcade of gifts was bestowed on the bride and groom. All of the gifts were impeccable. There were silver knives and gold jewelries. There were bottles of wine and examples of art. There was nothing lewd, grotesque, comical, or personal: no lingerie, no cash, no recordings of jazz, no books. Every gift pointed toward a useful, lavish life.

Presiding over the night was six-foot-seven Sherman Wolf. True, Alex Cohen had footed the bill, but that was nothing magnanimous. It was Sherman who imbued the night with class: he sank his teeth into steak tartare, he danced with wives, he shook hands with his cousin Ida to end a long-standing feud. Above all, Sherman was happy. No goofy jingle writers had appeared—Sherman had feared there might be a union of them—to sing stupid songs or snort laughter. For the evening's end a limousine had been hired to pull up to the front doors of the Plaza and spirit Jacob and his bride off to an Adirondack mountain resort. Finally, in the reception's pièce de résistance, the governor himself appeared for fifteen minutes. He kissed the bride, pounded the groom's shoulder, then took Sherman aside for some intimate words.

Amid all this wonder was Jacob Wolf, twenty-eight, newly married and utterly dismayed. Jacob sat at the head table beside Rachel and watched the night go unhappily by. The Plaza was glorious, of course. The food was glorious, and the lighting, and the violin music, and even Jacob's snot-nosed cousin Lucy from New Haven had somehow lost her baby fat and vulgar tongue and become glorious too. But Jacob was not built for glory. He'd known this all his life. He smiled at his and Rachel's guests because they wished him well, but in his heart he was terrified of these people. Contrary to myth there was nothing pretentious or phony about them. They were everything they believed themselves to be. They were rich, shiny, intelligent, and, Jacob guessed, they were moral champions of every perseverance. It was exactly their goodness that chilled Jacob's heart. For he knew himself to be a flawed, simple man. He wrote breezy, foolish song lyrics for a living and was content to do so. He took long walks in Central Park, not so as to appreciate nature or become fit, but rather for no reason whatever. He'd chosen Rachel as a wife because she'd been an easy catch. She'd walked up to him at Duranigan's, and, through body language and the English language, made it known to Jacob that she was available. They dated for a month, and Rachel said things that made Jacob laugh. She had a capable body, as did Jacob—though they didn't sleep together before their honeymoon—and Rachel neither loved nor disdained the jingles Jacob wrote. Out of what might have been joy but was certainly relief, Jacob asked Rachel to be his wife. She immediately said yes, and that was that.

Or perhaps not, thought Jacob, looking out at his reception. Perhaps the power and vibrance that shone so exquisitely in these guests lay dormant inside Rachel too. Jacob lived in the Preemption apartment building on West Eighty-second, and he planned for Rachel to move in with him after the honeymoon. But how long would she be content there? Maybe a month into the marriage she would demand magic: a move to the Upper East Side, tickets to *Carmen*, papaya for breakfast. What if she suddenly decided that California was an important place? Or craved oysters? Or wanted to discuss Churchill?

Rachel squeezed Jacob's hand. "You look worried."

"I'm not," said Jacob.

"You're lying. Stop worrying."

Jacob looked at his new wife. He looked at her sparkling gown, her cleavage, her rather ugly eyebrows.

Rachel shrugged. "I'm just a girl," she said. "You're just a guy."

Thank God, thought Jacob.

The legend of Jacob's bath began later that night, in the mountains.

Jacob and Rachel's honeymoon lodge was called Blackberry House. It was a compromise between a Vanderbilt retreat and a contemporary bed-and-breakfast. The house itself was vast and wooden and just an hour south of Canada. The ground-floor common room was paneled and studious. It featured bearskin rugs, racks of antlers, and a chessboard with pieces cut from tusk. The bedrooms, however, were warm and dear, with quilts on the beds, lighted candles, and, in the bathrooms, free-standing tubs with brass lion's feet. In Jacob and Rachel's room—the Blackberry Room—there was an antique loom, and a giant dormer window that looked out over Raquette Lake. Outside this window, on the roof, in the moonlight, was a skunk.

"There's a skunk out there," said Rachel. She still wore her wedding dress. She pointed at the roof, looked out at the night. It was spring in the Adirondacks, but the windowpanes were cold.

"It's two in the morning," said Rachel. "There's a skunk outside our window."

Perhaps Jacob should have been thinking about consummation. Instead, he was wondering how a skunk could possibly scale a three-story building.

"*Mephitis mephitis,*" said Rachel. "That's Latin for the common skunk."

For the *Times,* Rachel had once checked animal facts.

"How'd he get up there?" said Jacob.

The man and his bride watched the skunk. The skunk was black and white and did not currently smell bad.

Rachel removed her shoes, rubbed her feet. "I don't know how romantic this is. A *Mephitis mephitis* outside our window on our honeymoon night."

Jacob didn't reply.

"I'm going to take a bath," said Rachel.

She went into the bathroom, closed the door. Jacob stayed looking at the rodent. The skunk wasn't moving. It was planted five feet from the window, in plain view of Jacob and Rachel's nuptial bed.

Jacob heard the chirp of pipes, the running of water. His wife, he knew, was up to something feminine. As he thought this, Jacob decided to get rid of the skunk.

"Honey?" called Rachel. "What're you doing?"

Steam leaked from the crack under the bathroom door.

"Nothing," said Jacob.

He removed his good leather shoe, put it on his left hand like a shield. With his right hand Jacob opened the window, slowly, just a few inches. He stuck his left hand outside.

"Go away, skunk," whispered Jacob, waving his shoe. "Hit the road."

The skunk looked at Jacob. It seemed terribly bored.

"Fuck off," hissed Jacob. "Scram."

He glared at the skunk. He waved his shoe carefully.

"Shoo, now," he said.

Jacob kept waving his shoe. He didn't want the skunk to fall to its death, necessarily. He just wanted it to move to a different part of the roof, to eavesdrop somewhere else. As it turned out, the skunk did neither of these things. Instead, it pulled a one-eighty and sprayed Jacob's shoe.

"Oh, shit."

Jacob pulled his hand out of the shoe, yanked himself back inside. He closed the window as quickly as he could, leaving his shoe outside. But it was too late.

"Uh-oh," said Rachel from the bathroom.

"I'm sorry," called Jacob.

He stood up, plugged his nose. The stench was unbearable.

"You'd better come in here," said Jacob's wife.

I've ruined it, thought Jacob. I've ruined our honeymoon.

"Come on," said Rachel.

She was standing, wrapped in thick white towels. One towel wrapped around her hair, turban style. The other was fixed over her breasts and came down to her thighs. There was a scab on her knee.

"We'd better plug the door," said Rachel. She took an extra towel from a shelf, laid it across the crack under the door.

"I tried to get rid of the damn thing," said Jacob. "It sprayed my shoe."

Rachel had been in the tub. She was wet beneath her towels.

"I'm sorry," said Jacob.

"It's all right," said Rachel.

The air was fogged. The tub was still full. Jacob looked at his woman, at the way she'd wrapped herself in towels. It was a manner in which women often wrapped themselves in towels, one for the hair, one for the body. It wasn't original, but it was something men never did. Jacob liked it.

"Um." Jacob blushed. After all, under the towels was his wife.

"He only sprayed my shoe," said Jacob. "He didn't get me."

Rachel giggled. She wrinkled her nose.

"He got you," she said.

Jacob laughed. Rachel laughed too. They fell silent, watching each other.

"Maybe you should get in the tub," suggested Rachel.

Jacob panicked. He'd heard about women who made love in bathtubs.

"I don't know about that," he said.

"You smell," said Rachel. "Undress, and get in the tub."

Rachel smiled. Jacob took her smile to mean she wouldn't get kinky. So he relaxed. He undressed slowly, letting her see him. He got in the tub.

Rachel picked up Jacob's clothes, threw them outside the door. She closed the door, knelt by the tub.

"You're . . . um." Jacob was eye level with Rachel's bosom. "Are you going to . . ."

"I'm not getting in there with you," said Rachel.

"Oh, fine," said Jacob quickly.

"I've already had my bath."

"Exactly."

"I don't take long baths."

"Yes. No problem."

Rachel laid her cheek on the side of the tub. She looked at Jacob's body in the hot, clear water. She saw all of him.

"Rachel," said Jacob. He was embarrassed now, sitting in the tub, water to his neck. He felt like a boy.

Some of Rachel's hair fell from her towel, mingled with the water. She reached out, stroked Jacob's neck.

"I love your neck," she said. "Your neck and your jaw."

Jacob let her touch his face. She was his wife.

"I love you," he said.

Rachel sighed happily.

"I do," said Jacob.

Rachel stopped rubbing Jacob's jaw.

Now what? thought Jacob.

Rachel picked up a white cotton washcloth. She lathered it on a bar of soap. The soap smelled like wintergreen.

"What're you doing?" asked Jacob. He kept his eyes on the washcloth.

Rachel rubbed the washcloth till it foamed. She arranged

the cloth over her hand, dipped her hand under the water. She massaged her husband's chest.

"Be quiet," said Rachel. "I'm going to give you a bath."

Jacob obeyed his wife. He remained quiet, and she did what she said she would. She gave her man a bath.

In the bath's early stages Jacob laughed. He had ticklish underarms, and he was self-conscious about his body. But as Rachel proceeded to wash him head to toe, Jacob stopped laughing. His wife was committed to her action. She scrubbed her new husband carefully. She was firm with his hands—which had been tainted by skunk—and hard on his feet. She worked thoroughly on his torso, but she was tender with his groin. Finally, overwhelmed with the care being shown him, Jacob closed his eyes. A mellow joy stole over him. For weeks he'd been planning for tonight—for his conquest of Rachel's body—but now his plans faded. He still wanted to make love to her in the bed, but right now something simpler was happening. Rachel's fingers were tending his skin, grooming him wetly, kindly.

"You like this?" whispered Rachel.

Jacob kept his eyes shut. His body had gone over to goose bumps, and his mouth came open in surprise. Jacob felt sure, suddenly, that Rachel had never bathed another man.

"Hmmm." Rachel's throat was pleased.

"You like this," she whispered.

The bulk of Jacob and Rachel's honeymoon was their business. But one warm fact remained: after a meal and a walk in the forest Rachel gave Jacob a bath every night. Within three days husband and wife were hooked on the ritual. They came to enjoy it not as a luxury, a sign of some new, candied life, but as a necessity. It was as if Jacob had been climbing a mountain all his years and had come now to a decent peak, where there was a woman and a well of water. The woman was there to strengthen the man, to quench his thirst, and the man loved the woman and he was grateful. It wasn't about equity: Jacob never bathed Rachel. He was ready to perform a lifetime of chores for her, but this isn't about that. This is about the bath: the legend.

Jacob and Rachel returned to Manhattan. Rachel returned to checking facts, Jacob to writing jingles. They moved into Jacob's place in the Preemption apartment building.

The Preemption was located at West Eighty-second and Riverside Drive. It was a cryptic old brownstone, with gargoyles on the roof, and it loomed over the Hudson River like a watchtower. Inside, the Preemption was special for three reasons. It featured the oldest working Otis elevator in Manhattan, a hand-operated antique with mahogany doors at each floor. The Preemption also featured a peculiar doorman, a Negro man named Sender. Sender was tall, wiry, and dignified. He wore a blue suit like a train conductor, and he never seemed to age or leave his post. Some Preemption residents guessed that Sender was not quite fifty, some that he was over one hundred, but nobody could beat him at arm wrestling. He had an oval scar on his forehead between and just above his eyes. Whispers went around every October that Sender had been born with a third eye, and that the doctors had removed it from his forehead when they cut his umbilical cord.

The third, fatefully unique characteristic of the Preemption was the fact that Elias Rook, the building's original designer and owner, had installed freestanding bathtubs in every apartment. Elias Rook finished the building in 1890, but he was an endowed, strict Presbyterian, and he had eternity in mind when he fashioned the Preemption. As a result the apartment floors and walls were cut from the sturdiest oak. The glass on each vaulted window was inches thick. The tubs, however, were the masterpieces. They were cast iron with white enamel coatings, brass pipes, and brass fittings. If a fact checker like Rachel ever bothered to research the Preemption, she might discover the incredible truth that not a single resident had ever, in half a century, suffered foul water, broken pipes, or even crumbled enamel in their tubs. Of course, over the years, most tubs had been converted into showers, Jacob's included. It was against Preemption rules to remove the original tubs—which were cemented into place anyway—so most residents hired plumbers to raise a pipe like a mast and fit the mast with a shower head. These people—the majority—then fenced their tubs in with plastic curtains, showered quickly, and returned to the world. But a few Preemptioners never erected showers. They stewed themselves slowly in their tubs, their old-fashioned cauldrons, and they thought of Sender, and they pondered the Preemption's elevator, which also never broke, and they were not afraid.

The day Jacob and Rachel Wolf returned from the Adirondacks, Jacob dismantled his shower. From then on, every night of their marriage, Rachel bathed Jacob. She bathed him on November 20, 1953, the night their first son, Elias, was born. It wasn't something Rachel told her family or the doctors at St. Luke's Hospital. She just did it: she checked into St. Luke's in the morning, gave birth to Elias, and was home by nightfall to bathe her husband.

Rachel made it home to bathe Jacob, too, on April 8, 1956,

the day her mother died of a brain aneurysm. She bathed Jacob on every Sabbath, and on Jewish holidays. She bathed him during full moons and the World Series, bathed him when she was angry and when he was cruel. Jacob, for his part, made it home for his bath every night. On July 30, 1958, the night he received an award at Rockefeller Center for his Jeremiah's Mustard jingle, Jacob refused a fifth beer at Duranigan's and caught a cab home for his bath. On August 23, 1969, in a hotel room at the Plaza, fifty-year-old Jacob Wolf ended his affair with Broadway pianist Melodie "Three-Four Time" Sykes. He rushed home, convulsing with sobs, and climbed into the tub for his wife.

For decades nobody knew the secret, the private font, of Jacob and Rachel's marriage. Their parents didn't know. Neither did their neighbors, or their children, Elias and Sarah. These latter figured, all through their adolescence, that their parents were simply horny. They watched Jacob and Rachel disappear every night into the master bedroom, which connected to the bathroom. When Elias and Sarah heard tub water running, they assumed that sex was being achieved, and that they themselves had been conceived in warm water. This led to some teenage confusion for Elias, who deduced that young women were at their most pliable and libidinous if you scuttled them into a shower and soaked them down. Sarah, of course, was like minded, right up until college. If a boy or man ran hot water anywhere within two rooms of her, she collapsed into giggles or scampered off in fright.

The legend of Jacob's bath went public in January 1991. Jacob was seventy-two, Rachel was sixty-five, and the Gulf War was on. Jacob's mother had died five years before, and his father, the mighty Sherman Wolf, was ninety years old. Sherman had shrunk almost a foot. He lived now at Benjamin Home, a convalescence house on the Upper East Side. The facilities at Benjamin Home were extravagant. The beds were firm, with good wooden frames, the halls were carpeted, the nurses kind. Sherman Wolf growled at the old women who played canasta in the lounge. He followed the war proceedings religiously on his television and in the papers. In his heart, though, Sherman was anxious. The world had remained Big and Tall, but he had not. His lungs ached when he took deep breaths. He suffered from arthritis, poor hearing, and cold spells that made his limbs shiver. On top of it all there was a madman in Iraq, and Sherman was convinced that this madman would soon attack Benjamin Home and, more specifically, Sherman himself.

"Dad," said Jacob. "No one's going to attack you."

"What?" Sherman glared at his boy, not comprehending. "What're you handing me?"

Jacob visited Benjamin Home every Sunday, and often during the week.

"Nobody's going to hurt you, Dad. I won't let them."

Sherman stared at Jacob in disbelief.

"You?" he muttered. "You can't stop the madman."

"Don't worry about the madman." Jacob arranged a quilt on his father's shoulders. It was a quilt Jacob's mother, Amy, had made.

"You." Sherman looked away and sighed. "You jingle writer."

Jacob's bath became famous because of Susan March, Rachel's maid of honor and colleague from way back. They'd started out together as fact checkers at the *Times*. When Rachel left work to raise Elias and Sarah, Susan March stayed in news. She worked at the *Times* for five decades, writing her way through Watergate, breakdancing, the Troubles in

Belfast. By the late 1970s Susan had her own biweekly column, "March Madness." The column ran the gamut from political satire to denouncements of fashion. Typically, Susan would send up some grotesque: a world figure of freakish disposition, or some no-name with a startling agenda. It was in "March Madness" that America first heard interviewed Dana Smith, the lover of accused serial killer Bobby Bobbington.

"I'll only talk to Susan," sobbed Dana, and she meant it.

Susan March also took swashbuckling offense to Denmark's 1986 Mongoloid Crisis—to the point, some said, that she swung key Senate votes on the issue. All in all, Susan's career attested that she had an eye for what mattered to the world, or at least to America. Susan had, apparently, a prudent heart, a savvy pen, and a willingness to touch the morally electric.

The catch came on New Year's morning, 1991. Susan March was in a cab, traveling down Fifth Avenue. It was four in the morning. Susan was returning home from a party, and she was drunk. It was one of those nights when alcohol had made her perceptive and depressed, and Susan gazed forlornly at the city as the cab sped along. It was snowing outside. There were very few other cars. The cabbie had figured Susan for a tourist and was narrating the sights of Fifth Avenue.

"There's Trump Tower," said the cabbie. "There's St. Patrick's Cathedral. There's two people fucking."

Susan started, blinked, looked hard. There indeed, on the steps of St. Patrick's, were two teenagers in the snow. The cabbie had slowed down to get a good look, so Susan got one too. She wished she could've said the teenagers were making love, ringing in the New Year with healthy abandon, but the cabbie was right. The teenagers were fucking. The girl's face winced. The boy had bunched the girl's dress and coat up around her neck, but his own pants were only at his thighs.

The nakedness, the snow, and the pain all belonged to the girl, and Susan was about to roll down her window and cry rape when the girl smiled. It was a hideous smile, Susan thought: permissive, rude, greedy, not to mention sacrilegious.

The cabbie shrugged.

"On we go," he said.

Susan couldn't sleep when she got home. She kept thinking about the teenagers. In her younger, brasher years she would've dashed off an angry column about public mores, about sex, privacy, decency. The trouble was, Susan herself felt suddenly, completely indecent. Everything about the previous night had been unhealthy: not just the teenagers, but the party Susan attended. It had been a gathering of heavyweights: news anchors, models, actors, some respected journalists, and even a supposed hit man named Mr. Bruce. What disgusted Susan wasn't the gin and cigars, or the presence of a killer, or even the rutting of a girl. What disgusted Susan was that she'd made a life out of embracing these things, giving them credence by writing about them. She was well into her sixties, and she'd never married, or been to Disneyland, or learned to sing. Instead, she'd drawn a bead on the large, savage habits of the globe: murder, extortion, hatred, crimes against women and the earth. She'd stared long at these awful truths. The problem was, as Nietzsche said, when you look long into an abyss, the abyss also looks into you. That New Year's morning Susan March made a terrible realization: she craved baseness. Some fiber of her soul longed to kill, as Mr. Bruce did, or to cleanse countries with napalm, or to be taken viciously by a man on the steps of a church. Not only did Susan want these atrocities, she wanted them so badly that she'd never erected the means to fight them off. She had no husband, no children, no balm to ease her days. And her arrogance, her pride in her lifelong, clear-eyed independence, died hard that New Year's morning: or so Susan thought, anyway.

Susan threw up. She wept and shook. She tried to remember the lyrics to an Irish lullaby and couldn't. She stared at her bathroom mirror for an hour, repulsed by the creases in her face, the marks of what she'd once considered wisdom. By nine A.M., Susan was on her couch, sniffling, clinging to Biter and Beater, her two cats, when the phone rang. Susan was in no shape to speak, but when she listened to the voice on the machine, she sighed with relief. It was Rachel Wolf calling, reminding Susan of their annual New Year's brunch appointment at Duranigan's. It was a ritual they'd kept up for twenty years.

"See you at eleven," said Rachel's cheerful voice. The machine clicked off.

Susan dried her eyes. She lay on the couch, recovering, thinking.

Brunch, she thought. Brunch, what a wonderful word.

It's so simple, Susan thought. She believed she was having an epiphany.

Brunch, Susan thought. Brunch and tradition and talking with a friend. Could a sixty-five-year-old, hungover woman write about such things, perhaps, instead of railing against misery?

Susan hugged Biter and Beater. She took a shower.

"What'd you do last night?" asked Rachel. She was eating eggs and potatoes with garlic and parsley.

Susan ate cinnamon toast. "Party. Uptown."

Rachel smiled.

She has a good face, thought Susan. Warm and wholesome, like toast.

"The jet set?" asked Rachel.

Susan nodded. "What'd you do, Raych?"

Rachel's hair was entirely gray, but long enough that she could still pull it back. Like a young girl's hair, thought Susan.

"The usual," said Rachel.

Susan leaned forward. "And what is the usual?"

Rachel smiled. "Oh, you know."

Susan shook her head. "No." Her voice quavered. "No, Raych, I really don't."

Rachel looked at her friend. Her face became serious. She was a mother of two and a grandmother of five. She could see when someone she loved was in trouble, in need.

"Well, Jacob fixed us two porterhouse steaks, like he always does on New Year's Eve. We had a little wine. Then Elias called, and later Sarah."

Susan waited. "And then?"

Rachel hesitated. It had been forty-three years, and they—she and Jacob—had never told anyone about what they did every night. But no one had ever needed to hear it, and now here was Rachel's friend. Here was Susan March, with a black death in her eyes that Rachel had only seen once before: when Elias had been admitted to a psychiatric ward for three months, suicidal over the loss of a woman. That death, that hole in the desire to live, made Rachel shiver for her friend as she had for her son. It was all she needed for a forty-three-year secret to end.

"And then," said Rachel simply, "I gave my husband his bath."

Out came the legend. With the drive of a child Susan asked questions. Rachel answered them. She told the story of her honeymoon. She told about the skunk and the bathing. As she spoke, she forgot her eggs and potatoes. She related the days and nights of her marriage plainly and truly, without sentiment. She told how Jacob's bath wasn't about sex, but about devotion, and love. She even admitted, because she thought her friend needed her to, that Jacob had once had an affair, an affair she'd known about the entire time it went on.

"She was a girl in an orchestra," Rachel said. "Jacob met her for her lunch breaks, and they'd go to hotels."

"The bastard," whispered Susan.

Rachel stiffened. "He was home every night for his bath."

"But he lied to you! He was cheating!"

Rachel stared at her friend, who didn't understand men.

"I was devoted to him," she said evenly. "I was his wife, and I loved him. The affair stopped."

Susan licked her lips, astounded, thirsty.

"And you still bathe him every night?"

"Every night."

Susan's eyes brimmed. "That's so beautiful."

Rachel rolled her eyes. "Don't cry, Susan."

"But it's so beautiful." Susan March sighed.

Rachel frowned. For the first time she sensed the danger of what she'd said and to whom she'd said it.

"It's just my life," she said.

"But it's so . . . so . . . *saintly*."

Rachel sat up straight. "For God's sake, Susan. I shouldn't have said anything."

Susan reached for her friend's hand. She reached for it earnestly, with the deep, soulful conviction of a person declaring war.

"But I'm so glad you did, Raych." She squeezed Rachel's palm. "I'm so glad you did."

Susan March devoted one day of her column to the legend of Jacob's bath. In what she thought was an act of homage she used Jacob and Rachel Wolf's real names and told their intimate tale to the world. It was a column, Susan decided, that hallmarked her new hope in mankind. No more would she rage against the irrational, the evil, awful, and absurd. There was another option, she said in "March Madness," for the true rebel, and that option was radical decency. Like Jacob and Rachel Wolf, people had but to choose a simple, decent action and devote themselves to it daily, entirely, without fail. It was the key to happiness, wrote Susan.

"Oh my God," whispered Jacob. He was reading the paper, reading about himself, his nightly bath.

"I'm sorry," begged Rachel.

"She even gave the name of our building." Jacob's voice shook with fury.

Rachel hung her head.

The Wolfs got letters. If Susan March had devoted a day of her column to a couple's bathing ritual, then that couple and that ritual deserved scrutiny and laud. One curious married couple even cornered Jacob in the Preemption's lobby.

"You could form a spousal cleansing club," said the husband.

"No, I couldn't," said Jacob.

"You could inspire the elderly," said the wife.

"Go to hell," said Jacob.

There were critics too. A few acquaintances shook their heads sadly at Jacob and Rachel, convinced that the Wolfs had been hushing up decades of perversity. There was speculation that Elias and Sarah had been psychologically warped by their parents' habit, and were even now practicing similar rites with their loved ones. The worst of this came from Sherman Wolf.

"What're you handing me?" Sherman was wrapped in his quilt, glaring at Jacob.

"Dad," began Jacob.

"No." Sherman made a bony fist. "There's a madman in Iraq, and my son is taking baths with his wife. I read this in the paper."

"I don't take baths with Rachel," explained Jacob. He was blushing, though, livid inside. Some nurses had smiled at him today. They knew.

"She gives me baths," said Jacob quietly.

"Shut your mouth," said Sherman.

"All right, Dad."

Sherman hunkered down in his quilt. He coughed feebly.

"You were never a man," he croaked.

Jacob set his jaw. He thought of a jingle he'd once written for a greeting-card company. He thought of the myth of Pandora, and the way Rachel never got soap in his eyes.

"I'm sorry, Dad," said Jacob.

The assault lingered in Jacob's mind, turned to a paranoia. Each night he still climbed naked into his tub, and Rachel still washed him. She sang him bits of songs he loved and petted back his hair. But something had died. Jacob felt it. Whether they'd mailed him letters or not, certain inhabitants of the island now considered him and Rachel to be profound. Strange couples that they'd never met were surely aping them, Jacob thought. Men were submerging themselves in hot water, and women who loved these men were washing them. If such bathing had been brainless, coincidental—just a man and a woman and soap and water—Jacob could have stood it. But he knew what the world wanted. It wanted glory. It wanted the act of a wife bathing her husband to be capable of banishing adultery, impotence, boredom.

"I can't take it." Jacob stood abruptly, climbed out of the tub.

"What?" Rachel wrapped a robe around her husband, tried to calm him.

Jacob paced. He wasn't articulate.

"People," he said. "I can't take people."

Rachel hugged her husband from behind, stopped his movement. The back of his neck was crazy with gray hairs. She nuzzled these.

"I love you," she said.

Jacob wasn't caving so easily.

"Susan March is an intrusive bitch," he said.

I've ruined it, thought Rachel.

"Yes," she said.

They stood there, Rachel holding Jacob. Jacob's knees were gangly, dripping.

"I love you," said Rachel.

Jacob sighed. He wanted there to be a fight. But there wouldn't be.

"I do," said Rachel.

His wife's hands were belted together on Jacob's stomach. He covered them with his own.

"I love you too," he said.

The phone rang. Jacob left the bathroom, answered the phone.

"Hello?" he said.

"Good evening," said the phone. "This is Benjamin Home. Is this Jacob Wolf?"

Jacob closed his eyes. He got ready.

"Yes," he said.

Jacob and Rachel went together. Jacob's father had had a stroke. The left side of his face and body were paralyzed, and he couldn't speak. He could hear, though.

"I'd like to see him alone first," Jacob told Rachel.

They were at Benjamin Home, standing outside Sherman's room.

"All right," said Rachel.

Jacob went in.

Sherman looked terrible. There were tubes in his arms. Half of his face had fallen: the skin slacked, the eye lolled in its socket, the left side of his mouth sagged. His living eye, his right eye, looked radically, pleadingly afraid. It was fixed on a nurse, a young woman sitting at Sherman's bedside. She whispered kind words to Sherman, and with a washcloth she wiped off his chin the drool that poured from his addled lips.

It was very simple. Jacob walked to the bedside, took the cloth from the nurse.

"I'll do that," said Jacob. "I'm his son."

The nurse nodded, left.

"Dad," said Jacob.

Sherman's eye panicked, roamed.

"Sherman Wolf." Jacob moved his face closer. "Dad."

Sherman's eye found Jacob. The old man's lips tried to work. The drool came forth, spilling down Sherman's neck.

"No, Dad," said Jacob. "No talking."

Jacob settled his father's head on the pillow. He swabbed drool off his father's chin, neck, shoulder.

Sherman's eye tried to rally its forces. It tried to resist. But in the end it relaxed, and the son moved the cloth over his father, tending him in a manner that would become a habit.

Fourth Angry Mouse

Jeremy Jax wanted to be funny, like his grandfather.

Jeremy's grandfather was Robby Jax, the famous comedian. In his seventies—which also happened to be the 1970s—Robby Jax was still performing at Cherrywood's Lounge, on Forty-second Street, and Jeremy attended the shows with his parents. Jeremy was ten, and when he sat on the couches in Cherrywood's, he expected someone might read aloud to him from *The Chronicles of Narnia*. Bookcases lined the room. There were studs on the walls on which men hung their hats. The smoke in the air had a blue glow, and the smoke seemed to remain in the room, day or night, even when no pipes were lighted. At Cherrywood's women drank coffee with amaretto, and men drank ale. When someone sank a shot at the pool table, the ball fell snugly into one of six leather pouches.

In one corner, between two bookcases, was a small hardwood stage bearing an upholstered chair. In this chair, drinking century-old Scotch, was Robby Jax. He sat down around eight on a Saturday night, drank silently until nine, then began to speak. If you were new to Cherrywood's, you wouldn't even know at first that a performance was under way. It would dawn on you gradually that the woman whose eyes you meant to seduce was having none of you. She was staring at the old gentleman in the corner, the one with the furry eyebrows. Everyone was staring at the old gentleman and beginning to smile, and the lights in the lounge had dimmed.

"And so," sighed Robby Jax, "I told Emma Jean Bryce of Vassar College that she reminded me of a stalk of celery. And Emma Jean Bryce of Vassar College looked at me quite seriously and said 'Robert, I don't know what that means. I honestly don't.' " Robby Jax sipped his Scotch. He glanced slowly around at his audience. He adjusted his vest over his thick middle. "And I said to her . . . I said . . . 'Emma Jean. A man can do many things to a stalk of celery. But one thing a man cannot do to a stalk of celery is make love to it, Emma Jean.' "

The audience laughed.

Robby Jax shook his head. "The women at Vassar College," he said sadly, "are virginal stalks of celery."

The audience kept laughing.

"I'm in my first year at Vassar," called out a girl, "and I'm not a virgin."

"Not yet you aren't," said Robby Jax.

The audience roared.

Jeremy didn't understand how it happened. None of the things his grandfather said were actual jokes. They were just stories, little pieces of life that sounded true. For all Jeremy knew, his grandfather made them up as he talked. But, somehow, the Scotch and the smoke and his grandfather's tweeds warmed people up, got them laughing.

"What's the secret?" Jeremy demanded one night when he was twelve. His grandfather had just finished a set at Cherrywood's. He was drinking Scotch at the bar, and whispering to a young woman in black velvet. The woman had a southern accent.

"Well?" said Jeremy.

"The secret to what?" said Robby Jax.

"How do you make people laugh?" Jeremy had his arms folded.

Robby Jax scowled. He loved Jeremy, but he was a widower and young women in velvet were rare occasions.

"What's the secret?" persisted Jeremy.

Robby Jax bent to his grandson. "Relax, kid," he whispered.

"What's the secret?" Jeremy whispered back.

Robby winked. "I just told you. *Relax.*" Robby stood back up, held his palm open toward the woman. "And now, Jeremy, I'd like to introduce you to one of the finest creations Our Lord ever set down on earth. She is called a brunette."

The young woman giggled. "Hush, Robby."

Relax, thought Jeremy. *Relax, relax.*

He thought this all through high school. He thought it when he worked stage crew for the productions of Smile and Frown, his high school's drama club. Jeremy would've auditioned himself, but his voice cracked into falsetto when he got nervous. Jeremy figured that once he was eighteen, officially a man, his voice would be strong. Plus, he'd be at college, away from Manhattan. He could relax and become a brilliant comic actor.

Jeremy's chance came in October of his freshman year at

Hobart College. He saw signs around campus advertising an annual student talent show called the Follies and he decided to audition. There were slots for student singers, musicians, and performance artists, but the most coveted position in the Follies was master of ceremonies. It was in this role that Jeremy planned to make his comic debut.

The auditions were held in the Hovel, the on-campus student pub, on a Thursday night. The Hovel was dark and crowded. On most nights it was a pit where students sought drinks and laughs. Tonight, though, it was meant to be a charmed, bewitching cave, full of human art.

"Don't suck," said Patrick Rigg. Patrick was Jeremy's roommate, along for moral support.

"I won't," said Jeremy.

Patrick and Jeremy sat in the corner. Jeremy wore his black suit, the one that matched the color of his hair. This suit, Jeremy believed, made his green eyes look jovial and menacing, as if he were a funny but dangerous man, like Lenny Bruce. It was this sinister edge, this tiny malevolence within himself, that Jeremy planned to exploit as a trademark of his performing style. Still, as a nod to his grandfather, the more traditional storyteller, Jeremy ordered Scotch at the bar.

"No Scotch," said the bartender.

"Perhaps Crown Royal?" said Jeremy.

The bartender snorted. "Perhaps beer," he said. "Perhaps Jägermeister."

Jeremy ordered the Jägermeister, which was served in a plastic cup. He returned to his corner to watch the competition.

A quick-eyed juggler performed onstage. A dancer danced. Three frat boys in Marx Brothers garb jabbered and received applause. An awful singer named Freida forgot her lyrics and wept and ran away.

"Jeremy Jax," said the judges. "Auditioning for MC."

Jeremy took the stage. He set himself down in a chair amid the footlights. He smiled wearily at the audience, the way his grandfather always did. He drank his Jägermeister. Directly before him was a table where three judges sat.

"Say something," suggested a judge.

Jeremy nodded. He understood what was required of him. However, he hadn't planned any material. He'd expected a perfect, spontaneous anecdote to rise within him, but it wasn't happening. A minute passed. Jeremy gulped at his Jägermeister.

Relax, Jeremy told himself.

A judge wrote something down.

"Um," said Jeremy.

His heart lurched. He saw Patrick frowning. People stirred in their seats, whispering. Jeremy stared at the drink in his hand.

"What's the deal with malt liquor?" he stammered.

One of the kinder judges smiled. "We don't know," she called out. "What is the deal with malt liquor?"

Jeremy didn't answer. He sat motionless in his chair. There was a riot in his stomach, in his mind. He tried to think of a story, any story.

"Jägermeister," he said, "is German for Master Hunter."

Someone in the audience sighed. Seconds passed.

"Women are celery," blurted Jeremy.

The Hovel fell silent. Patrick Rigg left. People looked at the floor.

"Thank you," said the judges.

Outside the Hovel, in the darkness, in a clearing of trees, Jeremy came to himself. His first instinct had been to run from the pub, to get out into the October air. He'd expected himself to throw up or cry or gnash his teeth. He was perhaps on the verge of doing these things when he made out another figure in the dark beside him. It was a girl kneeling on the ground, her face in her hands. It was Freida, the awful singer.

"Hey," whispered Jeremy. "Hey, there."

Freida looked up. Her face was miserable, splotchy with eye shadow.

"Are you great?" She sniffled.

"What?"

Freida pointed at the Hovel. "I—I meant, were you great. In there. Onstage. Were you great?"

"No," said Jeremy. His voice was hard. "I sucked."

As he said this, Jeremy felt a chill inside himself. It was a cold, new rage of some sort. It was painful, but somehow good. It made him feel capable of startling feats, like bludgeoning his grandfather.

"I'm Jeremy Jax," said Jeremy. He was practically shaking. "I'm terrible."

Freida shivered. She wiped her face, took the hand of the furious young man.

"I'm Freida," she said. "Come on."

They went to Freida's dorm room. In what seemed an implicit, mutually understood gesture, Jeremy removed Freida's clothes. He did so violently, as Freida expected. Then they lay down.

Jeremy stared deep into Freida's eyes as they screwed. He wielded his body into hers, taking a certain vengeance on the night. Freida made awful noises that weren't so different from the awful noises she'd made at the Hovel. When it was over, they lay there. Jeremy's hands shook at his sides. Freida's eyes were closed. Jeremy tried to think of something to say, but couldn't. So he got up, dressed, and left.

When he was twenty-three, Jeremy Jax returned to Manhattan. He had, by that time, a degree in Russian literature, a head of graying hair, and an apartment in the Preemption apartment building on West Eighty-second and Riverside. He also had a job as assistant to the director of the Lucas, a theater on Fifty-first Street that he admired for its history.

The Lucas was a dying theater. It had ruled Broadway in the 1930s, staging the world premieres of several famous productions, including Hunter Frank's *Killing Me Lately* and Dazzle MacIntyre's *Eight Boxes*. These plays and the Lucas itself had been renowned for their raw, aggressive candor. *Killing Me Lately,* in fact, had been investigated by the New York City Police Department in 1938 because the character of the murder victim was played by a different actor every night, after which that actor vanished from the cast. The owner of the Lucas at the time, Sebastian Hye, claimed it was merely a gimmick to fascinate the bloodthirsty. New Yorkers, of course, took the bait and bought tickets in droves.

By the early 1990s, when Jeremy Jax took work there, the Lucas had fallen from the grace of its early decades. The physical plant was in disrepair. The black plush seats needed reupholstering and the ceiling was full of echoes. Also, Michael Hye, the current owner and director of the Lucas, no longer wanted to produce sensationalist, frightening plays.

"Satire, fine," said Michael. "Irony, great. But no existentialism. No amorality. No ennui."

Michael was in his office, speaking on the phone to the playwright of the Lucas's latest show. Jeremy Jax sat in his cubicle outside Michael's office, eavesdropping.

"Now, then," said Michael, "there are flaws in *Of Mice And Mice*."

Jeremy sighed. *Of Mice And Mice,* the Lucas's new show,

was scheduled to open in one month. It was a departure from traditional Lucas fare. It was a play in which all of the actors were dressed as giant mice.

"Act One is fine," said Michael. "It's Act Two. What's driving the mice in Act Two?"

Jeremy sighed again. Since its birth the Lucas had been owned by the Hyes, a famous Manhattan theater family. The Hyes had always served as the producers and directors of the shows, and sometimes even as the editors of the playwrights. It was an unusual relationship, but Lucas Hye, who founded the theater in 1890, had been unusually wealthy and could afford to be overbearing. The contemporary Hyes could afford it too.

"Fine," said Michael Hye into the phone. "I want the revised script by tomorrow." The phone clicked.

Jeremy sighed one final time.

"I heard that," called Michael. "What's your problem?"

"Nothing," muttered Jeremy.

Michael appeared in the doorway. He was six feet tall, like Jeremy, but pudgier and fifty years old. He had muttonchops and halitosis.

"Let's hear it, Jax," said Michael.

Jeremy had no love for Michael. However, Michael gave Jeremy good money, and decent hours, and when Jeremy sat in on rehearsals, Michael often asked him what he thought.

"It just sounds," said Jeremy, "like you're trying to make *Of Mice And Mice* funny, and it's not supposed to be funny."

"Question," said Michael. "Is Jeremy Jax the expert on funny?"

"No," said Jeremy.

"Question," said Michael. "Was Ionesco's *Rhinoceros* funny?"

"Well . . ." began Jeremy.

"No," insisted Michael. "I saw it in London in seventy-nine. There were twenty people on that stage dressed as rhinoceroses and there wasn't a chuckle in the house." Michael put his hands to his hips. "The mice aren't funny. The mice are *dire*."

"Whatever," said Jeremy. "Forget I mentioned it."

In college, after his disastrous audition, Jeremy had turned his back on comedy. He found a home in Dostoyevsky and Chekhov. Russian writers, Jeremy felt, understood melancholy. They could be wry, but they believed in the Devil, and you didn't have to like black clothes or coffee to get their darkness. In what he considered a kindred Russian spirit, Jeremy had embraced the darkness he'd discovered in himself during that night years ago, his one night with Freida.

They'd never had a relationship, Jeremy and Freida. They'd come together once, as failures, and fucked each other as failures, and avoided each other thereafter. Jeremy remembered Freida as a ragged, tragic figure, like a doomed Karamazov or a Faust. He thought of her sometimes after work when he walked down Broadway to Cherrywood's Lounge, his late grandfather's haunt.

Jeremy drank Cutty Sark at Cherrywood's, sitting at the bar, glaring at the stand-up comedians who tried to take Robby Jax's place on the stage. The comedians were male, in their mid-thirties, with thinning hair and decent suits. They rolled their eyes and quibbled about women.

"Comedians aren't men," said Jeremy Jax. He was speaking to his old Hobart roommate, Patrick Rigg. Patrick was on Wall Street now. He lived in the Preemption apartment building, he was famous for his handsome bones, and he carried a gun.

"Russians are men," said Jeremy.

Patrick shrugged.

"Look at this guy." Jeremy nodded toward the stage, where the comedian was making baby sounds in the microphone.

"He's doing a bit about dating," explained Patrick.

Jeremy sucked ice and Scotch. He sucked till the cold hurt his teeth.

"He's mocking idyllic romance," said Patrick.

Russians, thought Jeremy, do not do bits.

It was on an ordinary Wednesday that Jeremy Jax became Fourth Angry Mouse. It happened quickly, and if Jeremy had had time to consult the darkness within him, he probably would have refused the role. But he was groggy from lunch when Michael Hye ran into the office.

"Call an ambulance," panted Michael. "Fourth Angry Mouse is down. Unconscious."

"What happened?" said Jeremy.

Michael shook his head. "He was berating First Kindly Mouse, and he collapsed. Hyperventilated or something."

Of Mice And Mice had eight characters, Four Kindly Mice and Four Angry Mice. All eight actors wore identically sized mouse outfits, but the mice were distinguishable by the colors of their trousers and their habits of movement. Second Kindly Mouse, for instance, was partial to softshoe. Third Angry Mouse rode other mice piggyback.

It turned out that things were serious. Fourth Angry Mouse, a habitual smoker, had suffered a collapsed lung.

"Jeremy." Michael pulled Jeremy into the office. It was

four o'clock, still Wednesday. The ambulance had come and gone.

"Jeremy," said Michael. He spoke quietly, reverently. "The Lucas needs you."

"How's that?" said Jeremy.

Michael gripped Jeremy's arm. "You've got to be Fourth Angry Mouse."

"Like hell I do."

Michael's face was grave. "We have no understudy. The show opens Friday."

"Call Equity," said Jeremy.

Michael frowned. "Whenever it's possible, the Lucas does things in-house."

"Whenever it's possible," said Jeremy, "I don't play rodents."

"Don't be flip, Jeremy." Michael punched a calculator. "I'll give you one hundred and fifty dollars a night till we can train a professional in the role, if that's necessary. It's virtually a nonspeaking part, it's only a two-month run, and you know the show cold. Plus . . ."

"Plus what?"

"Plus, I suspect you understand Fourth Angry's sensibility."

"He doesn't have a sensibility, Michael. He's a fucking *mouse*."

Michael snapped his fingers. "That. Right there. The way you just spoke to me. That's Fourth Angry's tone. His Weltanschauung."

"Forget it," said Jeremy.

"Three hundred a night," said Michael.

"Done," said Jeremy.

Rehearsals began twenty minutes later. Jeremy suited up in a giant mouse outfit and took the stage. The other mice gathered around.

"Who's this guy?" they asked.

"It's me," said Jeremy. His breath felt warm and close inside the mouse head, which was held to the costume's body by hinges. Jeremy's eyes peeked out through a grille in the costume's mouth.

"I'm Jeremy Jax," said Jeremy.

Third Kindly Mouse put his paws on his hips. "Michael. This is absurd."

"Yeah," said First Angry Mouse. "We're professionals. You can't just stick some random employee into—"

"The kid knows the part," said Michael Hye. "Besides, Fourth Angry only has one line."

Fourth Kindly Mouse patted Jeremy's back. "Let's give him a chance."

"What's his background?" said Third Angry Mouse.

"He's Robby Jax's grandson," said Michael.

The mice all nodded, impressed.

"Let's hear him," said First Angry. "Let's hear him try his one line."

Michael urged Jeremy onto the roof, which was a giant promontory piece of the set. It was from this roof that Fourth Angry Mouse proclaimed his line.

"Go on, Jax," said Michael.

Jeremy climbed the roof, looked out at the empty seats of the Lucas. A spotlight came on in the ceiling, singled him out.

Three hundred a night, Jeremy told himself.

"Do it up, kid," yelled Fourth Kindly Mouse.

Jeremy took a breath.

" 'I have arrived!' " he shouted.

Within two weeks an extraordinary thing happened. New York City fell in love with *Of Mice And Mice.*

There was no rational accounting for it. Manhattan's theater tastes had ranged over the preceding decade from men drenched in blue paint to maniacs thumping garbage cans, so the popularity of eight giant mice was perhaps only a matter of savvy timing. On the other hand, *Of Mice And Mice*'s playwright was furious. He'd intended *Of Mice And Mice* as a somber allegory about the divisiveness of the human heart, and audiences were finding the play outrageously funny. Children and adults loved the show with equal ardor, the way they might a classic Looney Tunes. Susan March, who wrote the editorial column "March Madness" for *The New York Times,* claimed that "these eight mice show us, with their tongues in their divine little cheeks, how laughable are all our attempts at serious human contention. Who would've expected such charm from the Lucas?"

Receiving particular laud was the character of Fourth Angry Mouse. He wore unassuming blue trousers and had only one line, but there was something about his befuddled manner, his confused scampering to and fro among his fellow mice, that endeared him to audiences and won him standing ovations.

"Fourth Angry Mouse," wrote Susan March, "is petulant, skittish, bent on private designs. But he is so convincingly lost in his own antics that we can't help but laugh at the little guy. He could be any one of us, plucked off the street, tossed into public scrutiny. Would any of us seem less goofy, less hysterically at sea?"

Compounding the intrigue around Fourth Angry Mouse was the fact that the program listed his actor's name as

Anonymous. This was unheard of. Benny Demarco, the character actor of film and stage fame, was carrying the role of First Kindly Mouse, and garnering good reviews. Trisha Vera, as First Angry Mouse, had some brilliant moments, including a Velcro routine on the walls. But it was the unknown man behind Fourth Angry Mouse that Manhattan wanted to meet most. Some critics speculated that it was Christian Frick, reprising his Tony-award-winning role as the Familiar in *Coven*. Most reviewers, though, suspected that a newcomer lurked behind Fourth Angry Mouse, a dark-horse tyro with few credentials beyond instinct.

As for Jeremy Jax, he was flabbergasted. He tried in each performance to implement the critical notes he'd been given by Michael Hye and *Of Mice And Mice*'s livid playwright. However, Jeremy was no actor. He had no knack for detail, no timing, no sense of his body as perceived by others, and so no clear motives for how to move when dressed as a seven-foot mouse. He got upset at the laughter he aroused—he didn't want his fellow mice to think him a showboat—but the more upset he got, the harder people laughed and the more money the Lucas made.

Relax, Jeremy told himself. *Relax.*

But Jeremy couldn't relax. His fame was a farce to him. He wanted no one to acknowledge it until he decided if it was shameful. If he'd been a praying man, Jeremy might've consulted the spirit of his dead grandfather directly for some assurance that he was authentically comic. Instead, he stood in the lobby of the Preemption, staring at the four portraits that hung on the wall over Sender's desk. These portraits were of the Rooks—Elias, Hatter, Joseph, and Johann—who had, in succession, owned the Preemption since Elias Rook built it in 1890. The portraits showed four men of unsmiling German lineage. Jeremy respected their shared, serious countenance and the fact that they all looked like svelter versions of his grandfather Robby. Each Rook wore a dark suit or tuxedo, and each, except Johann, had his date of birth and death engraved beneath his name.

Jeremy was particularly taken with the portrait of Johann Rook, the Preemption's current owner. This man was known for his secrecy and spectacular wealth, and his image carried a severe aspect. He had a full head of shock white hair, and wore a black tuxedo, and rumor went that Johann Rook traveled the world under various aliases, now practicing medicine in Paris, now mining diamonds in Johannesburg, and occasionally intervening in the lives of his Preemption residents. Jeremy, though, studied Johann's portrait only because, of the four Rooks, this man looked most like Robby Jax, the one soul whose approval Jeremy most craved.

Am I funny? Jeremy thought, staring at the portrait when the lobby was empty. Deep down, am I?

Of course, he got no spoken answer from Johann Rook. So, frustrated, Jeremy got drunk at Cherrywood's with Patrick Rigg.

"You no longer suck," said Patrick. "Why not spill your name?"

"Because," hissed Jeremy. "Because I'm a fucking mouse, that's why."

Patrick shrugged. Outside of Michael Hye and the other cast members—whom Michael had contracted into secrecy—only Patrick knew Jeremy's alter ego.

"You might be a mouse," said Patrick, "but you're definitely the man. Everybody loves you."

Jeremy scowled. If I were a man, he thought, I'd be drinking vodka in Siberia. I'd be living on tundra, with a beefy wife.

To cheer his buddy up Patrick dragged Jeremy to Minotaur's, a basement nightclub in the meatpacking district. Minotaur's was a labyrinth of halls and dark corners. There were doors off the halls, some of which led to rooms of bliss. Other doors led nowhere. If you got separated from someone at Minotaur's, you might not see him or her till morning or ever again. The idea, though, was to dabble in as many corners as you could, then follow the maze to its center, a wide clearing called the Forum. In this room were several bars, a high ceiling, a dance floor, and a stage that had revolving entertainment: house on Mondays, blues on Tuesdays, swing on Thursdays, ska on Fridays. Patrick brought Jeremy to the Forum on a Wednesday. Wednesday was Anything-Can-Happen Night.

Jeremy groaned again. "Why am I here?"

Patrick whinnied a high, eerie laugh. He pointed at the stage.

"Watch," he said.

Jeremy watched. A person named Harold read erotica. A girl named Tsunami danced.

"They suck," said Jeremy.

"Watch," insisted Patrick.

"Ladies and gentlemen," said the MC, "please welcome back to Minotaur's The Great Unwashed."

A whoop went up. The lights dimmed. Three young women took the stage, one at the drums, two on guitar. The girl on lead guitar had long black hair combed over one eye in a sickle that hid most of her face. Seconds later she and her band were at it. They played simple, throbbing music, but what got Jeremy's ear was the singer, the lead guitarist. Her face was hidden by her sickle, and her voice was awful but arresting, like Lou Reed's. She told lyrics in a simple monotone, then her words rose and cracked and broke your heart. Jeremy felt the hairs on his neck ripple. He turned to Patrick.

"She's . . . she's . . ." Jeremy wanted to say she was terrible. He wanted it to be a compliment.

"She's Freida," said Patrick. "Freida from Hobart."

Jeremy's mouth opened. Patrick was right. It was Freida.

"She's great," whispered Jeremy.

"I know," said Patrick. "I saw her here last month."

"Why didn't you tell me?"

Patrick grinned, sly and easy. He knew things about Manhattan that only dead people should know.

Jeremy found Freida after the show. She remembered him, and shook his hand. They went through a door, bought some drinks, went through another door, sat on a couch.

"I can't believe it's you," said Jeremy. "You were great out there."

Freida brushed back her sickle. "Your hair got gray," she said.

"So what do you do with yourself now?" asked Jeremy.

Freida tapped her guitar. "I do this, stupid. I sing."

"Full time?"

"Well, I'm a saleswoman at Saks. But who cares about that?"

Jeremy stared at her. He wanted to tell her how supple her thighs looked under her miniskirt, how terrific it was that she was profiting from her awful voice.

"What are you doing?" asked Freida.

Jeremy downed some Ballantine. "I'm assistant to the director at— Well, I work at the Lucas Theater."

Freida nodded. "The Mouseketeer Club."

"Ha," said Jeremy. He took another look at Freida's thighs, which, if he remembered right, had a tiny spray of freckles on them up around the hips. He remembered his grandfather, who'd loved whispering to pretty girls. Jeremy glanced around. The room they were in was dark and empty.

"Freida," he whispered. He placed his hand on her thigh.

Freida immediately removed it. "Nope," she said. She smoothed her skirt, and looked at Jeremy, her eyes all business.

Jeremy was surprised. He'd heard anything went in the back rooms at Minotaur's, and he'd once taken this girl quite aggressively. He reached toward Freida's lap again. Freida slapped his hand easily away. She made a little sound that could have been a laugh, then stood up.

"What's wrong?" demanded Jeremy.

Freida shook her head. "Nothing's wrong, stupid." She picked up her guitar and walked away.

The more Jeremy thought about Freida, the madder he got.

"She called me stupid," Jeremy muttered. "Twice."

"What are you mumbling about?" asked First Angry Mouse.

The mice were backstage, in the green room, stretching, getting their heads on straight. The Saturday-evening curtain was rising in five minutes, and rumor had it that Mayor Fillipone was in the audience.

"Nothing," snapped Jeremy.

"Hey, Jax," said Benny Demarco, "don't step on my tail during the butter dance."

"I won't."

"Well, you did this afternoon."

"Bullshit," snapped Jeremy.

Michael Hye popped his head in the door. "Places," he said.

Jeremy sighed heavily.

"What's your problem?" said Michael.

"Fourth Angry's pissed off," said Benny.

Jeremy gave Benny the finger.

"All right, all right," said Michael. "Everyone, relax. We've got the mayor out there. Places."

The mice scurried out.

Jeremy moved upstage to the giant cheese grate, took his position behind it.

The curtain rose. The audience applauded. The mice began their story, strutting and fretting upon the stage. Jeremy remained cloaked in darkness. He didn't appear until twenty minutes into Act One. Most nights, while he stood waiting, he peeked through the cheese grate and scanned the audience for famous people. Tonight he looked for the mayor. What he discovered instead was a young woman in the tenth row with a sickle of hair across her face.

"Freida," whispered Jeremy.

She wore a crimson gown, and gloves that came up her forearms. Beside her was a handsome man in a tuxedo who had one hand locked around Freida's wrist. With his free hand, using his fingertips, he stroked her biceps casually, possessively.

Jeremy scowled. *Relax,* he told himself. *Relax, relax.*

But he couldn't relax. Not only had Freida called him stupid, she'd laughed at him, laughed at the immense, sexual, Russian darkness inside him. And now here she was, the lead singer of The Great Unwashed, hiding her awful voice behind her crimson dress and her sickle of hair. Freida was a celebrity, apparently, a healthy Manhattan aesthete out on the town with her lover. It made Jeremy furious.

He rushed into view, two full minutes ahead of cue. The audience exploded with applause. The other seven mice stared at Jeremy.

Michael Hye stood at the back of the Lucas.

"Oh, no," he whispered.

Jeremy panicked. He squeaked loudly, twice, which was the signal for the butter dance, which wasn't even part of Act One. Chaos ensued. Half of the mice followed Jeremy's lead and improvised a makeshift butter dance, while the other mice threw up their paws in protest. The audience laughed.

Benny Demarco, as First Kindly Mouse, leaned close to Jeremy.

"You're ruining it," he hissed.

Out of frustration Benny gave Jeremy a kick in the ass. Fourth Angry Mouse responded by shoving Benny into the butter churn.

The audience roared. The playwright, standing beside Michael Hye, seethed and cursed.

First Kindly Mouse began chasing Fourth Angry Mouse. The chase rambled through the butter dancers, over the cheese grate, onto the lower portion of the roof, off of which Jeremy flipped Benny. Benny landed on top of two other mice, collapsing them to the floor.

The crowd was in stitches, even those who'd seen the show before and knew a bungle was under way.

Jeremy stood panting in his mouse outfit, his face—his human face—gone beet-red.

Relax, he ordered himself. *Relax.*

But, even as he thought this, Jeremy caught Freida's face in the crowd. Her mouth was thrown open, bucking with laughter. Her teeth seemed to eat the air ravenously as she howled. The mouth of her lover was howling too.

Jeremy closed his eyes, hard, hating what he was: a funny man. He was funny in a tense, awful way, a way that infuriated him and delighted others. These others, the audience, were delighted even now. They laughed, pointing at him. He couldn't bear it. He ran to the top of the roof.

"I have arrived," hissed Jeremy.

He put his hands to his mousy head, tried to unscrew it. He cuffed at his face, boxed his ears, yanked at his headpiece.

"What's he doing?" squeaked the mice below.

Michael Hye and the playwright caught their breath.

"Oh God," whispered Michael.

The audience hushed. Fourth Angry Mouse was clawing at his cheeks, apparently trying to tear his own skull off.

The other mice dashed for the roof.

"Don't do it," squealed Third Kindly.

"Wait," barked Third Angry.

"I have arrived," warned Jeremy. He swatted stubbornly at his neck, loosening the hinges there.

First Kindly Mouse was only feet away.

"Character," hissed Benny. "Stay in character."

"I have arrived," shouted Fourth Angry Mouse. He popped the final hinge in his neck.

No, prayed Michael Hye, but it was too late. In a beheading that shocked the masses, Jeremy Jax revealed his feeble self.

The Opals

James Branch discovered the opals in Manhattan, underground. He came upon them in a charmed, perhaps fated manner. It happened like this:

James was twenty-five, single and shy, with sleepy blue eyes and straight teeth. He worked as an accountant on Wall Street and he lived in the Preemption apartment building. Every evening after work, before taking the train north, James caught a cab to Flat Michael's, an East Village restaurant where he ate dishes called Bison, or Snipe, or the chef's specialty, a strange concoction known simply as Vittles.

Dinner was the one flavorful hour of James's day. After crunching and tallying numbers from eight to six, he abandoned the abstract and indulged his senses. He was not a talker, a drinker, a clubgoer, or an athlete, so his indulgences almost exclusively were meals, and James loved the unpredictable offerings at Flat Michael's. In the last year he'd feasted there on Possum, Gilthead, Rarebit, Neck, and Rattler. He savored the names of these dishes almost as much as the dishes themselves. For James was a lover of simple detail, a fan of wrought-iron fences and haiku. He felt that the dishes served at Flat Michael's—in their ingredients and in their names—possessed an Old World, elemental quality of romance, as if some medieval knight-errant had gone hunting and laid the spoils on James's table. James was also a recovering stutterer, and between the ordering of his meal and its arrival, he would practice his skills.

"Langostino. Langostino." Each night, James whispered the title of his forthcoming entrée as if it were an incantation or the name of a woman he hoped might join him.

"Souvlaki," whispered James. "Calamari."

This quiet habit gave James great satisfaction and, somehow, comfort. It gave an order and a voice to his day, and it lent him a place among the patrons of Flat Michael's. The restaurant catered to the eccentric and lonesome, so the tables filled quickly each evening, and James tried always to arrive by six. One October night he worked late and reached the restaurant after seven.

"One-hour wait, so sorry," said Juan at the door. Juan was James's favorite waiter.

"A little purgatory," chuckled Juan. He was foreign and religious. Purgatory was a word he could pronounce.

"Even for a regular?" whispered James.

Juan sighed sadly. "One-hour purgatory, Mr. James. So sorry."

James went back outside, wandered the neighborhood. He was a creature of ritual, uninterested in other eateries, so he decided to while an hour strolling. On one corner he listened to a vagrant street singer he knew from the subways, a lanky, black-eyed guitarist named Morality John. Walking on, peering through glass windows, James studied the ferrets at Tandy's Pets, the pastries at Let Them Eat Cake, the leather boxer shorts at Barby's Bondage. James had never entered this latter establishment, but he stopped before its open doorway to blush at some chain-mail brassieres on a rack inside. It was the kind of store, James guessed, that his housemate, Patrick Rigg, might frequent.

"You like?"

James whirled. Beside him stood a red-haired woman in skimpy silver bikini armor and black battle boots, smoking a cigarette. She had goose bumps on her naked arms and thighs, and cemented onto her smiling front teeth were the golden letters B-A-R-B-Y.

"Um . . . I," sputtered James.

"I was on my smoke break." Barby dropped her cigarette, ground it under a heel.

"Well, sure," said James.

Barby danced playfully toward James, swaying her hips, making James stumble back into the store. Barby sashayed inside too. She pulled the door shut behind her.

"Whew," she said. "Cold out."

"Um," said James.

Barby kept herself between James and the door. She turned a pirouette, tapped her chrome panties. "Pretty cool, huh? We're having a sale. The theme is 'The holidays are coming, so you should too.' "

James's cheeks flushed. "I . . . wasn't really shopping."

"Balls and chains are marked down," explained Barby. "So are nipple clamps."

James glanced around nervously. The walls were covered with masks and gags and dangerous-looking whips.

"I just need a rest room," lied James.

"Sure. Long as you buy something." Barby yawned and pointed. "See that shelf labeled Orifice Fucktoys?"

A squeak came out of James's mouth.

"You all right?" said Barby.

"I just . . . swallowed my gum."

"Anyway, past the Fucktoys there's a stairwell. Bathroom's one floor down."

James sprinted for the stairs, hurried underground. At the base of the stairs he caught his breath, wiped perspiration from his temple.

"Jesus Christ," whispered James. He stifled an impulse to laugh at himself, at his prudish embarrassment. Looking around, he was surprised to find himself in a dank concrete hallway of some length, with several doors leading off of it. The doors were pink and each bore a word or phrase in neat black paint. One said BARBY'S, another said FOR SLEEPING, a third said LAV, and a fourth said PRIVATE. At the far end of the hall opposite James stood a closed black fire door, hinged on a track. Scrawled across it in drippy pink letters were the words JOHN CASTLE'S NOMADIC.

James glanced back up the stairs. Barby wasn't in view and there weren't any other patrons around. James wasn't normally an adventurous fellow—at this hour he was usually sipping ginseng tea and paying his Flat Michael's check—but something inspired him now to tiptoe to each door and put his ear to it. He heard nothing through any of them except the last, the fire door. There seemed to be some clanging going on behind it, some meeting of metals, as if swords were being smithed. Also, the closer he stood to the door, the more he sensed that a warmth—perhaps a literal fire—was alive on the other side.

James stepped back. The fire door was crude, thick, and ancient. It was made of steel and iron, and for some reason it reminded James of the antique but operable Otis elevator in the Preemption. He would have guessed that the fire door hadn't been opened in decades except that the pink painted letters on its surface looked fresh.

"John Castle's Nomadic," read James. "John Castle's Nomadic."

He stared at these words, whispered them over and over. He couldn't make sense of them, but the rhythm of their syllables in his mouth and the ping and tong of whatever metalwork was under way behind the door proved too much to resist. James grabbed the handle hook on the door and put his weight to it. The door slid easily aside on its hinges.

What he saw inside looked half like a blacksmith's shop and half like a storage cellar. It was a large room mostly in shadow, with a glowing orange kiln and small furnace against the far wall. Beside the kiln stood a tall bookshelf, two stools, and a wooden table. The ground was concrete. The thirty yards of floor space between James and the kiln were crammed with weathered cargo trunks. A path that stretched from the fire door to the kiln had been cleared between these trunks, like a church aisle leading to an altar. As James stepped down this aisle, a scented steam rose from the furnace, and the kiln fire flickered like a great, quiet candle. Also, the clanging had ceased as soon as James opened the door.

"Hello?" called James.

As his eyes grew sure in the darkness, he stopped walking. The beaten cargo trunks around him were opened and turned toward the aisle like display cases. Within them, on beds of black velvet, lay the most stunning, prodigious collection of gems that James had ever seen. There were diamonds, fat as fists, and inch-thick emeralds cut in squares, like portions of some sweet, gelatinous dessert. There were amber stones, mica-thin but pancake-wide, set on golden saucers. The facet of a ruby, shining in the kiln light, showed James the entire glimpse of his profile.

"Whoa," whispered James.

"Who sent you?" boomed a man's voice.

James jumped in place. "Whoa," he said again.

"Who sent you?"

James turned one revolution, scanning the darkness for the speaker. "N-nobody sent me. I just . . . wandered in."

"No one just wanders in. People are sent."

James heard a scrape behind the bookshelf. "Where are you?" he asked.

A severe-looking man appeared from behind the stacks. He had a full head of shock white hair, but stood with such firm, healthy carriage that James couldn't say he was elderly. Also, the man wore a black tuxedo with the sleeves rolled up to his elbows, as if he'd been engaged in some physical labor. In fact, he held an enormous hammer in one hand and a thin gold necklace in the other, and James surmised that the recent clanging had been the work of the hammer.

"I—I'm sorry if I disturbed you. Are you John Castle?"

"Never mind about that. Come over here."

The man's voice had a resounding quality, as if he were calling out within a cave. James moved closer to the kiln, inside which he could see white-hot rocks or embers. He could also see clearly now the eyes of the white-haired man. They were brown eyes, rich and earthy like soil after rain, and they were watching him closely.

"Hmm." The man set his hammer and necklace on the table. He took James's right hand, inspected the palm.

"Oh," said James. "Well. Hello."

The man dropped James's hand. He sniffed the air, as if to place where he might have smelled James before.

"Hmm," said the man. "Who'd you say sent you?"

"Nobody. I don't know. Barby?"

The man shook his head. He situated himself on one stool, nodded at the other.

"Perhaps you'd like to sit down," said the man.

"Well . . ." began James.

"Sit down," said the man.

James sat. He looked at the man, and the man looked at James.

"Barby doesn't send people. And people don't just wander in." The man tapped the table. "So who sent you?"

James stared back at the fire door. Through it he could see a square of normal light, a peek of the stairway. But for some reason he was not afraid to be where he was, in this strange room with this stranger. James liked happening upon odd corners of Manhattan. He liked this cellar the way he liked Flat Michael's or the Cloisters or the Otis elevator in his apartment building. Plus the white-haired man beside him seemed calm but deeply sure of himself, like a Supreme Court justice.

"I don't recall having been sent by anybody," said James honestly. "I was just waiting to eat dinner. I was looking around." James peered at a trunk full of diamonds. "I guess maybe I sent myself."

"Good answer," said the man. "Bravo."

The fire crackled. The stools had no backs, yet the man

opposite James sat with fine posture, his hands on his knees. James waited to see what would happen next. Apparently, he and this stranger were going to sit on these stools beside this furnace.

"Um. My name is James Branch."

"Yes, I know. It's a good name."

"Thank you. Um. How do you know it?"

"Never mind about that."

James waited to be offered the man's name, but he wasn't. He stole glances at the stranger's white hair and strong jawline. His face had a hard dignity that James seemed to recognize, as if the man were a veteran film star whose picture James was used to.

"Have we met somewhere before?" asked James.

"Hmm," said the man.

James rubbed his neck. He cast his eyes over the opulence around him, the trunks of gems. He wondered if the man had gathered this treasure to himself in some grand, death-defying manner. Or maybe, James thought, he just forged them out of thin air in his kiln.

"So the sign on your door," said James. "John Castle's Nomadic. What's that supposed to mean?"

The man didn't smile. "It means I get around."

"Oh. Are you franchised?"

"In a manner of speaking."

James decided to try a joke. "And are all your places in sex-shop basements?"

The stranger shrugged. "I am where I am." He stood and clapped his hands, as if some preliminary negotiations had been settled. He beckoned James toward a chest of gems. "So, what can I interest you in tonight, Mr. Branch?"

James sighed. He'd been happy just sitting. "Well. Thanks, but I don't know that I need any . . . you know, diamonds or whatnot."

"You might soon. Perhaps you should have a look?"

"I don't think I—"

"Have a look," said the man sternly.

James obeyed. He didn't know why, but he felt compelled to follow the older man's lead. So he crossed to the chest and inspected its contents. This particular chest contained gems fashioned into jewelry. Lining the edges of the chest was a string of pearls long as a lasso. Coiled double around any woman's neck, James decided, these pearls would still droop to her waist. Besides the necklace there were brooches of amethyst, moonstone finger rings, and baubles whose origin or application to the human frame James could not discern. One ankle bracelet was a thick gold chain loaded with chunks of topaz so large that the bracelet might have been a manacle, designed to restrain or delight a queen.

"You may touch them," said the white-haired man.

Once again James obeyed. His fingertips descended, glided shyly over smooth, cool surfaces.

"That one is heliotrope," said the man. "These are garnets."

"But . . . I don't have a girlfriend," said James.

"This is onyx."

James kept his fingers moving. The man in the tuxedo turned the chest toward the kiln, let more light spangle off the stones.

"Beryl," he said, pointing to what James touched. "Cat's-eye. Agate."

James nodded. Quietly, almost without his noticing, his

lips began repeating the names of the gems, as if he were sitting in Flat Michael's, whispering for his dinner.

"Jasper," prompted the man.

"Jasper," said James.

"Hyacinth."

"Hyacinth."

After a while James became silent and just touched the stones, let their winking in the kiln light wash over him like a spell. He admired coral, turquoise, lapis lazuli. It suddenly seemed correct to James that men had slaved for centuries to mine these precious things from the earth and offer them to women. Whether a shopgirl wore chain-mail brassieres or a bride wore her diamond ring, it struck James as lavishly proper that women should flaunt the strong, sturdy stuff of the universe in a way that men couldn't.

All at once a great sadness rose in James's heart. He knew that he couldn't afford the treasures spread before him, but what struck him now with a pang was the fact that even if he could gather a trove of rubies or sunstones, he had no one to give them to.

"I don't have a girlfriend," he said again. The revelation sounded half right, so he tried it once more.

"I don't have a *woman*," he affirmed.

"You might soon," said the white-haired man.

James blinked. Lost in epiphany, he'd forgotten the man.

"What?" asked James.

The man in the tuxedo stood tall behind the chest. "Let's imagine, James Branch, that a woman was coming into your life sometime soon. If you loved her and you could give her any one of the items in this chest as a gift, which would you choose?"

James bit his lip. He gazed around at the cellar, the furnace, the door.

"How do you know my name?" he asked, for the second time.

"Never mind about that. What one thing in this chest would you give the woman you loved?"

James studied the man's face. He searched again for some clue as to how he knew this person. He also tried to find any malice in the stranger's gaze, any sneer to his lip that would reveal whether he was toying with James, testing him merely for sport. But the man seemed earnest.

James lowered his eyes. He felt embarrassed. "I—I couldn't afford a single thing you have."

The stranger sighed patiently. "Say you could, though. What would you give her?"

James couldn't help looking. The gems were lovely. All right, he told himself. All right, what the hell.

"Um," he said. His eyes browsed the chest. Not the snake of pearls, he thought. Not the topaz anklet. James had seen such accoutrements in Madison Avenue bars, heaped on the necks and limbs of fashion models. He liked it more when a woman wore just one piece of jewelry, something simple and elegant.

"Maybe this," he said, lifting a small silver bracelet. Strung along the bracelet were tiny jade dolphins.

The white-haired man took the bracelet from James, slipped it into a pocket. "Sorry. This one's reserved for a different party. Choose another."

"Um. Weren't we only speaking hypothetically?"

"Choose another," ordered the man.

James surveyed the gems. He considered an egg-sized ruby, a pyramid-shaped diamond. They were all too giant, too oppressively wonderful, to suit any woman that might date James. In one corner of the chest, though, stuck between two ripples of velvet, lay a pair of small earrings. The settings were plain gold, and the stones were a polished, muted white. James picked the earrings up.

"What are these?"

"Opals," said the man.

James turned his palm toward the kiln. When firelight struck the opals, tiny prisms came to life inside them. James got a glimpse in his mind of a woman with warm skin and hair the color of honey. He pictured the opals against her skin.

"I'd give her these," declared James.

The white-haired man nodded curtly. "Good answer. Bravo."

James stared at the little white worlds in his hand. "They're beautiful," he said.

"They're yours."

James looked up. "What's that?"

"You heard me. Keep them somewhere safe. You'll know when to give them to her."

James looked back and forth from the opals to the man. "You—you don't understand. There is no her."

Just once the man's face softened. He smiled like a parent lifting a curfew.

"There will be soon," he said.

For a moment James loved the conviction in the stranger's voice. He thought of the women he worked with, of Barby, of the woman who'd just popped into his mind, the one with honey-colored hair. Then he shook his head.

"B-but," he stammered, "you still d-don't see. Even if I had somebody, I couldn't really afford to buy—"

"This transaction is complete." In a nimble move the stranger kicked shut the trunk of jewelry at his feet, knelt, and locked it. The opals still lay in James's palm.

"But there hasn't been any transacting," complained James. "I haven't paid you any money. I can't. You haven't even told me how much these are."

The man sighed, his face stern again. "Money, money. Listen, James Branch. If I need something out of you, I'll ask for it. In the meantime, go eat your Tilapia or Dingo or whatever it is you order up there. There ought to be a table coming free around now. Good-bye and good luck." The stranger moved back toward the kiln, toward the hammer he'd left on the table.

"Hey. Sir?" James cleared his throat loudly. He glanced at the closed trunk on the floor. He still hadn't closed his fingers around the opals.

"Um," he said, "you're very kind to offer me these, but I'm not entirely comfortable taking them without—"

The white-haired man turned on James. The hammer was back in his hand, and, suddenly, some acute, terrifying purpose flashed in his eyes, as if the work he was resuming was none of James's business.

"W-whoa," whispered James. His spine trembled. Without another word, and feeling like a thief, he turned and fled.

All the next day James pondered what had happened. He brought the opals to work with him, took them slyly from his pocket, gazed at them during lunch. But he showed them to nobody and told nobody about them. He suspected that the manner in which the opals had come to him and the man who'd delivered them were powerfully inscrutable. He'd heard a story once about a hiker on some mountain who'd been struck by lightning from the only cloud in an otherwise blue sky. The man survived, having felt only a momentary sizzle in his brain and his toes. James felt like that man. He worried that if he spoke of the opals or showed them around to just anybody, they might vaporize in his hand.

He did stare a bit more boldly that day, though, at the earlobes and haircuts of his female coworkers. He imagined the opals against each woman's skin, asked himself if she could be the one.

The other slightly bold action he undertook that evening was to return to Barby's Bondage. Something told him not to push his bravado by entering the basement, but he did approach Barby herself, as she was stocking dildos on the Fucktoys shelf.

"You again." Barby was dressed like a civilian now, in blue jeans and a cotton sweater, though her teeth still professed her name.

"Hey," said James.

Barby wore a sour look on her face. James wondered if her sale was going poorly.

"You sure blew out of here fast last night," sniffed Barby.

"Yes. Um. Sorry about that. Listen. I have a question." James drew a breath. He knew what she would answer. "Um, is there a jewelry store in the basement of your shop? You know, past the bathroom, behind the black fire door?"

Barby stood and faced James. She blew a strand of hair out of her eyes. "What the hell are you talking about?"

James stood his ground. "Is there?"

"No, there's no jewelry store downstairs. I tell you what is downstairs, though. My personal fucking space. Is that what you were doing last night, poking around in my rooms?"

"And you've never heard of a man named John Castle?"

"Who?" Barby crossed her arms on her chest.

James nodded. He didn't have to check. He knew she was telling the truth.

"Hey. Mr. Questions. How about you buy some Bondage or hit the bricks?"

James took a step backward, pointed toward the street. "I'll, um—I'll hit the bricks."

"Damn straight."

James headed toward the door.

"Creep," yelled Barby.

But James Branch was already grinning, moving into the street, fingering the opals safe in his pocket.

Kissing in Manhattan

Rally McWilliams was profoundly lonely. She wanted to believe that she had a soul mate, a future spouse gestating somewhere in Nepal or the Australian Outback. But in Manhattan, where Rally lived, all she found were guys.

"Guys." She sighed.

"Yeah," said Kim. Her voice was dark. "Guys."

Rally and Kim lived in a SoHo loft. They were both thirty-one. They worked and dated guys. Rally never knew the names of Kim's guys. There was a Republican, an electrician, and a doctor that Kim called Dr. Charm. Rally, for her part, had slept with a guy named Paul for three years in her early twenties, until he moved to Idaho. Then came Sam, who was sensitive and kind, and who'd once eaten lime-green Jell-O out of the hollows of Rally's collarbones. Rally had figured that was the start of something extraordinary, but when Sam finished his Jell-O, he only burped and went to sleep.

"My mom," explained Kim, "says you can't love a man till you learn to love yourself."

Rally threw up her hands. "What does that mean? Learning to love yourself?"

Kim shrugged.

Rally was a travel writer. She wrote for *Five Kingdoms* magazine, and she was routinely sent to locales that she classified as exotic or lame. Exotic places that she'd covered included Capri and Dublin. A lame place was Moab, Utah, where Rally met nobody wonderful and almost got bitten by a snake.

"I have to meet at least one wonderful person," Rally told Kim. "Otherwise, a place isn't exotic."

"Isn't it hit or miss, though?" said Kim. "I mean, what if you're only in a town for a weekend and all the wonderful locals are away?"

Rally had stunning honey-colored hair that tumbled to her waist and got her free drinks. When she and Kim talked at night, they sat together on their couch, and Kim, who was a salon stylist, fooled with Rally's hair. Kim never left Manhattan.

"If I were wonderful," said Kim, "I wouldn't go parading in front of some travel-writing chick. I'd stay in and order Chinese and learn to love myself."

"Sooner or later," said Rally, "you'd go out. I'd catch you."

Rally was obsessed with what made people wonderful. It was usually what she least expected, but she knew the truth when she found it. In Dublin she'd hoped to meet blue-eyed men, raconteurs who would buy her pints and tell her stories. Instead, it was the Irishwomen who fascinated Rally, the young ones with babies, or the ones with pale skin and cigarettes.

In Montana, Rally had talked to countless cowboys—men with blue jeans and money—hoping to sniff out the spirit of the West for a piece she was writing. But it was in Glacier National Park, listening to a park ranger named Russ, a little barrel of a fellow with a lisp, that Rally felt the stubborn inconsequence of men in the wild. What startled Rally, and kept her traveling, was this: when the wonder of an individual human being struck her—when an Irishwoman took smoke in her mouth, or a park ranger's voice broke—Rally felt a throb of loneliness and wanted to kiss that person. Sometimes she wanted only gentle contact, a brushing of her lips on the stranger's cheek. Other times she wanted violent, total commiseration. Park ranger Russ must have been sixty, but he had such a noble manner and was so committed to the things he said about ice and bears, that, given the moment, Rally would have pressed her mouth to his, kissed him deeply, tried to entwine her solitude with his.

In actual fact, Rally hardly ever spoke to these strangers, much less kissed them. She told no one of her impulsive desires, because they struck her as amoral and frightening. She imagined conversations with a phantom psychiatrist, always a man.

I want to kiss the smoke in that Irishwoman's mouth, she confessed.

Why? asked the man.

Because she is sad, said Rally. *And she's tired of Dublin. And she'll never have that particular smoke in her mouth again.*

Are you a bisexual? asked the man. *A swinger?*

No, Rally answered. *But I can't kiss the smoke without kissing the woman. Don't you understand?*

Of course, Rally's phantom psychiatrist never did understand, and, deep inside, neither did Rally. So, rather than understand herself, she took the wonder she felt around certain strangers, her desire to kiss them, and wove it into the stories she wrote for *Five Kingdoms*. When she wrote about Capri, Rally thought of the old woman she'd helped up a stairway there. As she described the Blue Grotto or the cliffs or linguine with clams, Rally kept her mind on the old woman and fashioned each sentence as if it were a dignified kiss to the old woman's forehead. Somehow, such kisses came through in her writing, because Sabrina, Rally's boss and editor, loved Rally's stories.

"You have a gift," said Sabrina one night. "An absolute gift."

"Aha." Kim held up her hand like a crossing guard. "Rally McWilliams has a gift. But does she love herself?"

"Screw you," laughed Rally.

Rally, Sabrina, Kim, and Dr. Charm were at Minotaur's, a basement nightclub. Kim and Rally were there because it was Friday, and because Rally knew Half Stack, the Minotaur's DJ. Sabrina was there because she was single and pretty. Kim wanted to dance, so she dragged Dr. Charm to the mosh pit. Rally and Sabrina stood at the bar, drinking champagne, talking about France. Rally was flying to France in November to do a piece on Beaujolais nouveau.

"*Five Kingdoms* will pay for ten days," said Sabrina. "Just don't spend the whole time drinking Beaujolais on our dime."

"I don't want to drink it," said Rally. "I want to know why everyone freaks about it."

A song Rally loved came on. A guy with pink hair asked Sabrina to dance. Sabrina consented, and the guy waltzed her off. Rally was left alone at the bar.

"You shouldn't wear your hair like that," said a man's voice.

Rally turned.

The man was wearing a black jacket and spooning sugar into a glass of whiskey. He had short, sharp black sideburns, and a slight bulge in the left rib cage of his jacket near his heart. Rally thought the bulge might be a gun.

"Me?" said Rally.

The man surveyed Rally's outfit. She wore blue-jean overalls with a white T-shirt. Her hair was in two pigtails that sprouted up, then back, then down.

"You should wear one long braid down the middle of your back." The man kept sugaring his whiskey. "Simple, classic. None of this little-girl business."

Rally raised her eyebrows. The man seemed in his early thirties. He had handsome cheekbones, and jungle-green eyes. Rally smiled.

"I thought guys liked the little-girl business," she said.

The man stirred his drink. When he stopped stirring, the liquid still had crystals in it.

"I'm Patrick Rigg," said the man.

Rally checked the dance floor. Sabrina and the pink-haired man were still a couple. Kim and her doctor had vanished.

"I'm Rally McWilliams. I'm a travel writer." She tapped his glass. "What's with the sugar?"

Patrick shrugged. "It's what I like."

Rally felt a vibe under her skin, an alert. She looked more closely at Patrick's sideburns, decided they were a safe length.

"Whatever happened to straight whiskey?" she teased. "You know. Simple, classic."

Patrick sucked the knuckle of his thumb, as if he'd recently banged and hurt it.

"This is what I like," he said, holding up his glass.

At the end of the night Rally gave Patrick her phone number. Back at the loft she told Kim about him.

"He works on Wall Street," said Rally, "and he may carry a gun. He had a strange bulge in his shirt."

"Amen to strange bulges," said Kim, and Rally blushed.

Patrick didn't call for a week. When he did call, it was on a Friday in mid-September, just past four in the afternoon.

"Meet me at Saks at five o'clock," he told Rally. "Take a cab so you aren't late. Wear your overalls, a plain white T-shirt, and a strapless bra. French-braid your hair, and don't wear a coat."

"Who made you commandant?" said Rally.

Patrick hung up. Rally looked at the phone in shock.

Presumptuous bastard, she thought.

But it was a warm evening, with an orange, autumn tint in the clouds. So Rally dressed as Patrick asked, except she chose a T-shirt with a large, smiling Tweety Bird on the front.

When the cab pulled up to Saks, Patrick was waiting on the curb. He wore a black suit, and his eyes, in daylight, were even greener than Rally had hoped. As she stepped out of the cab, Patrick paid the driver.

"You're on time." Patrick pointed at Rally's T-shirt. "But I told you, no decals."

Rally put her hands to her hips. "Tweety was all I had," she lied.

Patrick took Rally to the dress department. He had her try on ankle-length silk dresses, none of which cost less than a thousand dollars.

This is crazy, thought Rally. He doesn't even know me.

But she liked the way the saleswoman handed her the dresses.

"That one," said Patrick, when Rally came out in a svelte black Narciso Rodriguez with spaghetti straps.

Rally stared at herself in the mirror. She felt smooth in the dress: shivery and good.

"It's thirty-five hundred dollars," she said.

"It's perfect." Patrick turned to the saleswoman. "She'll wear it out."

The saleswoman nodded.

Rally's eyes were wide. She came close to Patrick, touched his sleeve.

"You don't even know me," she whispered.

"Leave your overalls and such in the dressing room," ordered Patrick. "They'll be disposed of."

Rally drew in a breath. For the first time she sensed that Patrick was ushering her into a new country, a realm where objects, probably even humans, could be purchased and discarded easily. She felt a thrill in her loins.

"I'll need shoes," she said firmly.

Patrick bought Rally a pair of heels as black, unadorned, and indulgent as her dress. He paid for her makeover at the Glorybrook cosmetic counter, which was run, as far as Rally could tell, by well-dressed, well-paid witches. These women put fine shadows over Rally's eyes, drew bloodred lipstick across her mouth, misted her with a perfume called Serendipity. Rally endured all of this quietly, like a child being bathed. She kept her eyes on Patrick, who stood at the end of the Glorybrook counter, staring at her. His eyes, Rally saw, had a proprietary cast to them, a pitched look of want.

He's going to devour me, thought Rally.

The witches kept scratching and rubbing Rally. When they finished, Patrick tipped them each one hundred dollars, which only made Rally hornier.

He's going to devour me, she thought, and I'm going to let him.

They dined that night in the upstairs room at Duranigan's, which Rally had heard was the exclusive haunt of mobsters and beautiful people. Patrick and Rally ate quail, and arugula basil salad, and Patrick ordered Rally champagne made by monks. Patrick himself drank what he always drank, an old-fashioned with Old Grand-dad whiskey and sugar. Rally noticed again the discreet bulge close to Patrick's heart. It made her ask questions.

"Tell me about your work," she said.

"No," said Patrick.

"Your family, then."

Patrick's teeth were busy with quail, but he looked at Rally as if she were insane.

Rally frowned. "How about college? I mean, you went to college, didn't you?"

"Stop it," said Patrick.

Rally swallowed hard. She crossed and uncrossed her legs beneath the table.

"Stop asking about stupid things," said Patrick.

Rally glanced around. There were several burly Italian men eating pasta at a corner table, but they didn't have bulges in their coats.

"Well." Rally looked back at Patrick, blinked her blackened lashes. "We have to talk about something, don't we?"

Patrick's lips curled. His suit fit him perfectly, he had broad shoulders, and he seemed to Rally absolutely content to reveal nothing about himself.

"Tell me something crucial, then," she told him. "Say something crucial."

Patrick sipped his whiskey. His eyes scanned the ceiling.

"Once," he said, "when I was five, I jabbed a shish kebab skewer through my brother Francis's hand."

"On purpose?" gasped Rally.

"We were playing acupuncture. Francis told me to do it. He was older. He said it would heal him."

Rally thought about that. "Straight through the hand?"

"Straight through. You could see the skewer on both sides. Like in a film where a cowboy gets an arrow through the leg."

"Jesus," whispered Rally. She was done eating now. A waiter took her plate.

"Was there much blood?" asked Rally.

"There really wasn't," said Patrick.

Who *is* this guy? Rally thought.

After dinner they went to Patrick's apartment. He lived on the Upper West Side, in a tall, looming brownstone called the Preemption apartment building. The Preemption had a splendid, ancient elevator, with mahogany doors, but Patrick didn't kiss Rally inside this elevator as she thought he might. He got her to his home, gave her a glass of water.

"Do you have a housemate?" asked Rally.

"Yes," said Patrick. "He works with me. His name is James Branch. Come see my bedroom."

Patrick's bedroom featured a queen-size bed and a full-length oval dressing mirror with an ornate wooden border. The wood of the border was fashioned into overlapping vines with thorns on them. Patrick took Rally by the shoulders, turned her body to the mirror.

"Stand still," said Patrick. "Cross your arms behind you."

Rally stood still. She waited for kisses.

"Watch yourself in the mirror. Keep your wrists crossed at the small of your back."

Rally was nervous, but she did it. The room was dark, but there was enough moonlight for her to see the slink of her figure, the red dash of her lips. Patrick stood behind her, half a foot taller than Rally, and his hands came around her shoulders to the front of her neck. One of his hands held, to Rally's surprise, a small, open jackknife.

She froze. "Hey."

"Stay still," said Patrick.

Very carefully, Patrick took the bodice of Rally's dress, just below the front of her neck, and cut a niche in the silk.

Rally's heart lurched.

"Patrick," she complained, "this dress cost you thousands."

"Be quiet and watch." Patrick closed the knife, dropped it in his pocket. He gripped Rally's dress at the neck, on either side of the niche. Rally felt the pressure of his elbows on her shoulders. Then his hands rent the length of her dress in two. The silk parted like curtains.

"Patrick," whispered Rally. She leaned back against him, but Patrick leveled her steady on her feet.

"Watch," he said.

Rally frowned, but watched, while Patrick wrapped the dregs of the dress around her neck, sashing it into a scarf that hung down over her breasts. All Rally wore now were her white bra and underwear and black heels and a pricey scarf.

"Patrick." Rally gripped his thigh. "Patrick, kiss me."

Patrick removed Rally's hand from his thigh. He held her wrists crossed firmly behind her. He was strong, and fully clothed.

"Now look at yourself," he told her.

Rally's skin went over to goose bumps. She wanted to be underneath Patrick, on his bed.

"Patrick, can't we just—"

"Be quiet and look." His voice was resolute.

Reluctantly, Rally stared into the mirror. She saw her pale, full-figured self in white-and-black trappings. She saw her bowleggedness, the way her knees never touched, no matter how closely together she rammed her heels. Her high-school track coach had told Rally her bowed legs gave her balance as a sprinter, but she wasn't a sprinter tonight. Patrick still gripped her wrists, and Rally was filled suddenly with hatred for him, anger at the fact that he wouldn't kiss her, that he wouldn't let her hands free to rip the black silk from her neck.

"What do you want?" she demanded.

Patrick tisked his tongue. "Look at yourself. I want you to see what I see."

Rally tried to turn around. "Are you going to hurt me?"

Patrick put one hand to Rally's chin, made her face the mirror. "This is how I see you," he said. "Look."

Rally thought she could get one hand free if she yanked, but she didn't try it. She didn't yank free, didn't reach for the scarf, didn't rip it off. She wanted to know if there was going to be kissing and lovemaking. She also wanted to know what she was going to wear home now that her overalls were the property of Saks Fifth Avenue and her new dress was in shreds around her neck. On the other hand, as Rally stared at the mirror—at her half-naked self and the shadow that held her—there was a quickness in her breathing.

"Do you . . . *want* to hurt me?" she whispered.

"I want you to look at yourself," said Patrick, "till you see what I see."

Rally glanced at the mirror. She had obviously fallen in with a pervert, or a prophet. She studied the cant of her hips, which she thought looked impressive, given the running she did three times a week. She also thought her biceps had some decent muscle on them. If she hauled off and smacked Patrick's face, she figured she'd leave a respectable mark before he strangled her to death. Rally giggled.

"Don't laugh." Patrick applied pressure to her wrists. "Just look."

"All right."

Patrick made a contented noise. He stared at the mirror.

Rally breathed in and out.

"All right," she promised. "I won't laugh."

The next morning Rally sat around her loft in a daze, unable to focus on her writing. Patrick had held her half-naked for an hour the night before, then dressed her in some clean sweatpants and a T-shirt of his, and sent her home in a cab without even a peck on the cheek. The night had been glorious, then kinky, then over.

"What the fuck?" said Rally, out loud, to no one. She said it several times.

Rally stared at her computer, which showed her tentative *Five Kingdoms* itinerary for France in November. Rally intended to write a piece not about Beaujolais nouveau, the wine itself, but about the culture surrounding the annual release of the wine, the way it was hailed and imbibed so quickly, for one short November week, then forgotten. However, on this particular morning Rally couldn't focus on wine. She was thinking about how she'd had four thousand dollars of Patrick's interest wrapped around her the night before, and there'd been no sex whatsoever.

"What the fuck?" said Rally.

The phone rang. It was Sabrina.

"Well?" demanded Sabrina. "How was he?"

Rally wondered what to say. Normally, she shared her dirty details with Kim and Sabrina. But this time, though she was dying to spill everything—especially the price of the Narciso Rodriguez—something told her not to.

"He didn't kiss me," said Rally.

"Huh," said Sabrina. "Well, how's the wine trip looking? Got your reservations? You psyched?"

"We didn't kiss," said Rally absently.

Rally saw Patrick seven Fridays in a row. Patrick never called Rally during the week. He phoned her each Friday, met her at Saks, spent thousands on her, took her to dinner, took her home to his bedroom, cut up her dress, and held her. Patrick, Rally discovered, followed unspoken rules in this ritual and expected her to follow them too. The dresses were always simple, pure-silk affairs by Badgly Mischka or Pamela Dennis. They were solid-colored dresses—black, midnight-blue, maroon—and they came chastely to Rally's ankles until they were cloven in two and wrapped around her throat in the moonlight. Patrick crossed Rally's wrists behind her back each time and held her in place for an hour. He never kissed her, never fondled her, never tried to remove her undergarments, never spoke crudely to her, and when the hour was over, Patrick sent Rally home in a clean pair of his sweatpants and a clean T-shirt.

Rally was frustrated and intrigued by Patrick. On their third date she tested his parameters. When she donned her dress at Saks, Rally kept her bra on but left her underwear behind. That night, when Patrick ripped her dress in two, he snorted and backed away from Rally, dropping the dress. Rally turned around and came close to him, tried to kiss him, to coax his hand to her lap.

"Come on," she whispered.

Patrick glared at her, pushed her away.

Rally came at him again. "Touch me," she whispered. "Have me."

"No," hissed Patrick. He crossed his arms on his chest.

Rally stood tall and vicious in her heels. "What the hell's this all about, then?"

Patrick stared at her. "It's about you doing what I say. Seeing what I see."

"Oh, really?" Rally crossed her arms now too. "What about you doing what I say?"

"If that's what you want, leave."

Rally felt embarrassment coming, or tears.

"I don't understand." Rally made her voice meek. "Aren't we ever going to . . . kiss? Make love? I mean . . . don't you want to?"

"Right now, I want you to leave," said Patrick.

Rally's mouth was open. "This isn't normal, Patrick."

Patrick's eyes lit up hard. "I said, leave."

So Rally left, and expected never to hear from Patrick again.

"Is he a good kisser?" asked Kim.

She and Rally were at home, on the couch.

"He's wonderful," lied Rally. Patrick had still never once pressed his lips to hers.

Kim stared at Rally's French braid, which had become a constant. Kim thought the braid was a shame. She thought Rally's hair had opportunities.

"You've seen him three times," said Kim, "and you're always coming home in his clothes. Are you guys doing it?"

It, thought Rally. It.

"Yes," she lied again.

Kim watched her friend. She waited for details, got none.

"Hey, Rall," she said. "You haven't said any more about France. You still going?"

Rally rubbed her forearms. They'd looked slender in Patrick's mirror the night before, like a ballerina's arms. She'd liked how they looked.

"Rall?"

"Hmm? What?"

"France. Are you still going?"

"Oh, sure," said Rally. "Sure, sure."

To Rally's delight Patrick called the next Friday, as if there'd been no breach between them. He ordered Rally to Saks and Rally went. She couldn't explain to herself why, but she went and didn't try any tricks that night as she stood before his mirror, her abdomen exposed, her knees cold. The torn dress around her neck was pale blue.

"Do you want me to dance for you?" whispered Rally.

"I want you to look at yourself," said Patrick.

Rally stared at her body. Outside the window red police lights flashed in the night. A fire truck blared by.

"Do you want me to speak?" asked Rally.

Patrick squeezed her wrists. "You know what I want."

By the fifth week Rally looked forward to Friday night. She understood that she couldn't call herself Patrick's lover, but she felt unique, like she was modeling something intimate and perfect for him, something that could only be achieved by the mix of her body with the colors Patrick wrapped her in. There was something flattering and lavish about Patrick's obsession with her. When she stood in the darkness, half naked in heels, held by him, not talking, Rally watched her form in the mirror and tried to behold what he beheld. She thought of little dollars transferring electronically from Patrick's bank account to the bank accounts of Saks and Duranigan's.

"Why me?" she asked him once, but Patrick laid his finger over her lips.

On their sixth Friday, Rally experimented with clichés. She sucked in her gut, thrust out her chest, pouted her lips, made her face scared but attentive. When Patrick didn't rape her, Rally changed tacks. She let her stomach sag, and her face slacken. When again Patrick didn't react, Rally ignored him and focused on the mirror. She studied the woodwork of the mirror itself, the thorns that surrounded the glass. Then she honed in on her image: the lift and fall of her ribs as she breathed, the slung-up poise of her breasts, the strapping of her ankles in her high heels. She loved how most of her skin was free to the air, but some of it was trapped and contained. She thought of the weave of her braid, that carefully wrought spine of hair.

Rally smiled. I'm good, she thought to herself.

The next morning, a Saturday, Rally went alone to the Cloisters museum. France was just two weeks away, and Rally always visited the Cloisters before a big trip to tone her people-watching skills. She considered people-watching a duty for a travel writer, and the Cloisters was perfect for practice. It was part museum, part church, part castle on the Hudson, and when people studied the art there, or strolled the ramparts, or just held hands, Rally found they were less self-conscious than in other places in New York. She could study strangers' demeanors and seek wonder—kissable wonder—among their faces and habits. Plus, the Cloisters was quiet, and Rally needed time to ponder Patrick Rigg, to decide whether he was wonderful and maybe her soul mate. A dangerous charm attended Patrick, and he dressed like a king, and he could laugh. The bewildering part was that whenever Rally started now to think about Patrick, she switched in her mind to thinking about herself, about her body in Patrick's mirror. She couldn't help it. When she dreamed at night, Rally saw herself as a nymph in a viny midnight wood, all breasts and legs and psychedelic eyes. She sometimes woke in the early morning, while it was dark, and crept into the bathroom of her and Kim's loft and stripped to her underwear. Patrick wasn't there, but Rally held her wrists behind her anyway, imagining Patrick's force upon them. She wore her bathrobe sash around her neck to simulate a torn silk dress, and admired her reflection until, to Rally's horror and delight, her groin went slick. It went slick, but where were Patrick's hands when she needed them?

"What are you thinking?" said a man's voice.

Rally started, blinked. She turned around, got her bearings. She was in the Cloisters' tapestry hall, standing before a tapestry at which she'd apparently been staring. Beside her was a slender young man with sleepy blue eyes and straight teeth.

"I'm sorry?" said Rally.

"I was just, um, wondering what you were thinking." The young man nodded at the tapestry. "You seemed so . . . engrossed."

Rally blushed. She focused on the tapestry. It showed a unicorn being hunted by men and dogs. The unicorn stood in a green clearing by a fountain, with two spears sticking out of its ribs, and blood trickling down its hide. The dogs and men surrounded the unicorn. The dogs had open jaws and the men, armed with more spears, looked grim and dedicated. The unicorn was obviously doomed to death or capture, and the pain in its eyes was anything but magical.

"It's terrible," said Rally.

The young man with the sleepy eyes studied Rally. He looked gentle, and doubtful.

"Is that really what you were thinking?" he said.

Rally looked away.

You're a stranger, she thought. *I'm* supposed to watch *you.*

"I like it," sighed the young man. He gazed sadly at the unicorn. "I—I probably shouldn't. Instead, I should think it's awful. Right?"

Rally paid attention suddenly to the sleepy young man, to the need in his voice. She reached out and touched his shoulder, just barely.

"No," she said. "No, not right."

For Friday number seven with Patrick, Rally wore very white underwear and a very white bra. Her dress was the color of light silver. It hung off her shoulders, a layer of thin, insubstantial armor. It was early November now, and cold in the city, so Patrick had bought Rally a black cape to go with tonight's dress. But Rally found herself anxious to get to Patrick's apartment, to shed both the cape and the silk. She ate her dinner at Duranigan's impatiently, and kept sneaking to the bathroom to admire the taut pull of her braid.

At the table, whiskey in hand, Patrick grinned like a wolf.

Rally touched her cheek, tested its softness. She was worried by Patrick's grin.

"What?" she asked.

"It's working," said Patrick.

"What is?"

"You know what." Patrick looked Rally up and down.

Rally sniffed haughtily. "What, you think I'm in love with you?"

Patrick shook his head. "Au contraire," he said.

That night, after he split her dress and made it a scarf on her neck, Rally told Patrick to cinch it tighter to her throat.

"And let it fall straight down between my breasts," whispered Rally. "Like a man's tie."

Patrick obeyed.

Rally stared at the mirror.

"I like how smooth my calves are," she whispered.

Patrick squeezed her wrists. He made a noise that could have been a snicker.

"And I like how they painted my mouth tonight." Rally turned her head side to side, profiling her lips in the mirror. All at once a great urge struck Rally as she stared at her lips. She could feel the urge deep in her diaphragm, even see it in her reflection. She sucked in her breath.

Patrick felt the change. "What?"

Rally shook her head. "Nothing."

Patrick's grip tensed. "You have to tell me."

Rally watched color rise in her cheeks. "It's not right. It's—"

Patrick moved closer to Rally. For once, her hands brushed his pants, felt an urgency there.

"I want to kiss myself," whispered Rally.

Patrick exhaled. He sounded like someone who'd been waiting a long time.

"I want to . . ." Rally loved her jawbone, the arc of her hips. She imagined her body in a wind tunnel, the kind they test vehicles in. She imagined air scooping over her, defining her.

"I want to kiss myself," she said. "All over."

Patrick pushed himself up closer to Rally. Her shoulder blades were against his chest now, but Rally kept her eyes on herself. Her groin tremored.

"I want to . . ." Rally fixated on the mirror. She tried to free her hands, to move toward herself.

Patrick redoubled his pressure on her wrists.

"You can't," he said simply.

Rally bit her lip. She closed her eyes, but when she did that, she couldn't see the nymph anymore. She opened them again, saw what she wanted. It was an impossible, wavering, trapped woman's body. Rally lurched toward it.

"I can," she whimpered. "I want to."

Patrick sniggered. His teeth flashed in the mirror, while his hands clutched Rally's wrists.

"Nope," he said.

Rally wrenched back and forth. Pressure built in her eyes and groin. She squeezed her thighs together, gritted her teeth, felt herself giving in to something unnameable.

"I can," she hissed. "I'm going to."

Patrick kept laughing. Rally's nails were digging at his hands now, clawing him. Her eyes were wide in the mirror, and her leg muscles were hard, twitching.

"Please," breathed Rally. "Yes. Yes."

"No," ordered Patrick.

Rally whimpered and fought. She had sweat on her brow, felt pleasure rising in her thighs.

"Please," she begged. Patrick stood firm, telling her no.

"Please," cried Rally.

But then, just as Rally's breathing hit its stride and her begging found a new pitch, Patrick released her wrists with a cackle. Rally stumbled forward, tripping to her knees, one of her heels flying off. Rally's hands splayed on the ground, arresting her fall.

"Ow."

Rally looked up at the mirror. She saw herself on her hands and knees, panting, her braid thrown forward over one shoulder, her breasts, cupped in white, pointing neatly down. Her scarf was still tight around her neck. It extended down to the floor and coiled there, but it looked awful to Rally now, like a leash. Patrick stood over and behind Rally, chuckling, his hands on his hips.

"Ow," said Rally again.

Patrick made no move toward her. His eyes blazed with a pleasure and a triumph Rally had never seen before.

"I hurt my knee," said Rally.

Patrick nodded. "I expect you did. You can go home now."

The lust drained from Rally's mind.

"What?" she whispered.

"You heard me," said Patrick sharply. "Go home."

Rally stayed on her hands and knees, wondering if he wanted her that way. Angry tears filled her eyes.

"What are you doing?" she whispered.

"I'm going to have a drink," explained Patrick, "as soon as you skedaddle."

"No," snuffled Rally. "What are you doing *to me*?"

"Go home," ordered Patrick.

Rally sat up. She turned her eyes from the mirror.

"Is this what you think about during the day?" she said savagely. "Doing this to me? Making me want . . . this?"

Patrick pulled sweatpants and a T-shirt from a drawer, dropped them on the floor near Rally.

"During the day," he said, "I think about money."

Rally got to her feet. She yanked the silk from her throat. She got furiously, shakily dressed, her mind throbbing with a redness, a color that could have been blood.

"Does it turn you on?" asked Rally. "Sending me home at midnight, then calling me again next Friday and doing it all over again?"

"I won't call you next Friday," said Patrick. "You'll be in France. Now, get out of here."

Rally's chin was quaking.

"You're a fucking nutbag," she said.

Instantly, Patrick was in Rally's face. He had rage in his eyes. He hammered one hand on his suit coat, thumping his chest over his heart.

"Do you know what's going on here?" yelled Patrick.

Rally gasped, backed away. She stared at the bulge in Patrick's coat, the lump she still thought was a gun.

"I'm sorry," she stammered.

"Do you have any idea who I am?" Patrick's voice was splitting. His shoulders were hunched like a bear's.

"Ye—yes. I mean, no." Rally ran from Patrick's room, out his apartment door, sobbing, *No, no, no.*

"Cut it off," ordered Rally.

Kim sat close to Rally on the couch. On the coffee table beside them were Kim's scissors and other salon weapons. Rally's hair was wet and she had a towel around her shoulders.

Kim stroked Rally's hair, which fell clean to the couch cushions, even covered them a little.

"Men are brutes," said Kim gently. She petted Rally's neck, rubbed Rally's back. "You don't have to do this."

Rally held herself archly, staring straight ahead. "Cut it off. Make it short and funky and whatever, but cut it off."

"Shhhh." Kim fought to make her voice soothing. She was trying to save something rare, something beautiful. "Just because some jerk liked your hair one way doesn't mean you have to—"

"Cut it off," shrieked Rally.

Rally went to Beaujolais, France. She walked down quaint, ancient streets, visited wine masters, tasted what they offered, floated from one vineyard to another. She sat on stone fences and gazed at sheep. She wore sturdy, roomy American blue jeans and baggy sweaters that didn't accentuate her figure. Her hair was cropped at the neck in a fashion that required no tending or thought. She spent each night in the restaurant of one inn or another, eating chicken and beef entrées, prepared with simple sauces. As she wrote and drank Beaujolais, Rally jotted down observations about the land and the wine. When it came time to write about the people, Rally did something she never had. She ignored the truth she saw around her and transformed everyone she met into a stock fairy-tale character. She wrote of polite men with wine-stained, crooked teeth, of buxom, helpful women, of children who carried baguettes and stomped on grapes. Everything was wholesome and pleasant and continental, until one night Rally drank far too much wine at a bar. She found herself dizzy and outside under the stars, her body being pressed against a rough-hewn rock fence by an eager young man named Olivier. Olivier kept making sexy French whispers and stroking the waistline of Rally's blue jeans. The mistake came when Olivier put his lips to Rally's, eased his tongue into her mouth, and kissed her. For a second Rally gave in to the swirling, crafted sky, and kissed Olivier back. She joined her mouth with a stranger's and tried to be a happy, fleeting thing, as fleeting as wine. But repulsion came. Rally was aware not only of her tongue, but of her entire self beneath her clothes, and she pulled herself away from the man, as if she'd betrayed a jealous, omniscient lord.

DUTY

My name is Patrick Rigg, and I'm thirty-three years old. I'm also a millionaire, because when I was six, my older brother, Francis Rigg, was killed unexpectedly by Guppy The Wonder Fish. My family lived near Chicago at the time, and Francis and I always begged our parents to take us to Guppington Estates, a theme park on the city's outskirts. Guppington Estates was one of these bizarre start-up American theme parks. Guppy, the central character, was a stout orange fish who wore a black tuxedo and a monocle. He spoke impeccable English and munched on pralines, but he also knew jujitsu. Guppy's afternoon cartoon show aired in Chicago and maybe everywhere. Each episode started with Guppy minding his own business, browsing through a bookstore, drinking latte, looking for collectible editions of Joseph Conrad titles. Usually, Guppy had by his side his classy fish girlfriend, Groupy. Groupy was incredibly well read, with a killer figure. She and Guppy would exchange witticisms and hold fins until the Largemouths showed up. The Largemouths were rough-cut, troublemaking bass, who, for reasons unclear to me as a child, followed and tormented Guppy every episode. They seemed to resent that Guppy was well born, and that he had a sexy girlfriend, while they were just punks as far as fish went. Bear in mind that none of this made any sense whatsoever. In any case, the Largemouths would pester Guppy and shove him around and call him a square, but their big mistake—which they made unfailingly every episode—came when they began insulting Groupy. As soon as that happened, Guppy would remove his monocle, hand it to Groupy, and say quietly: "This I cannot endure." Then, with lethal exactitude, Guppy would kick the living snot out of the Largemouths. He employed elegant, bone-crushing jujitsu moves, and when he was finished, there was a pile of dead fish carcasses on the floor beside him.

Francis and I worshiped Guppy. Francis, who was three years my elder, would sit with me every afternoon to watch Guppy on TV, and after the show we would act out the carnage we'd just witnessed. Francis was always Guppy by virtue of seniority, and I was a Largemouth. Basically, my brother and I just pounded on each other till one of us bled or cried or it was time for dinner, but I always resented being labeled a Largemouth. The punches I threw were real, indignant and sloppy, and they cost Francis one tooth and two black eyes in the years before our last trip to Guppington Estates.

The Estates was a fancy theme park. It featured the Hard Rock Bass Café, and Blowy's Bookstore, and all the other places that some marketing genius convinced me were normal fish hangouts. I might've asked my parents a million questions about why Guppy didn't live underwater and why he adored pralines, but I don't remember such questions. All I remember are the utterly kempt streets of Guppington Estates, and most especially, Guppy's mansion. The mansion was the coolest part of the park. Inside it were dazzling chandeliers and a wet bar where you could purchase pralines and imitation champagne. In the mansion's backyard was a giant Plexiglas fishbowl, Guppy's swimming pool. The bowl was probably thirty feet high and just as wide and it was filled with blue foam to simulate water. The idea was, your parents bought you a ticket and you were issued a Largemouth fish-head helmet. Then you climbed a staircase to the rim of the bowl and waited in line on a platform. Some guy in an eight-foot-tall Guppy suit stood at the head of the line. When you got up to him, you could throw a couple punches at Guppy and he'd fake some whimsical groans and moans, so your parents could get their money's worth. Then Guppy would holler, "This I cannot endure!" and swat you across the butt with a fin, sending you over the rim of the bowl into the pit of blue foam. You got to clown around in the foam for a while with other kids and then an attendant plucked you out.

If it sounds dangerous, it was. The platform was high, and poorly fenced in. Also, it's amazing that no kid ever asphyxiated in that foam. Bear in mind, though, that this was the early 1970s, and neither parents nor children were very clear about what the hell was going on. You had to be eight years old to dive into the bowl, and you had to wear a helmet, but that was it. I'm sure theme-park ordinances are far more rigorous now, but back then, standing on the rim of Guppy's sky-high fishbowl seemed like a perfectly sanctionable activity for a child. At least, it was sanctionable until Guppy swatted my brother Francis too hard and Francis glanced off the bowl's outer rim, plummeted thirty feet, and crashed headfirst into the ground in front of my parents and me. I'd been sulking around the base of the bowl, bitter that I was too young to be swatted by Guppy. Francis landed three feet from me. He was wearing his Largemouth helmet when he fell, but I heard his neck crack. It sounded exactly like it sounds in the movies, quick, clean, and sure, like a snapped wishbone. I knew he was dead as soon as I heard that sound and saw the weird twist in Francis's neck. I knew it before my mother screamed, before my father raced to his limp, fish-headed son. I knew my brother was dead, and in that moment I knew something else, something that a lifetime of nightmares and bullshit therapy and millions of sympathy dollars bequeathed to me by the defunct Guppington Estates Corporation has never been able to erase or rectify. My brother's death was absurd. It was an accident, yes, a progression of unforeseen, unfortunate split seconds in time, but when all was said and done, my brother was lying there dead with a fish helmet on, and his head was twisted in a silly way that heads shouldn't twist, and it was absurd.

Later, when I saw Francis in his coffin, I cried, because I understood that he would never punch me again. Today I live in Manhattan and trade millions of dollars in stocks every day, and Francis will never get to know this city—the glory of its money or the smell of its women. If your first temptation is to say, *How tragic,* my first temptation is to stick a gun down your throat and pull the trigger. You weren't there. You didn't see the twist of Francis's neck or his stupid fish helmet. Your mother didn't die of depression because of that twist and that helmet. Your father probably doesn't live as a recluse in his Adirondack hometown, and you probably don't send him checks every month to keep him in his deer-blind bliss. My brother's death wasn't tragic, it was ridiculous. It was point-blank absurdity, Francis's death was, and it wrapped itself around my life forever, like a straitjacket with clunky buckles.

So that's how I wake up every day, with the straitjacket—the absurdity of Francis's death and the absurdity of just about everything—tight around my skin. I brush my teeth, I eat Special K, I make money, I drink whiskey, and I'm capable of laughing. But none of these things ever loosens the straitjacket. There are only three things that accomplish that feat, three things that I take seriously, three things that let me relax a little. I do these three things without fail. Here is what I do. I carry a gun every day, I listen to a priest every evening, and, almost every night, I tie up beautiful women in my bedroom.

The gun's easy to explain. It's a licensed black SIG, and I carry it in the left breast pocket of whatever suit I'm wearing. My suits are expensive, always black or charcoal, and I'm handsome enough that people always check me out. They notice the bulge in the breast of my suit, the lump over my heart. They know it's a gun, and they watch me with fear and interest, wondering if I'll take out my gun and fire it. This doesn't thrill me, having strangers fear me, or knowing my coworkers worry that I'm packing heat. What thrills me is that I'm not what these people take me for. They believe I'm predictably dangerous—I can tell from their handshakes, their eagerness to accept when I insist on picking up the tab. They think me a strong, well-dressed character, a man of a certain code. I am cordial and principled, they think. They believe that I'm like Guppy, or some mobster, that I'll only resort to violence if my honor or the honor of someone I cherish is compromised.

My weapon, they suspect, is my instrument for executing justice.

Lucky for me, that is bullshit. What keeps me breathing in and out is knowing that I am not enslaved by principle at all. I can produce my SIG any time I want and snuff out the fourteen lives in closest proximity to me and still have one bullet left for myself. I can kill the Ukrainian woman sitting beside me on the uptown train, or Harrison Phelps, the shy man in my company's bonds department. I could buy a dozen roses for nobody, then plug a hole in the heart of the salesgirl who sold me the roses. With my SIG I can leap at any second into the absurd abyss that swallowed up my brother, and if you're too close to me when I leap, I might yank you in with me.

To which you undoubtedly reply that I am one twisted individual. Well, so what? If you're one of these people who feels he deserves a straight story, like I have some duty to enlighten or clarify, then go fuck yourself. How would you know the first thing about who I am, about what's choking me, about what I can or cannot endure? Maybe if your best friend gets his neck broken by a man in a giant Guppy suit, we can talk. Barring that, I humbly beg you to shut the fuck up. I'm trying to talk about my gun, and the priest and the women whose wrists I hold behind their backs. I'm trying to talk about things that are potentially absurd but that can also level absurdity, nullify it, if only for a moment.

So, the priest. His name is Father Thomas Merchant. He's the pastor at St. Benedict's Catholic Church, which is smack in the middle of Wall Street. Here's a big, fat surprise, I'm Catholic. That means that I know there's a God and that I grew up listening to inordinately bad acoustic guitarists every Sunday. Let's get one thing straight, though. My knowing there's a God doesn't change my brother being dead, and it doesn't stop the world from being full of pain. Yes, Jesus walked among us, and yes, you might get creamed in the street this afternoon by a delivery van carrying diapers or cherry cola. So I don't waste my time begging God to help me win the Lotto or to keep children from suffering or to play Mr. Fixit for life on earth. God's already proven He's not going to do that to anyone's satisfaction. Consequently, I feel quite free to say the word fuck whenever I choose, and to make and spend obscene amounts of money every day. I wear Armani suits, I read a tickertape the way doctors read an EKG, and I wait for that diaper van to run me down.

Father Merchant comes into the picture like this. Every evening, after work, I duck into St. Benedict's while Father Merchant is saying five o'clock Mass. I get there in time for the gospel and the sermon. I never sit down. Instead, I stand in back, in the shadows behind the candle trays, and I leave after the sermon. I never go to Communion, because not only do I carry a gun, but I love and need my gun in a way that God did not commission. I also never go to Confession because of what Guppy did to Francis. I can't enter utterly into the sober contemplation of my own faults while there are still men in fish suits breaking the necks of little boys.

I enjoy hearing Father Merchant, though. He's not one of these softy modern guys preaching milk and cookies and moral loopholes. He's got scraggly brown hair and strong brown teeth, like he's been eating sand in a desert.

"The Commandments come first," says Father Merchant. "The Beatitudes second."

What Father Merchant means is that it's no good worrying about meek, merciful peacemaking if you hate your parents, or if you're fucking someone you're not married to, or if you can't tell people the truth. Father Merchant, of course, is an unpopular preacher. He's got a gut, and his brown teeth are probably from cigarettes. Most nights I'm the only person under forty at St. Benedict's, and the handful of old women in the pews wouldn't exactly inspire the young or delight the weak. What I mean is, there are no frills at St. Benedict's, no cozy youth groups, no flautists, no epiphanies. Father Merchant represents a God who needs to be obeyed rather than embraced, and that happens to be the kind of God I understand, a God who is truth—even if it's absurd truth—rather than comfort.

Yahoo, you're thinking. I already mentioned that I tie women up every night, or hold their wrists behind their backs, so you're thinking, Enough already, get to the sexy stuff.

Fine, except I'm not sure you'll think it's sexy. It's sexy to me, though.

What I do is, I meet really beautiful women almost every day. I meet them in bars, on the subway, at bodegas, on the street. I am young, rich, handsome, unmarried, and often broodingly withdrawn into my thoughts, an irresistible combination for female *Homo sapiens.* Also, I have absolutely no compunction about saying whatever the hell I want, and most women adore that too. Either they adore it, or they're appalled but so intrigued that they can't help investigating me by accepting a date. I'll give an example. The following conversation took place three months back between myself and a young German au pair named Eva. Eva is nineteen, with a forest of lush black hair, and eyes just as black. She has very pale skin. She is not skinny, but she has a killer figure, and she is undyingly sensual. When I first saw her, she was standing in front of FAO Schwarz, holding the hand of a boy named Rusty, the boy she takes care of. They were looking together through the store window at a giant stuffed animal Triceratops, and a June breeze pushed Eva's short dress around her thighs. I walked right up.

"I'm Patrick Rigg," I said.

Eva looked me up and down. She saw that I was dangerous, but she yawned. Undyingly sensual women can yawn on command.

"Gee," said Eva. "Gosh. Golly. Wow."

"I'm Rusty," said Rusty.

I ignored the child.

"You're not skinny," I told Eva, "but you have a killer figure."

Eva stopped yawning. She frowned at me, tried to look naive.

"Killer?" she asked. "Figure?"

"You have a marvelous body," I said.

Eva's lips parted slightly. I had her now.

Rusty tugged on Eva's hand, tried to remind her of himself.

"Long ago," he said, "Triceratops roamed the earth."

I didn't take my eyes off of Eva.

"Rusty," I said, "if you go inside and leave us alone, I'll buy you that Triceratops."

Rusty raced inside.

"Hey," Eva called after him.

"Forget him," I said.

Eva watched her charge through the window. Rusty was poking a salesclerk on the arm, pointing excitedly at the dinosaur.

"You shouldn't lie to children," said Eva.

My God, women are lovely. They're lovely and prophetic. I could see from Eva's simple cotton dress, from the lack of sun in her skin, from the way the breeze blew her hair into her teeth, that she knew she'd be in my bedroom that very night. She was only nineteen, but she already knew how to deflect the conversation away from herself to something neutral and insignificant, like Rusty. She knew that if she did that, if she prattled stupidly for a while, she could relax and let me move her toward lust.

"I wasn't lying," I said. "I'll buy him the dinosaur."

Eva gazed through the window display. She knew not to look at me.

"That dinosaur," she said, "will cost hundreds of dollars. Maybe even a thousand."

"Good," I said.

Eva smiled, and that was that. She met me at Saks Fifth Avenue later that night, when she got off work. I spent four grand on a silk dress and heels and a makeover for her, then took her to dinner at Duranigan's, where I take all my women. By eleven we were back at my apartment, in my bedroom, in the dark. With a pocketknife blade I cut Eva's dress off her body and sashed it around her neck like a scarf. Eva stood expectantly in her brassiere and underwear, with the silk around her neck, waiting for me to remove all her clothing, lay her down, and take her. But I didn't do that. Instead, I held Eva's wrists behind her back and made her look at herself in my dressing mirror. I held her like that for an hour, until she was hot and bothered, then I dressed her in a pair of sweatpants and a T-shirt, got her a cab, and sent her home.

By now you're wishing maybe that there were a sexual 911, so you could phone in my psychosis. If so, you have no sexual imagination, and I'll leave you to your sorry missionary position. If you're intrigued, though, I'll tell you some secrets. One is that I don't fuck women, on God's orders. I'm not a virgin—I've had my slips—but I know the real rules as well as you. Following those rules or not is completely your affair, and if you're looking for an argument, find a Jesuit. What I want to talk about, what I want to honor, are the most beautiful creations on the planet, women's bodies. If you're a woman, and you're sick of hearing about how gorgeous you are, tough. I'm going to say what I want, and if you'd rather be demeaned or disregarded or merely endured, go find some stupid lover who will screw you blindly for his own pleasure, or maybe some drunk who will slap you around. I have a different aesthetic, and here it is. Women save me from absurdity. Think what you like about me, but when I watch the news and see thousands of Ecuadorians killed by a hurricane, or when a diaper truck flattens a pedestrian, or when I'm plagued by thoughts of my brother's fishy neck, I have to run to the nearest beautiful woman I know and lavish all the money and attention on her that I can. It's the only thing that helps, the only thing that loosens the straitjacket.

Why this is, I don't entirely know, and I don't much care. Some cynical scientist somewhere would surely cry biology in my face, and claim that my admiration for women's breasts and hips and haircuts is pheromone based and unconscious. Well, I've got a bullet for that guy too. Any man whose craving for women isn't rooted in his spirit will never be able to honor women the way I do. And any woman who can't learn to revel in her own body—who loathes being put on a pedestal by herself or by a man—isn't worth my time. I'm only putting her on the pedestal so I can join her up there, anyway. At midnight, in the room where I sleep, when I cross a woman's wrists at the small of her back, and hold her stripped to her underthings before a mirror, I'm asking her not only to feel the power I have over her, but to see and understand and love the power that she has over me. I want her to know that just being near her body, her gestures, thrills and pleases me, as much as and maybe more than plain old fucking would.

It takes a long while for most women to come around to my brand of intimacy, if they do at all. Like a painter who has models sit for him, I usually only hold my women for about an hour at a time, and I never have the same woman in my bedroom more than once a week. Still, many of them leave after that first hour—that first night—insulted that I haven't humped them. Trust me, the ones who run away that fast are lost anyway. They're doomed to futures and marriages barren of the long, slow sensuality that yields fire between men and women. The women who come back to my bedroom, though, are the glorious ones, the ones who are willing to endure the ache of detachment. I hold these women on their feet before my mirror, and they quickly learn the rules.

The rules are, the woman wears her brassiere and underwear and whatever dress I've bought her and shredded and tied around her neck. I wear and, at this point, never remove my suit. There are no kisses or caresses, no words exchanged, no laughter, no music. I hold the woman's wrists crossed behind her back, and I keep a ruthlessly tight grip. This way the woman knows she is helpless. She knows I can take her if I want to. But after a while—when she understands that I'm not going to take her, but keeps returning to me anyway—an amazing thing happens. The woman begins to forget that I'm there. She stares at herself, gets to know her body, and, hopefully, comes to love what she sees, comes to understand that the creature in the mirror is something extraordinary, elegant, wrapped in dignity, something not meant to be taken lightly or grabbed at and denuded too quickly.

Sometimes, women get wild over themselves. Some thrash and try to tear one of their hands free so they can jam it down between their thighs. I never let this happen. I want them to come just as much as they want themselves to, but I want to be part of it, and I want our joy to be enormous. So, after a month or so of half-naked nights in the mirror, I up the ante and move the woman to my bed. She often presumes the time has come to fuck, but she's mistaken. I'll tell you how it happened with Eva, just last month.

"Walk over to the bed," I told her.

Eva obeyed. It was a warm August Thursday—I always have Eva over on Thursdays—and Eva stood at the foot of the bed. A light midnight breeze from my open window blew Eva's silk scarf around her shoulders. The scarf was light gray. An hour before, it had been a dress.

I walked over, stood facing Eva. I'm a foot taller than she.

"Do you remember how much that dress cost me?" I asked.

"Twenty-two hundred and nine dollars and seventy-seven cents," said Eva.

Eva's perfume, Serendipity, was rich in my nostrils. All my women wear Serendipity.

"Are you impressed," I asked, "by the money I spend on you?"

Eva nodded. Outside my window there was moonlight on the Hudson.

"Are you worth it?" I asked.

"Yes," said Eva.

"Are you beautiful?" I asked.

"I'm breathtaking," said Eva. She didn't smile, and she

kept her hands at her sides while she spoke. She kept her eyes on mine. She was ready.

"Take off your underwear," I said, "and your brassiere. Leave your scarf on."

Eva obeyed quickly, then stood before me, hands at her sides. Eva's parents are both professional auto mechanics, so that meant that when Eva removed her underclothes in front of me, I saw a naked nineteen-year-old German au pair with hefty breasts who could sing sweet songs to children and weld a broken car chassis. Intoxicating.

"You're incredible," I said, looking her over.

"Are you going to touch me?" Eva asked. She knew by now not to assume.

I shook my head. "I'm going to tie you up. Lie down on the bed, on your back, with your head on my pillow."

Many women, quite content to be held, refuse to be lashed to bedposts. Eva's not one of them.

"Get your ankles and wrists as close to the four bedposts as possible."

Eva did this. I fetched some old ties from a box under my bed and tied Eva up tight.

"Now what?" asked Eva.

I smiled down at her. "Now I call my friends."

Gang rapist! you're thinking. Pervert and freak!

Listen, stop assuming you know me. I already told you that you can't relate because your brother was never Guppied to death. So, unless you're in the business of binding women to bedposts on a pretty much nightly basis, don't pretend to know how I go about it and why.

"Don't make a sound," I instructed Eva. "No matter what happens when the crowd arrives, don't make a sound."

Eva looked up at me. The gray silk was coiled around her

neck and one end of it had slunk down to her abdomen. She had some natural human fear in her eyes, but she nodded her consent. God, is Eva sensual.

I promptly left my bedroom, and closed the door behind me. I picked up the phone and summoned my friends, as I do most nights around midnight. A strange fact about me is that I require only about two hours of sleep a day, usually from six A.M. to eight A.M. This has been the case since the day Guppy killed Francis. I don't know whether my body feels it needs to be on alert for homicidal maniacs in fish suits or what, but the fact is, when night falls, I almost never get exhausted the way other people do. Usually, after I've held a stripped-down woman in front of my mirror and then sent her home, I just get bored, and I have to gather an artillery of characters to keep myself interested in living.

Here are the people I call. I call Jeremy Jax, my old college roommate, who's currently playing the part of a disgruntled mouse in an off-Broadway play. I've never seen the play and won't because seeing people dressed as giant mice would remind me of Guppy and I just might draw my SIG and start shooting. Jeremy, though, is amusingly morose, and hapless with women. It gives me great pleasure to chat and drink whiskey with Jeremy in my living room. He tells me of his nonexistent sex life, never knowing that I have a naked young woman bound and waiting for me in the next room.

I also call Nicole Bonner, a girl who lives many flights above me, and Walter Glorybrook, a hot-dog vendor who lives one flight down. My building is called the Preemption apartment building, and it's understood to be a gothic, nocturnal haunt, where commencing a party at midnight on a weekday is par for the course. I call this guy Checkers, a headhunter, and I sometimes wake my roommate, James Branch, a real loner, and force him to enjoy himself with others. I also call women, a clutch of beautiful Manhattan women, all of whom know when they come that I have one of their kind bound to my bed. Each of them has been bound for hours in exactly that condition, helpless, sworn to silence, forced to listen to clinking glasses while she dozes, watches the moon, curses me, pines for me, or pines for herself.

It's always the same. The women know my love and respect for their bodies, while the men know nothing about me, except that I like to drink with them and hear their stories. These men are nowhere near me in wealth, and if their endless ravings about pussy and politics reveal their true selves, they don't share my watchfulness for God and absurdity. This is fine with me. Just because I work to keep the Commandments doesn't mean I consider myself a judge of human character or anything approaching a mouthpiece for God. I'm far too singular in my obsessions, and my friends are free to snort cocaine or pillage or love Jesus as their consciences dictate. In any case, I'm only having these guys over for drinks and laughs. I believe they consider me a rich, sleepless, congenial vampire, a creature who's probably up to something shady that, luckily, doesn't involve destroying them.

As for the women, they have no need to dress seductively, but they do anyway. As I said, I usually invite only women whom I've held and bound in my bedroom, and gathering these veterans together thrills me to no end. Many of them show up repeatedly, despite knowing that all the other women there share the same physical past with me. At any moment these women might band together, charge my unlocked bedroom, and, in bacchic jealousy, tear to pieces whichever Eva or Julie or Justine they find bound there. However, this never happens. Instead, I *talk* with these women. I make conversation, something I've never done with them in the bedroom, something most of them crave more than sex. I might touch one woman's wrist as she's pouring herself a gin, and ask her whether she has siblings. I might sit down beside a woman on my couch, our knees bumping lightly, and ask her what music she loves. These questions—so trivial on most dates—carry weight and charm, because I've known these women so long. I've reversed the standard progression. I already know the woman's physical form so intimately despite never having fucked her—and she's gotten so comfortable with her body in my presence—that everything we say to each other now is a focused delight. We can talk freely, without convention or expectation, and I listen to the woman—who's already shown that she can be candid and vulnerable—and I begin to care for her immensely.

The last step of my night is this. After I've sent my friends away, and my roommate has gone to bed, and I've untied Eva or whomever and dressed her and sent her home, too, without even a kiss good-bye, there will be one woman left. She will be a woman whom, over the course of months, I have held before my mirror, and bound naked to my bed, and talked with at my parties. She will be a woman I've chosen earlier in the night to be the one. I'll have asked her upon her arrival not to drink anything alcoholic that night, to keep her mind and spirit free. She'll have hidden in the bathroom while I send away that night's bed-bound woman. Then, out of my bathroom, at five A.M., will come a woman who so knows herself and trusts my care for her that when she lies naked and unbound on my bed, and I—naked before her for the first time—join her and kiss her lips and put my fingers to the ribs over her heart, she can orgasm almost immediately, from the slightest touch. I am totally serious about this. Plenty more touching ensues, the nature of which it would be ungentlemanly to reveal. Suffice it to say that, without fornication or traditional intercourse, the woman and I reach sexual peaks and realms that would make angels want to be human. When we're satisfied and exhausted, then my two hours of sleep curl close to me, and I hold the woman tight and smell her hair and the pain in my chest, the death of my Francis, fades for a while.

Let the interrogation begin. Why? Why? Why? you ask. Why can't I resign myself to Francis's death? What would the Church say about my exploits with women? And why so many women? Why not choose just one, one who can make me happy, make me laugh, one whom I can marry? Well, to answer you honestly, how the fuck should I know? I'm only telling you what works for me, what keeps me from putting a bullet in my heart. As to Francis, I'm not going to elaborate on every plate of candy I ever shared with my brother, every memory I have of him, just to garner sympathy or paint a poignant background for my motives. In the first place, it would kill me to do so, and, secondly, I already told you I don't owe you anything. As to loving so many women, my basic understanding is this. When I meet the woman who'll make me need and want only her, then I won't need and want all the others. Maybe this particular woman, the one for me, is grown and gorgeous and right here in New York. Maybe she's barely eighteen in Tahiti. All I know is, when she meets me and stands before my mirror, she'll fall achingly in love with herself like no other woman has yet, and I will see this and pounce and never let her go.

As far as my sex life and Mother Church are concerned, I would say that, in the spaces between His commandments,

God allows us to proceed with as much tenderness and self-sufficiency as we can muster. Meanwhile, if you're looking for more character development on the Father Merchant front, you're shit out of luck. I know the man about as well as my male party guests know me, which is to say not at all. I'm not a full-fledged St. Benedict's parishioner, and I've never even seen Father Merchant except when he's in the pulpit and I'm in the darkness behind the candles. It's better that way. I'm detached from any sympathies Father Merchant might have for me, and it's his job not to get clouded by such sympathies anyway. When you're being charitable, or loving somebody, you're not supposed to let your right hand know what your left hand is doing. This means it's none of your business how much money I send my dad or give to Church organizations, and it's not my business to tell you. In fact, if I were a better man, I wouldn't have told you that I give anything at all. That's the problem with my confessing anything, whether it's to a priest or some random like you. I have to be ruthless with myself and not reveal too much about the way I kiss and cling to women, because you'll start thinking it's your job to understand or pity or fix me.

After all, I'm only human, and I might break all the rules I just told you I live by. With my gun and my sensitivity about Francis's death, I could get homicidal pretty quickly, if anybody ever really fucked with me. And you're probably thinking that with all these beautiful women I tie up, I could cross the line into rape at any second. Well, sure. I'm stronger than any woman I've ever held, and I could very easily pop Francis's fish-head helmet—which I keep under my bed—over some woman's head so she'd be blinded and confused and anonymous. Then I could bang away at her body to my heart's content. I could do it just as easily as I could shoot my roommate, and I'd be concocting absurdity if I did it. The woman might be begging me to stop, but if she had a Largemouth bass head, I'd have trouble respecting her argument.

He's psychotic, you're thinking. He's a freak and a monster. Well, I haven't done it yet, have I? I haven't raped or murdered anybody, have I? I've made many women happy, and even shared breakfast with some. Just this morning Eva was in my bed, and we were both sitting up, naked, with warm sheets and blankets heaped on our shoulders like we were king and queen. We were eating grapefruit and looking out the window at a bird who was chirping for the dawn to come. The sky was silver.

"What kind of bird is that?" asked Eva. "A sparrow?"

"It's a pterodactyl," I said.

Eva grinned. "Pterodactyls are extinct. They roamed the earth long ago, with Triceratops."

Eva and I each had our own grapefruit. We each had our own bowl and our own spoon.

"It's a phoenix, then," I said.

Eva nudged me. "Phoenixes are mythological. They burn themselves up, then rise from their own ashes."

The bird kept chirping. I kissed Eva's pale, warm shoulder.

"It's just a little sparrow," said Eva.

"No," I said. "It's something wonderful."

The Smoker

Douglas Kerchek taught twelfth-grade advanced-placement English at St. Agnes High School, on West Ninety-seventh and Broadway, and Nicole Bonner was the standout girl in his class. She was the tallest, at five foot ten, the oldest, at nineteen, and the smartest, with a flawless A. She wasn't the prettiest, Douglas thought—not beside the spunky nose of Rhonda Phelps or Meredith Beckermann's heart-shaped derriere—but Nicole was dangerously alluring. She had a chopped, black Cleopatra haircut, and wise blue eyes, and her recent essay on *Othello* had ended with this note:

Dear Mr. Kerchek:

Last night in bed I read Fear + Loathing in L.V. *It is puerile, self-involved gamesmanship. I suppose I don't love drugs enough, although my parents make me drink brandy with them every night. They consider it a gesture of affection.*

I saw you yesterday, outside the locker room, changing your shoes to go running, and your ankle looked quite blue. What did you bang it on?

Respectfully,
Nicole Bonner

This note caused Douglas some concern. He himself disliked Hunter S. Thompson, but Nicole had also written "in bed" and mentioned his bruise. It was Nicole's habit to do this, to call out random, intimate specifics from the world around her and bring them to Douglas's attention. She'd done it that day in class.

"Iago is filled with lust, Mr. Kerchek," said Jill Eckhard.

"He's a Machiavellian bastard," said Rhonda Phelps.

"You know what's an excellent word to say out loud repeatedly?" Nicole Bonner chewed her hair. "Rinse. Think about it, Mr. Kerchek. Rinse. *Rinse.*"

That evening, as always, Douglas walked home to his shabby studio apartment. Douglas was thirty-one. He lived alone, five blocks north of St. Agnes's, in an apartment building filled with Mexican men who drank Pabst and had boisterous poker games every night in the lobby outside Douglas's first-floor apartment. Their nickname for Douglas was "Uno," because whenever he sat with them, he had one quiet beer, then bowed out.

"Uno," cackled the Mexicans. "Come take our money, Uno."

A twelve-year-old boy named Chiapas rattled a beer can. "Come get your medicine, Uno."

Douglas grinned wanly, waved them off, keyed his door open.

Rinse, he thought, frowning. Rinse. *Rinse.*

After a quick sandwich Douglas corrected essays. He was a tough grader, and he had short black sideburns with streaks of gray in them. He also had a boxer's build, a Harvard Ph.D. in English literature, and no wife or girlfriend. All of these qualities made Douglas a font of intrigue for the all-female population of St. Agnes's—both the lay faculty and the students—but in truth Douglas led a sedentary life. He loved books, he was a passionate, solitary filmgoer, and he got his hair cut every four weeks by Chiapas, whose father ran a barbershop down the block. All told, Douglas was a quiet and, he thought, happy man. He was also the only male teacher at St. Agnes's. Cheryl, Audrey, and Katya, the three single women on the faculty, would have taken up the crusade of dating him, but he wasn't drawn to his coworkers. Cheryl wore electric shades of suede that confused him, Audrey had two cops for ex-husbands, and Katya, despite her long legs and Lithuanian accent, was cruel to the girls. So Douglas spent his nights alone, seeing films, correcting essays, and occasionally chatting with Chiapas and company. On this particular night Douglas was barely into his stack of essays when the phone rang.

"Hello?" sighed Douglas. He expected it to be his mother, who called weekly from Pennsylvania to see if her son had become miraculously engaged.

"Good evening, Mr. Kerchek."

Douglas frowned. "Nicole?"

"Yes, sir."

"How did you get this number?"

"Off the Rolodex in the principal's office. How's your ankle?"

Douglas sneezed, twice. He did this instinctively when he didn't know what to say.

"God bless you," said Nicole.

"Thank you," said Douglas. He glanced around, as if expecting his apartment suddenly to fill with students.

"How's your ankle?"

"It's . . . it's all right. I banged it on my radiator."

"Really?"

The truth was, Douglas had slipped in his shower like an elderly person.

"Yes, really. Nicole—"

"Do you know what's happening to *my* ankle, as we converse?"

"No."

"John Stapleton is licking it. He likes to nibble my toes too."

Douglas blinked several times.

"John Stapleton is a domestic shorthair. Sometimes he licks, other times he nibbles."

"I see," said Douglas. There was a substantial pause.

"John Stapleton is a cat," said Nicole.

"Of course," agreed Douglas.

"Do you enjoy gnocchi?"

Douglas set his essays on the couch beside him. "Pardon?"

"Gnocchi. Italian potato dumplings. We had them for dinner tonight. Father makes them by hand every Thursday. It's the only thing Father cooks, but he's good at it."

Douglas crossed his ankle over his knee.

"So, do you enjoy them?" said Nicole.

"Gnocchi?"

"Yes."

"Yes."

"Yes, meaning you enjoy them, or yes, meaning you understood what I was asking?"

"Yes. I mean yes, I like them."

Nicole Bonner laughed.

"When should I start hearing from colleges?" she asked. "It's nearly April."

Douglas was relieved at the topic. "Any week now. But you'll get in everywhere. It's all about what you want."

"I want Princeton."

Douglas imagined Nicole sitting on a dorm bed, reading, sipping soup. He imagined baggy sweater sleeves covering her wrists.

"Fitzgerald went there," said Nicole.

"Yes," said Douglas.

"He was a career alcoholic."

"Yes."

"Did you know that John Stapleton is toilet trained?"

Douglas laughed out loud, once. This usually only happened at the movies, if he was alone and the film was absurd.

"Toilet trained. Meaning what?"

"Meaning that he uses the toilet, like a human being. He crouches on the rim of the bowl and does his business and presses his paw on the flusher afterward. He's very tidy."

"Nicole," said Douglas.

"It's the truth, sir. It took Father eons to train him, but he did it. We don't even have a litter box. Father was a marine."

Douglas checked his watch. "John Stapleton's an unusual name for a cat."

"He's an unusual cat," said Nicole.

"I think maybe I should hang up now, Nicole. Why don't we talk in school tomorrow?"

"All right. I don't want to inconvenience you in your evening time."

"It's all right."

"Really?"

"Well," said Douglas. "What I mean is, it's no problem. But, um, we'll talk in school tomorrow."

"Inevitably," said Nicole, and she hung up.

Douglas had written Nicole a letter of recommendation for Princeton. In the letter, he'd said this:

> *Whether she's tearing across the field hockey grass, debunking Whitman, or lecturing me about Woody Allen films, Nicole exudes an irrepressible spirit and a generous, unguarded tenacity. She reads an entire novel every night, not to impress anyone, but because she loves to do it. She is organized, clever, and kind hearted, and once she knows what she wants, she will pursue a thing—a line of argument, a hockey ball, a band to hire for the prom—with a charmingly ruthless will.*

Douglas prided himself on such recommendations, on making his students shine on paper. It was one of the few vanities he allowed himself. When it came to crafting words, written or spoken, Douglas felt that he'd been blessed with a knack for always knowing what to say. That was why, the morning after his call from Nicole, Douglas awoke feeling flummoxed. He'd spent ten minutes on the phone with a nineteen-year-old girl and tripped over his tongue the whole time. During the night he'd also dreamed he'd been walking barefoot down a beach with Nicole. In the dream she wore a low-rider black bikini and a lovely blue scarf in her hair like Jackie Kennedy. Douglas, meanwhile, wore green Toughskins jeans and a shirt made of burlap. Every time the waves washed over their feet, Douglas scampered back and yelled: "Beware the manatees."

Ridiculous, thought Douglas. Embarrassing. He put on a smart coat and tie, and decided to give the girls a pop quiz that day.

At school, in the faculty lounge, Douglas forced himself to make small talk with Cheryl, the suede-clad mathematician. When the bell for his AP class rang, Douglas strode into his classroom with confidence.

"Mr. Kerchek." Meredith Beckermann jumped from her desk. "Jill's going to ask you to come watch softball today, but you *promised* to see our forensics meet against Regis, remember?"

"I remember," said Douglas.

"Suck-up," Jill told Meredith.

Meredith glared at Jill. "Avaunt, and quit my sight," she sniffed.

Douglas surveyed the room. His AP class consisted of six girls, the brightest lights in St. Agnes's senior class. There were Meredith and Jill, the arguers; Rhonda Phelps, the bombshell achiever; Kelly DeMeer, the agnostic; Nancy Huck, who was always on vacation; and Nicole Bonner, who sat by the window.

"Where's Nancy?" asked Douglas.

"Bermuda," said Rhonda. "Snorkeling, with her aunt."

Jill tapped her *Othello* script. "Can we discuss the last act?"

"Desdemona's a dipshit," said Meredith.

"Meredith," warned Douglas. He glanced at Nicole, then at Kelly. They spoke the least of the six, Kelly because she was cultivating spiritual fatigue and Nicole because . . . Well, thought Douglas, because she was Nicole. The look in her eyes when she stared out the window reminded Douglas of when he was a boy and he would gaze at his mother's dressing-room mirror, wondering who lived on the other side.

"Vocab quiz," said Douglas.

The girls whipped out pens and blank pieces of paper.

"Three synonyms, from Latin roots, for bellicose." Douglas thought out loud. "Two antonyms for abstruse. One example of synecdoche. Extra credit, list four books by Melville. You have five minutes."

The girls began writing immediately. Douglas watched them with fondness. They were gifted young women, and they would all conquer this class and every literature class of their futures. He passed among them, staring at their bent heads, at the roots of their hair and their earlobes, wondering how many had prom dates, how many might end up teachers, how quickly Rhonda would marry. He rolled his eyes at Meredith and Jill's papers: each of them already had seven synonyms for bellicose. Kelly was finished in three minutes, and was now drawing hangman nooses—her trademark—on all of her letter *T*'s. Then Douglas looked over Nicole's shoulder. Her paper was in a band of sunlight, and on it she had written no vocabulary words whatsoever. She was, however, busily churning out sentences. Douglas watched, then caught his breath. Nicole had written verbatim, from memory and without error, the entire first page of *Moby Dick,* and was still going. Douglas waited to see if she would run out of steam or turn her head to look at him, but she didn't. He tried to recall if he or any other St. Agnes teacher had ever asked the girls to memorize and recite Melville, but he knew this wasn't the case.

Douglas leaned down. He could smell Nicole's raspberry shampoo. He scribbled in the margin of her paper, *This isn't what I asked for.*

Without glancing up Nicole crossed out what he'd set down and wrote, *It is a far, far better thing that I do.*

"Pens down," said Douglas.

After school he performed his daily regimen, half an hour of free weights followed by a three-mile run in Central Park. He got back to St. Agnes's with just enough time for a shower before the forensics match. Outside the locker room, though, lounging on her back on a windowsill eight feet off the ground, was Nicole Bonner.

"How'd you get up there?" panted Douglas. He was winded from his run.

"Flew." Nicole sat up, studied her teacher. Douglas had a privileged view of her ankles, which were crossed and not at all blue. She wore her school uniform, and low black pumps.

"What'd you read last night?" he asked.

"*The Moviegoer* by Walker Percy. Did you know, Mr. Kerchek, that thousands of runners die every year from heart attacks in midworkout?"

"I don't think I run fast enough to induce cardiac trauma, Nicole."

The girl on the ledge didn't swish her legs.

"Trauma's an excellent word to say out loud repeatedly. Trauma. Trauma."

"I should shower," said Douglas.

Nicole pointed at him. "Give me one good reason why I should go to college at all."

"Tons of reading time," said Douglas.

Nicole jumped off the ledge, landed lightly on her feet a yard from Douglas.

"I'll accept that," she said, and off she walked.

It was three weeks later, in mid-April, that Douglas received the invitation. It happened on a rainy Tuesday, at the start of the school morning. Just before chapel Nicole Bonner poked her head in the faculty lounge, where Douglas and Katya Zarov sat beside each other on the couch. Douglas was reading the paper and Katya had just noticed a ladder in her stocking.

"Mr. Kerchek," said Nicole.

Douglas and Katya looked up.

"No students in here," said Katya.

"Mr. Kerchek, I need to speak to you privately." Nicole stood with her hands clasped in front of her. She wore her uniform, as always, and a silver bracelet with jade dolphins on it.

Douglas stood. Katya Zarov made a little snort.

Out in the hall Nicole flashed Douglas a smile.

"Princeton's taking me," she said.

Douglas had a fleeting image of hugging his student. He patted her once on the shoulder.

"That's wonderful," he said. "Congratulations."

Nicole nodded sharply. She had a Bible under one arm, which surprised Douglas.

"As a thank-you for your letter of recommendation, my parents and I would like you to join us for dinner this Thursday at our home."

"Well," said Douglas, "that's very kind, but there's no need."

"We'll be serving gnocchi that Father will have prepared by hand. I've assured Father that you enjoy gnocchi."

"Nicole . . ." began Douglas.

The bell for chapel rang.

"You told me that you enjoy gnocchi, Mr. Kerchek."

"Oh, I do," said Douglas quickly, "but—listen, Nicole, I'm very proud that you've gotten into Princeton, but you don't have to—"

"I'm reading the Book of Revelation." Nicole tapped the Bible. "In case you were wondering."

Girls surged past Douglas and Nicole, chattering, chapel-bound.

"Come on, Nicky," said Rhonda Phelps.

"Good morning, Mr. Kerchek," said Audrey Little, the horny health teacher.

Nicole cocked her head to one side. "Did you know, Mr. Kerchek, that there are creatures in the Book of Revelation covered entirely with eyeballs?"

Douglas shook his head. He felt slightly dizzy, in need of ibuprofen.

"My parents and I will expect you at seven on Thursday." Nicole stepped backward. "We live in the Preemption apartment building, West Eighty-second and Riverside."

"Preemption?" called Douglas, but Nicole Bonner had turned away.

On Thursday afternoon Douglas got his hair cut at the corner barbershop. Chiapas, who wasn't five feet tall yet, stood on a milk crate, moving an electric razor over Douglas's sideburns, grinning at Douglas in the mirror.

"You a week early, Uno. Hot date tonight?"

Douglas smirked. "Yeah, right."

Chiapas whistled a tune Douglas didn't know. Because Chiapas was only an apprentice, Douglas got his haircuts for free.

"Bet you got a date, Uno. Bet you and Grace Kelly going out for oysters."

"Uh-huh."

Chiapas knew Douglas's movie addictions.

"Ow." Douglas flinched, and Chiapas pulled the razor away. Douglas turned his head. Two inches below his part the razor had bitten his hair down to the scalp.

"Whoops." Chiapas shrugged. "Sorry, Uno."

Douglas fingered the gash. "Chiapas. Today of all days."

The boy's eyes lit up. "You do got a date."

Douglas blushed. "I do not."

Chiapas inspected Douglas's head. The cutaway hair was in the shape of a question mark without the period. "Don't worry, Uno. It's cool. She'll love it."

"There is no she," insisted Douglas.

At seven o'clock Douglas arrived at the Preemption apartment building. He wore a camel's hair sport coat, and he carried a German chocolate cake from Café Mozart. He'd thought first to bring wine, then decided it was inappropriate, since Nicole was his student.

In the lobby Douglas was met by a tall black doorman with an oval scar on his forehead. Also in the lobby, sitting in an upholstered corner chair, was a young man wearing a slick black suit and an expression of profound malevolence.

"Douglas Kerchek?" said the doorman. "This way."

Douglas followed the doorman to an ancient Otis elevator, the hand-operated kind. From the corner of his eye Douglas watched the seated young man, whose lapel was flapped slightly open. If Douglas wasn't mistaken, there was a gun inside the young man's coat.

"Top floor. Penthouse." The doorman ushered Douglas into the elevator, pulled a lever, stepped out. *"Bonne chance."*

The elevator doors closed, and Douglas was alone, moving. He glanced around. The elevator was antiquated, with mahogany walls that smelled like something Douglas couldn't place, a medieval monks' library maybe, or the inside of a lovely coffin. When he disembarked the elevator, the door to the Bonner penthouse was already open. Nicole stood leaning against the jamb.

"Good evening, Mr. Kerchek."

Douglas made an effort not to widen his eyes. Nicole was wearing the most exquisite black silk evening gown he'd ever seen. It lay along the lines and curves of her body in a fashion so perfectly tailored that the material might have been woven around her as she stood there in the doorway. The gown was exactly as black as her hair, and, for a fantastic second, Douglas imagined that crushed black diamonds and the ink of several squid had gone into making the silk. Around her wrist was the bracelet of jade dolphins.

"Hello, Nicole," said Douglas. "You look . . . really nice."

"You have a question mark on your head," said Nicole.

Douglas sneezed, twice. Nicole blessed him. A man and a woman appeared behind her.

"My parents," said Nicole, not looking at them.

"Samson," announced the man.

"Paulette," smiled the woman.

"Douglas Kerchek," said Douglas.

Samson Bonner resembled a gigantic bass instrument. He was well over six feet tall, and although his torso sloped forward around the abdomen, it appeared to be formidably muscled. His voice was resoundingly deep, almost a shout, and his eyes were black. He was a renowned lawyer of unwavering, conservative politics.

His wife, Paulette, was as skinny and straight as a flute.

"The teacher, the teacher," chirped Paulette. "Come in, come in."

They all moved inside. Samson Bonner shut the door. Paulette whisked Douglas's cake box off to another room.

"Cocktails," boomed Samson.

Douglas looked around. The Bonner penthouse was the kind of lair that nefarious urbanites like Lex Luthor occupied in films. The huge main room had a high ceiling and a marble floor. Lining one entire wall were shelves bearing leather-bound tomes that might have come from the same monks' library he'd smelled in the elevator. Also in the room were two hunter-green couches, a hearth with a fire, a glass table laid for dinner, an oaken door that opened into a study, and three tall windows. Through these Manhattan could be seen, laid out like a map on which schemes were planned. Douglas guessed that the exterior dormers of these windows held gargoyles, and he was right.

Paulette Bonner swept back into view, carrying a tray of glasses and a cocktail shaker. "Sidecars, sidecars." Paulette set the tray on an end table by the couches.

"We're a brandy family, Douglas," said Samson. "We have a gusto for brandy."

"Ho ho," said Douglas. He'd meant it to sound chipper and hale, but it didn't.

Drinks were doled out. The women sat on one couch, the men on the other. Samson Bonner wore a fine bone-colored suit. His wife, who had black hair like Nicole's, wore a gray dress. The fire crackled. Douglas sipped his drink, which tasted like limes. In his hometown, Allentown, Pennsylvania, very few drinks contained limes.

"I'm so proud of Nicole," said Douglas. "Um, you must be too."

"We are, we are," breathed Paulette.

"Well, hell." Samson Bonner punched Douglas on the shoulder. "Just because Princeton has a white-boy hoop club doesn't mean they can't compete. Am I wrong?"

"No," said Douglas, whose shoulder now hurt.

"So they're pick-and-roll," declared Samson. "So they're old-school back-door. So what?"

"We're so pleased you've come," said Paulette.

Douglas glanced back and forth between the parents. Despite their bookshelves he couldn't tell yet whether they were literary, like their daughter.

"How's your sidecar, Mr. Kerchek?" asked Nicole.

"It's brandy and Cointreau," explained Paulette.

"And limes!" shouted Samson.

Douglas smiled and nodded.

"Anyway," said Samson, "let's hear from the man." He patted Douglas's back.

A silence happened. Douglas grinned around foolishly until it hit him.

"What, you mean me?"

"Sure you," bellowed Samson. "Absolutely you."

The Bonners sat waiting, looking at Douglas.

"Well." Douglas scratched his recently botched head. "What would you like to hear about?"

"Hell, we don't know." Samson har-hared.

"You want to hear about me? That I'm from Pennsylvania, that kind of thing?" Douglas looked at Nicole.

"Nah," said Samson. "Teach us something."

"Yes." Paulette's eyes flashed.

"Teach us something," said Samson, "or else no gnocchi for you."

Douglas laughed. No one joined him.

Nicole cleared her throat. "Father's serious, Mr. Kerchek."

Douglas stopped laughing. "How's that?"

"He gets like this," said Nicole. "You have to teach him and my mother something or the evening can't progress."

Douglas gazed at his student. He saw that she was in earnest, then looked quickly away. Nicole's hair was pulled back taut to her head tonight, and Douglas feared that if he stared too long at the taper of her temples, her father, the marine, would notice.

"Um. What would you like to learn?"

"Hell, we're easy." Samson punched Douglas again.

"Teach them a word," suggested Nicole. "Something quick. I'm hungry."

Douglas moved to the edge of the couch, out of Samson's fist range. He thought of things he knew well. He thought of books.

"I suppose," said Douglas, "I suppose I could tell you why I think Shakespeare named King Lear King Lear."

Paulette looked anxious, as if Douglas were in peril.

"*Leer* is the German word for 'empty.' And *King Lear*'s an existential play. The title character ends up mad, out in the wilderness, living in a hovel, like Job. He's a man stripped down, all alone with the truth of himself." Douglas raised his eyebrows. "An empty man."

"Bravo," shouted Samson. He jabbed toward Douglas's shoulder, but Douglas stood up quickly. He poured himself a fresh sidecar.

"Empty, empty." Paulette sounded delighted.

Nicole narrowed her eyes. "You never taught us that."

"What?" said Douglas.

"We read *King Lear* last November. You never taught us about the German. About the name."

Douglas shrugged. He set down the cocktail shaker. "Well, it's just a theory I have. It's nothing proven."

"Wrong." Samson pointed at Douglas. "It's the truth. I know the truth when I hear it."

"Well," said the teacher.

"It's the truth and you found it." Samson gave Douglas the thumbs-up. "The evening can progress."

Nicole stood. "I think it's damn selfish, that's what I think." She glared at Douglas.

"What is?" said Douglas.

"You," sneered Nicole. "You, keeping your precious little theory all secret from your students."

"Now, wait a minute," said Douglas.

"No." Nicole crossed her arms under her breasts in a manner that Douglas could not ignore. "You're our teacher, Mr. Kerchek. You're supposed to lay bare your thoughts on behalf of us girls."

"Looks like he kept some thoughts for himself." Samson winked.

"It's just a *theory,*" emphasized Douglas.

"Hmph." Nicole raised her chin, which made Douglas see her neck, the shadowy knife of her cleavage. "I am absolutely disappointed," she said icily, "and I will not speak again tonight until the salad course."

"Nicole," said Douglas.

But Nicole left the couch, took her place at the table.

Samson rubbed his hands together. "Let's eat," he cried.

During the shrimp cocktail appetizer Douglas related much of his life to the Bonners. He was nervous because Nicole was moody and silent, and he ended up blurting the stories of his postgraduate year in Japan, his bout with mononucleosis, his disastrous senior prom with Heather Angelona.

"You're feeling all right now, though?" said Samson.

Douglas looked up from his salad. "Sir?"

"You've recovered, I mean. From the mono."

"Oh. Yes, sir. I had it thirteen years ago."

"Bravo." Samson wolfed a chunk of cucumber. "Look, no more of this 'sir' business. I'm Samson, dammit."

"All right." Douglas tried to catch Nicole's eye. She sat across from him, while Samson and Paulette sat at the long ends of the table. When Nicole only stared into her salad, Douglas's gaze slid to the book wall behind her.

"So, Samson," said Douglas. "Paulette. Those are some wonderfully bound books, there. Have you read most of them?"

Samson stared hard at Douglas. He let ten seconds pass.

"Douglas," said Samson. "I have read each and every one of them cover to cover."

"Really?" Douglas scanned the shelves again. "That's unbelievable."

Samson scowled. "Oh, is that what it is, Mr. Harvard? Unbelievable?"

"I'm sorry," said Douglas quickly.

"You're a contentious bastard," declared Samson.

Douglas's stomach bottomed out, the way it had in high school before his boxing matches. "Samson. Mr. Bonner. I certainly meant no insult."

"Ha," shouted Samson. "Got you!"

Douglas looked at the Bonner women, who wore thin, knowing smirks.

"What?" said Douglas.

Samson punched Douglas's shoulder. "I was giving you the business, Doug. Had to test your mettle."

"Oh." Douglas took a gulp of his wine. "Ha, ha," he said weakly.

"I shall now rejoin the conversation," said Nicole.

"Hell." Samson pointed his fork at the books. "I've never read a single one of those things, Doug. They're a priceless collection."

"They're heirlooms," said Paulette.

"Right, heirlooms." Samson chewed and swallowed. "Nicole reads them. They belonged to my ancestor, Vladimir Bonner. He was a prince from the Carpathian Mountains or some crazy bastard place." Samson waved his hand dismissively. "The point is, he was a prince, and these are his books."

"The point is, Bonners are royalty," said Nicole.

Samson slapped the table. "The gnocchi," he bellowed. "I made it myself." He glared around, as if expecting dissent.

Paulette served the main course, which Douglas had to admit was delicious. He sipped his wine, and the conversation mellowed. Samson spoke of common concerns, the mayor, the weather, the stock market. Douglas complimented Samson on the gnocchi. When Samson asked about his Allentown boyhood, Douglas mentioned the Eagle scout he'd been but did not mention the chipmunks he had killed with firecrackers. Paulette asked Douglas about his favorite films, and Douglas answered. Every time Douglas looked at Nicole, she looked right back at him. All in all, Douglas was enjoying himself. The Chardonnay settled lightly in his head, and he found himself wondering random things, like how the Yankees would do this season, how cold it was outside, how curvy Nicole had ever emerged from beanstalk Paulette. The gnocchi plates were cleared.

"Well, girls," said Samson, "let's cut to the chase."

Paulette placed a snifter of brandy before each person.

"Which chase is that?" smiled Douglas. He wiped his mouth with his napkin.

"We feel that you should marry Nicole," said Samson.

Douglas sneezed four times in a row. Everyone blessed him.

"Pardon?" said Douglas.

"Paulette and I would like to arrange a marriage between you and our daughter here. Our only child."

Douglas stared at the Bonners. They were all seated in their chairs, smiling politely. Nicole wore the look that she always wore just before she aced a test. Nobody laughed.

"You're kidding, of course," said Douglas.

"Oh, no." Samson Bonner sipped his brandy. "I'm not giving you the business, Doug."

"He isn't, Mr. Kerchek."

Douglas got the boxing feeling in his stomach again. When he was young, he'd participated in the Friday Night Smokers, weekly events at the Society of Gentlemen club. The Gentlemen were hardworking Allentowners who drank whiskey and played cards on Friday nights in a furnished warehouse. Every weekend they brought in a select crew of boys from area high schools. To earn themselves ribeye steak dinners the boys donned gloves and duked it out in a lighted canvas ring in the center of the club while the men drank and cheered. To be picked to box a Smoker was the highest honor an Allentown boy could receive, and Douglas had been chosen fourteen times to fight in his weight class. He'd won twelve of those fights, one by knockout, and he'd never had his nose broken. Some nights even now, just before he slept, Douglas remembered himself in the ring, fighting Heather Angelona's brother, Carmine. Carmine had ten pounds on him, and he was beating Douglas on points till the third round, when Douglas delivered an uppercut that jacked Carmine right off the ground and dropped him unconscious. The men in the room roared like lions. The bell clanged. Douglas remembered cigar smoke in his nose, blood on his own face, and, strangely, no blood on Carmine's. Watching Mr. Angelona revive his son with smelling salts, Douglas had wanted simultaneously to vomit and to shove his tongue into Heather Angelona's mouth.

Douglas shook his head, cleared it. He stood up.

"Nicole," he said severely. "What's going on? Is this some joke, some bizarre family hoax?"

"No." Nicole rested her fingertips calmly on the table. "My parents would honestly like you to marry me. So would I."

"Please sit down, Douglas," said Paulette.

For once her tone had no levity. Douglas sat.

"This—this is nuts," he said. "We're just having dinner."

Samson Bonner rapped the table with his knuckles. "Hell, son, Paulette and I have been happily married for twenty-five years, and guess what? My father set the whole thing up. He and Paulette's father were law partners."

"My maiden name is Depompis," explained Paulette.

"Right," said Samson. "Depompis. Anyway, our fathers saw that Paulette and I would stack up together. Well, we feel that you and Nicole stack up too."

Douglas's head was swimming. "You've discussed this? As a family?"

"Sure," said Samson. "Every night for a week."

"Excuse me, Mr. . . . Excuse me, Samson, but you don't even *know* me."

"Oh, hell." Samson swatted the air as if it held gnats. "Nicole knows you. She says you watch a movie every night just like she reads a book every night."

"It's adorable," said Paulette.

Douglas stared at his student.

"Nicole," he said. "You're nineteen."

"Twenty in September," said Nicole.

"We held her back," said Paulette. "In third grade."

"Well, twenty, then," said Douglas.

"She struggled with phonics," said Paulette.

"Excuse me." Douglas cleared his throat loudly. The Bonners hushed themselves.

"Listen," said Douglas, "you've—I've— This has been a lovely meal, but—well, aren't you all being quite preposterous? As I was trying to point out—"

"Young man," said Samson, "do you not find Nicole attractive?"

Douglas shut his mouth. He kept expecting a game-show host to spring out from behind a curtain, but none did. Directly across the table from Douglas sat Nicole in her impossibly black dress, watching him with her relentless blue eyes. For the first time Douglas honestly considered what it would be like if she were his. He thought of Lillian Marx, the last woman he'd dated, who'd adored jazz music. He imagined holding Nicole's hand, driving with her to Montauk in a convertible, the radio playing the bizarre punk bands he knew she liked. He blushed.

"Religion's not an issue," blustered Samson. "Nicole assures me that you're high Episcopal, same as we are. She admires your intellect, and you always give her an A. So, what's your problem, Doug?"

Douglas pressed the corners of his eyes with his thumbs. "It just . . . seems a little sudden, sir."

Samson snorted.

"Douglas," said Paulette. "We're really very impressed with you. Especially now that we've met."

Douglas sat up very straight. "Yes. Well. As I was trying to say, Nicole's eleven years younger than I am. Doesn't that seem . . . problematic?"

"No," said Samson. "I've got twelve years on Paulette."

"Mr. Kerchek," said Nicole. "Did you know, Mr. Kerchek, that in centuries past a girl was often married and birthing offspring by fourteen?"

"Let's not rush into any birthing," chuckled Samson.

"This isn't the Middle Ages, Nicole." Douglas swallowed some brandy after all. "You haven't even been to college."

"Well, I'm going, aren't I?"

"Of course she is." Paulette sounded offended. "No daughter of mine will be denied an education because of her husband."

"Now, hold on," said Douglas.

"Hey," growled Samson. "You can have my daughter's hand, Doug, and we'll give you some starting-out money, but Princeton's nonnegotiable. Don't try to weasel her out of that."

"I wasn't."

"No weaseling," said Nicole.

Douglas sighed heavily. "I need to use the bathroom," he said.

"Well, hell," said Samson. "Who wouldn't?"

Paulette pointed to a hallway. "Third door on the right."

Douglas strode quickly out of the room. His mind was a blur. He thought of his unserved, uneaten German cake. He recalled a teaching class he'd once taken, where the instructor had told him to watch out for female students and their crushes.

Is that what this is? thought Douglas. A crush?

The door to the bathroom was slightly ajar. Douglas was about to push it fully open when he heard a toilet flush from within.

"Excuse me," said Douglas automatically. He stepped back, surprised. Moments later the door nudged open and a black cat stepped out of the bathroom. It stopped at Douglas's feet and looked directly up at him.

"John Stapleton," whispered Douglas.

"Mrow," said John Stapleton.

Stunned, Douglas stood very still. John Stapleton nibbled briefly at the toe of Douglas's left shoe, as if testing for taste. Then the cat proceeded down the hall, disappearing into the shadows.

This is nuts, thought Douglas. This night, this family, this cat, all of them are certifiable. But the cat seemed like an omen, somehow, and as Douglas washed his face and hands in the bathroom sink, as he studied his goofy haircut and took deep, weight-lifting breaths to compose himself, he thought of Nicole. He thought of the simple silver post earrings she always wore. He recalled the Melville she'd committed to memory, the respect she had for Graham Greene novels, the merciless grip she kept on her stick when she played field hockey. Her favorite film was *The Philadelphia Story,* a tough favorite to argue against. He'd heard her rail passionately against the death penalty once during an ethics class debate, and he'd seen her hold a faculty member's baby in her arms.

"I'd like to talk to Nicole alone," said Douglas, when he rejoined the Bonners.

"Of course you would," said Samson.

"Alone, alone." Paulette smiled wearily at Douglas.

"Use my study." Samson stood up, shook Douglas's hand.

They were alone. The study door was closed. Nicole sat on a daybed, her shoes off, her calves drawn together and to one side. Across the room Douglas sat on the edge of a wooden chair, the top crossbar of which was embossed with a crest. Douglas thought that it might be the Bonner family crest, but he didn't ask.

Nicole cracked her knuckles. "In a minute I'm going to start calling you Douglas instead of Mr. Kerchek."

"Oh, really?"

Nicole sighed. "Mr. Kerchek, please just listen. I'm going to say some things."

Douglas collected his thoughts. Outside the door were a married couple on a green couch, drinking brandy, perhaps petting John Stapleton. In the study with him was a headstrong young woman.

"Mr. Kerchek," said Nicole. "You know that I'm smart. That I can think and read well, like you could when you were nineteen. But I also know what the world is like, Mr. Kerchek."

Douglas watched Nicole. She's serious, he thought. She's deadly serious.

"I know," said Nicole. "I know how long people go in this city without finding someone to love. I'm young, but I understand loneliness, and how sad it is." Nicole rubbed her feet. "I know a guy in this building who ties girls up to his bed because he thinks it will cure his loneliness. That's the kind of sadness I'm talking about."

"Fine, Nicole. But what does that have to do with us?"

Nicole put her finger to her lips. "Listen. I know I can be irrational, Douglas."

Douglas caught his breath. He felt something in his spine, fear maybe.

"Like tonight," said Nicole. "That King Lear business. But here's something you probably don't know. I saw you at the Film Forum last week."

Douglas blushed again.

"They were showing *The Gunfighter,* with Gregory Peck. It was last Tuesday, the nine o'clock show. I saw it advertised in the paper, and I just knew you'd be there. So I went."

Douglas tried to remember what he'd worn out that night, what candy he'd brought with him. A flannel shirt? Gummi Bears?

"I sat five rows behind you and watched your silhouette. I saw you admiring the guy who played the bartender. You know, the guy from *On the Waterfront.*"

Douglas closed his eyes. She's right, he thought. She's nineteen, and she's right.

"Anyway, whether you marry me or not, this is what I want to tell you." Nicole exhaled. "It's no good, Douglas."

Douglas kept his eyes closed. He was listening.

"It's no good, the way you're living. All those weights you lift, all those miles you run, all those movies you see. It isn't right. It's lonely."

Douglas looked at her, then. He saw her curves and her temples, but something else, too, something that lived behind her eyes.

"You're a good teacher and all, but you're just killing time, Douglas. I can tell."

Bullshit, thought Douglas. Then he thought, How? How am I killing it?

"I can tell from the books you assign, the ties you wear,

everything." Nicole was not chewing her hair. "You're ready, Douglas. For *the* woman, the one you're supposed to marry." Nicole shrugged, just a little. "And I think she's me. I've dated some guys, and I know what's around, and—well, I just know what I want."

"How?" blurted Douglas. His hands trembled on the snifter, so he put it down. He felt like he might weep, but he refused to. "How . . . are you saying all this?"

"I just am." Nicole gazed at her teacher.

"Are you in—" Douglas changed phrases. "Do you love me?"

Nicole petted her neck, sipped her brandy. "Look. I've got Princeton to go to. And I've got that huge heirloom library out there to read. I'm just saying that you should have a woman with you at the movies, and she should be me. I'm ready for her to be me."

Douglas couldn't sit still any longer. He stood up and paced, the way he always had in the locker room before a fight. He wanted to shout or punch or be punched. He wanted something reliable, something he knew the feeling of. He stalked over to Nicole, unsure of what to do.

"Easy, Douglas." Nicole moved back on the daybed.

"No." Douglas shook his head, kept pacing. "No 'Easy, Douglas.' You have to tell me something, here. I'm thirty-one, and I'm—I'm your *teacher,* for Christ's sake. I mean—is this—look, answer me, now, Nicole."

"Okay," she whispered. "I will."

"Is this real? I mean, are you . . . in love with me?"

"I'm ready to be," said Nicole. "And I mean this as a compliment, but I've got nothing better to do."

Douglas stopped pacing. "I'm going crazy," he said softly.

"I'm standing here, solidly, on my own two feet and I'm going crazy."

Nicole smiled. She took his hand.

"Listen," she said. "I have the prom in a month, which my cousin Fred's escorting me to, and graduation's two weeks after that. It'll be hectic for a bit, but as of the first week of June I'm prepared to become completely infatuated with you."

Douglas laughed out loud, once, at the practicality in her voice. He thought of his mother, of Chiapas and the Mexicans, of the unbroken chain of essays that he'd corrected for the past six years. There might have been a thousand of those essays. And there might have been a time in history when all people spoke like Nicole Bonner.

"I can commute to Princeton," explained Nicole, "or else just come back to you on weekends. My family's a little eccentric, and I am, too, but—well, there it is. What do you think?"

Douglas pulled Nicole to her feet. He felt giddy, vicious. He didn't know what he felt. Like an animal he set his teeth for one last stand.

"Nicole." His voice was low, almost mean.

"Yes?"

"I'm—I'm only going to ask you this once more."

"All right."

"If you're kidding about all this, and you tell me tomorrow that you're kidding, then I'll—I'll . . ." Douglas clenched and unclenched his fists.

"I'm not kidding," said Nicole.

Douglas looked out the window at New York City. He looked back at Nicole.

"You're sure?"

Nicole reached up, trailed one hand lightly over Douglas's haircut.

"Domestic short hair," she whispered.

Douglas took both her hands in his. He was beaming. He felt slightly nauseous. "All right. All right, if you're serious, then I want you to do something for me."

Nicole frowned. "No sex till we're hitched. A kiss, maybe."

"Be quiet and listen." Douglas's voice quavered with pleasure. "I don't want you to kiss me. I want you to hit me."

"What?"

Douglas couldn't keep the grin, the old, triumphant sass, off his face.

"I want you to punch me in the stomach as hard as you can."

Nicole stepped away. "You're insane."

"No." Douglas took her by the shoulders, squared her off facing him. "Trust me. If you do this, I'll know that we're—I'll just know."

Nicole laughed, just a little. "You're a freak."

"Hit me."

Nicole angled her head to one side. "You're serious."

"Give me your hand."

Nicole held out her right palm.

"Make a fist. No, like this, with your thumb outside. Good."

"How do you know how—"

"Shut up and hit me." Douglas sneered at her. "Come on. Let's see what you got."

A wicked joy stole over Nicole's face. "You better watch it."

"Hit me."

"I'll do it, Douglas," she warned.

"Go ahead."

Nicole drew her fist back to her hip. Her eyes checked the door that was hiding her parents. She looked to Douglas as if she would erupt with laughter, or something else, something he couldn't predict.

"Come on, punk," Douglas dared her, and that was it. Nicole shot her fist forward and showed him what he, what the both of them, were in for.

Serendipity

Leonard Bunce wanted one woman, but he planned to use another. Leonard worked in Manhattan, as a lawyer for Spuck and Hardison. The two women were paralegals for the firm. The woman Leonard wanted was Hannah Glorybrook, and the one he planned to use was Alison Shippers.

Alison was five foot three and thirty-five years old. She was plump, busty, and strong in her body, but shy around men. She'd grown up in Maine, and she looked built for lighthouse keeping or work in a cannery. She had an apartment in Gramercy Park, and she wore suits to the office that did not capitalize on her womanhood. On Thursday nights Alison treated herself to sushi, her one urban indulgence, then gave herself a mudpack and watched television. On Saturday nights Alison wept herself to sleep.

Hannah Glorybrook worked two cubicles away from Alison. Hannah was a blond, graceful five foot seven, with sharp cheekbones and a come-hither gap between her two front teeth. She was twenty-six, and an only child. Her mother was dead, her skin was perfect, and her father owned Glorybrook Perfumes and Cosmetics, an expensive, successful line of products sold in New York and Paris. Hannah had the kind of body for which such goods are forged. Whether she had tousled hair or pigtails, whether she wore a gown or a rain slicker, Hannah charmed the streets of Manhattan. She consented to the trap of her good looks and trimmed herself daily in black seductions: berets, dresses, thigh-high stockings, buttoned-up vests. Hannah held a degree in political science from Tufts, and she was rich from her father's most famous perfume, Serendipity, which she wore daily. She'd worked six months at Spuck and Hardison, where she did her paperwork, then read novels at lunch. At night and on weekends she drank beer and wore sixties-style black-rimmed glasses that made her look savvy and feline.

Meanwhile, Leonard Bunce was a bitter bachelor. He was forty-three. In high school he'd collected trophies in quiz-bowl contests. He aced college, won a Rhodes scholarship, and was now one of Spuck and Hardison's premier trial lawyers. Leonard's bitterness, however, didn't rise from intellectual condescension. It stemmed from a giant birthmark on his right temple. This birthmark was a red, raised splash of skin that made it seem as if Leonard's brains were exploding out of his skull and leaking down into his right eye. Leonard hated his birthmark, and the women and friendships he was sure it had cost him, the privileges and challenges it afforded him. It nauseated Leonard to stare into a juror's eyes and see sympathy for his client building or dying as a result of his own visage. It sickened Leonard to believe that Hannah Glorybrook, the bombshell on the fourth floor, would never lavish her ecstasies upon him because of a physical branding he couldn't control. Whether the world, and women in particular, deserved Leonard's suspicions or not didn't change Leonard's demeanor. He curled his lip at beauty and truth, always wanting to conquer and wield them, never confident that he could.

Every evening, hands deep in his pockets, Leonard stalked the streets of midtown, craving half the women that passed him. He lusted after young mothers with wholesome hips, college girls in miniskirts, skinny models on billboards. At night, alone in his apartment, with his fists clenched, Leonard watched films with Ann-Margret, Raquel Welch, and Katharine Ross. It seemed to Leonard that God had created women for men to squeeze and spend money on, and that if only a man could be well paid and free of blemish, the graces of women were his to hunt and gather. The woman Leonard most wanted to squeeze, the one whose graces he most wanted to tap, was Hannah Glorybrook. However, out of livid conviction in his shortcomings and a basic desire to get laid, the woman whose desk Leonard approached was Alison Shippers.

"Ms. Shippers," said Leonard, "have you finished the Kowalski brief?"

Alison looked up. She had a round face with obvious features, like a man-in-the-moon caricature. Also, she wore a white blouse with a gold pin on the bust. The pin was a heart on a stick.

"Almost, Mr. Bunce."

Leonard checked his eyes east and west, scanning for eavesdroppers.

"Ms. Shippers," said Leonard, "will you join me for dinner tonight?"

Alison blushed. "Why, Mr. Bunce . . ."

She's got a pent-up, New England libido, thought Leonard. She'll fuck me like a sex-starved rabbit.

"Duranigan's at nine o'clock," he said. Two cubicles away he could see Hannah Glorybrook's neck and shoulders. Peeking out from under Hannah's dress was an indigo bra strap.

At promptly nine that evening Alison and Leonard dined at Duranigan's Restaurant on Madison Avenue. Alison wore perfume that smelled of berries and a tasteful white dress that came to her calves. She smiled meekly through her lobster cocktail and osso buco, while Leonard eyed her sturdy biceps.

"You played sports in college?" he guessed. "Rowed crew, maybe?"

"You must be psychic, Mr. Bunce."

By eleven-thirty that night Leonard had Alison alone in her apartment, where he filled her with wine and asked her questions. By twelve-thirty Leonard had his face in Alison's thighs.

"Why, Mr. Bunce," breathed Alison. She wondered if she'd done particularly good work on the Kowalski brief.

Leonard kept himself wedged where he was, flicking his tongue out at Alison like a serpent. He glared up at her torso, her pink brassiere. When he satisfied a woman this way, no talking was necessary. Alison couldn't witness his birthmark, and he, unable to see her face, could pretend she was a slender, conquered Barbarella.

At work the next day Alison made eyes at Leonard. She brought him coffee and touched his wrist.

"I'll make you dinner tonight," she whispered.

Gullible cow, thought Leonard.

Hannah Glorybrook strolled by, wearing high heels and a plaid Scottish miniskirt.

Leonard smiled thinly at Alison. He could still smell her awful berry odor.

"Dinner it is," he said.

It went on for a month. Leonard spent his days trying to approach Hannah Glorybrook, to find some pretext to speak to her. But whenever he got close to her cubicle, Hannah made some unconscious feminine adjustment—smoothing the lap of her dress, tucking her hair behind her ear—and Leonard's heart seized up, and he touched his birthmark and walked away. After such moments Leonard tried every means possible to expend the energies that Hannah stirred in him. He crucified his opponents in court, then waged war on the body of Alison Shippers.

On a warm Thursday night in August, Leonard Bunce was at Cherrywood's Lounge on Forty-second Street, taking the night off from Alison's meat loafs and thick ankles. Cherrywood's was a cozy bar that featured fine Scotches and live storytellers. It was the kind of dimly lighted establishment, Leonard thought, where a man could drink alone and have his place.

Leonard ordered Glenfiddich over ice, and sat in a booth, his birthmark toward the wall. He was well into his second Scotch when a smell reached his nose that had no trace of berries. Leonard looked up.

"Well, well, well," said Hannah Glorybrook. "Lenny Bunce."

Leonard's face creased with pleasure. Holding a pint of

Guinness and a cigarette, Hannah stood in a black shift that slit up one side all the way to her waist. She had her blond hair collected in a wispy beehive, and she wore cat-rimmed black glasses that Leonard had never seen on her. Strangely and, to Leonard, thrillingly, Hannah was barefoot and free of jewelry or makeup. Best of all, she was alone.

Hannah dragged on her cigarette, exhaled. "Hello, Hannah," she prompted him. "Good evening, Ms. Glorybrook."

Leonard stood with a fluster, banging his knee on the table. "I'm sorry. Ow. I'm sorry, hello."

Hannah slid into the booth across from him. Leonard sat back down. His right hand instinctively faked a scratch on his forehead to cover his birthmark.

"I don't really go by Lenny," he said.

Hannah held Leonard's glass to the light. "Scotch," said Hannah. "Yuck." She drank from her pint.

Leonard glanced around. Several men at the bar had looked up from their whiskey and were watching Hannah. Also glaring at her were two wives, three girlfriends, and the six single women who were lounging near the billiards table. These women had come from viewing Broadway plays and musicals, and they were adorned with pearls, diamonds, lipstick, and, to the last woman, heels.

"I'm surprised you got into this place," said Leonard.

Hannah blew smoke out the gap in her teeth. "I'm twenty-six," she said.

"You're barefoot," said Leonard.

"Yep."

"Are you meeting someone here?"

"Would you prefer that I were?"

Leonard blushed and, once again, scratched a phantom itch.

"I'll bet you're meeting someone, Lenny," smiled Hannah. "I'll bet you're meeting a sexy little trollop. A tramp."

Leonard imagined Alison facedown in a gutter.

"A hussy," said Hannah. "A harlot."

"You use a lot of big words," said Leonard.

"Only till a man vanquishes me. Then I'm docile. Pliable. Reticent."

Leonard turned even more crimson.

Hannah held up her empty glass. "I need a pint."

Leonard hurried to the bar, ordered a Guinness and another Glenfiddich. In his mind he reviewed his day at light speed, searching for whatever deed he might have done to earn this company. When he returned, Hannah was lighting a fresh cigarette.

She's staying, rejoiced Leonard. Even through the smoke he could smell the scent Hannah wore. It smelled finely of liquor, or a midnight breeze.

Hannah jutted her chin around. "These women are staring me down. They don't like how I'm dressed. They think I'm all about sex. They're jealous."

"Well, do you always walk around downtown without shoes?"

Hannah drank her stout. "Lenny, let's talk about something besides my feet."

"All right." Leonard thought madly of topics. He thought of the Certs breath mint he'd crunched down on the way into Cherrywood's.

"Do you believe in God?" asked Hannah.

"Yes."

"What's the coolest place you've ever been?"

"New Zealand."

"What's the best sport in the world?"

"Soccer."

"Wrong," said Hannah. "Hockey. Who's the most beautiful woman on the planet?"

Leonard thought of actresses he adored, a cheerleader he'd once lusted after, the mother of his boyhood pal, Johnny Wuggs. He wondered if Alison Shippers could ever be in a film, even as a supporting role. A toll-booth attendant, maybe, thought Leonard. A crossing guard.

"Time's up," said Hannah.

"Wonder Woman?" said Leonard.

Hannah laughed. Under the table she touched her foot to Leonard's calf.

"Me, silly," she said.

Leonard blushed. His hand flitted over his birthmark.

Hannah drained her pint. She leaned forward. "Don't I look like a naughty librarian, Lenny?" Hannah kept her voice low. "Like a woman who's smart but who loves men to fuck her?"

Leonard couldn't believe what he was hearing. But he didn't dare speak, afraid to break whatever psychedelic ride he was on.

Under the table, Hannah put her hand on Leonard's knee. "Who's the most beautiful woman on the planet?"

Leonard remembered his tongue, the serpent that lived in his mouth.

"You are," he hissed.

Hannah squeezed Leonard's knee. "And wouldn't you love to take me back to my apartment and fuck me?"

Leonard's loins ignited. "God, yes."

"Come on," said the paralegal. She pulled the bewitched Leonard Bunce to his feet.

Hannah's apartment was on the sixth floor of the Preemption apartment building. The building itself was a tower of darkness and intrigue on West Eighty-second and Riverside Drive. It had a luxurious, hand-operated elevator, and the hallways were lighted by wall-mounted oil lamps. Hannah's apartment was similarly ornate. Hannah's father, Gerhard Glorybrook, used his olfactory riches to fund big-game hunting expeditions across the world, and he often bequeathed to his daughter the spoils of his recreations. As a result two giant beasts, caught in the thralls of taxidermy, loomed in the main chamber of Hannah's apartment. Suspended by wires from the ceiling was an enormous bird of prey, while a full-grown black panther crouched, ready to pounce, beside a daybed.

"Wow," said Leonard Bunce.

Hannah turned on no lamps, but lighted four tall candles, one in each corner of the room. She stood beside the panther, stroking its head.

Leonard peered nervously at the candles. He figured he was in for some Tantric sex, perhaps with a voodoo theme. He pointed up at the bird, whose wingspan was six feet.

"Condor?" he guessed.

"That's a harpy eagle." Hannah wasn't smoking now. "My father killed it in the Amazon."

"Wow."

"Its cousin is the monkey-eating forest eagle of the Philippines."

"Ah," said Leonard.

"Remove your clothing." Hannah unzipped her shift.

Leonard's groin hardened. "What?"

Hannah's shift fell to her ankles. "We're going to fuck in the elevator."

Leonard's mouth went dry. Standing before him, in a black brassiere and skimpy black underwear, was the goddess he'd worshiped for six months. I'll fell her, Leonard thought, I'll take her as my prey. He stripped to his shorts.

Hannah crossed her arms, jutted her chin at Leonard's boxers. "Those go too."

Leonard hesitated because of his erection. Come on, he told himself. You're a predator. With a deep breath Leonard shucked off his shorts. He was naked.

"Good," said Hannah, "let's go." She led him to the apartment door, stood holding it open.

Leonard touched the back of Hannah's arm, stared at her midriff. He breathed her in.

"You first." Hannah patted Leonard's ass, ushered him toward the hall. "Chop-chop."

What the hell, thought Leonard. He leapt out into the hall, landed on all fours. He grinned back at Hannah and roared like a beast.

"Come on, baby," he growled.

Hannah shut the door in Leonard's face. Leonard heard the bolt shoot home. His face fell.

"Hey," he said. He was still on all fours. He still had an erection. "Hannah?"

"Yes?" said the door.

"Come out here."

"Nope."

Leonard looked to his left and his right. There were twenty doors on the hallway, and five lighted oil lamps.

"Hannah?"

The door remained closed. "Yes?"

"I thought we were going to . . . make love in the elevator?"

"Actually, I said we were going to fuck in the elevator."

"Right." Leonard grinned, waited. After a while he stopped grinning.

"Hannah?"

"Yes?"

"Aren't we going to fuck in the elevator?"

"Ha."

Leonard moved close to the door. He pressed his palms and his ear to it, like a safecracker. "Hannah? I'm naked out here."

No answer came. Leonard heard a dragging noise. He jiggled the door handle, but it was locked. There was a thin sliver of light at the door's base, and when he leveled his eye to it, Leonard thought he could see Hannah's feet.

"I've pulled my black panther over to the door," explained Hannah. "He's facing you. I've removed all my clothes, and I've mounted the panther like he's a horse."

It's a joke, thought Leonard. It's foreplay.

"My pubic hair has nestled in with the hair on the panther's back. It feels good."

"Hannah," began Leonard. "Is this a joke?"

"Imagine how sexy I look, Lenny, straddling this stiff, stuffed panther, with my perfect tits hanging naked where any man could grab them."

"Let me in," pleaded Leonard.

"I'm not pale either," chatted Hannah. "If you were guessing I'd be pale under my bra and underwear, guess again, buster. I've got a totally even tan. I sunbathe naked on the roof."

"Hannah." Despite his nakedness Leonard tried to sound suave. "This is foreplay, right?"

"Nope. It's candid conversation."

Leonard pounded with his fist. "Open this freaking door."

"Lenny? Lenny." Hannah's tone was even, reasonable. "Unless you want to walk home naked across Central Park, you'll collect your wits and listen."

Leonard stood up, paced back and forth in front of Hannah's door, his penis dangling between his legs. He glared at the door. As soon as Hannah opened it, even a crack, he would burst in and mount her.

"Lenny? Have you collected your wits?"

"You whore," hissed Leonard.

Hannah tisked her tongue loudly. "Sounds like you need a moment. In the meantime I'll rock myself back and forth on my panther, letting his stiffened back muscles thrill my naked loins."

Leonard kept pacing. He looked up and down the hall for a carpet he might wrap himself in, but there was none. He checked his watch, the one accessory left on his person. It was nearly midnight. Leonard had a meeting at eight-thirty the next morning with a wealthy, important client, Joanna Krickmire. Mrs. Krickmire, the CEO of Krickmire Stocks, was divorcing her husband of twenty-one years and expecting to pay him not a single penny. She'd asked Spuck and Hardison to retain for her their man with the blood-colored birthmark, because she expected the trial to be nasty and brutish, and she wanted appropriate representation.

"Mmm." Hannah's voice had a sexy timbre. "Mmm. Ohh."

Leonard pondered the paths across Central Park. On a warm summer night every one of them would be filled with lovers and brigands.

"Yes," whimpered Hannah. "God, yes."

Leonard stopped at the door, put his ear to it. He heard a sliding, scratching sound, like claws on linoleum.

"Hannah? Are you really getting yourself—"

"Mmm," moaned Hannah. "Not now, Lenny, I'm busy."

Leonard heard more scratching. He pictured Hannah's thighs pressed against the panther. He knocked on the door.

"Hannah," he whispered. "Hannah, let me in. Let me . . . do that to you. Please."

The scratching stopped. "Have you collected your wits?"

"Yes."

"Are you still engorged? You know, erect?"

Leonard blushed.

"It's nothing to be ashamed of, Lenny. It happens when a man hears a woman in the throes of passion."

"I'd rather see than hear you," whispered Leonard. "Let me in."

"Nope."

"Why not?"

"Because, under the current circumstances, you'll converse with me candidly. It's cruel but necessary."

"I can converse with you candidly inside."

"Lenny." Hannah's voice was a tease. "Considering the humiliation I'm putting you through, if I opened this door and you saw me naked, would you converse with me or fuck me?"

Leonard stared at the oil lamps down the hall, considered snuffing them out. "I might try to . . . consummate our evening."

Hannah giggled. "Uh-huh."

Leonard scowled. His groin throbbed. "I'd fuck you. Hard."

Leonard heard the sound of two hands clapping.

"Bravo," laughed Hannah. "By the way, you're probably

thinking of snuffing the lamps to cloak your nakedness. My stern warning is this: Don't snuff the lamps. If you do, my doorman, Sender, will appear. You don't want that."

Leonard scowled again, but sat still, his back against Hannah's door, his arms crossed on his knees. He'd heard the rumors about the Preemption's doorman.

"Also," said Hannah, "don't try to summon the elevator. It's closed between midnight and one."

"What do you *want*?" said Leonard.

"You mean, what are my demands. When a person takes another person hostage, she's expected to have demands."

"I'm not your hostage. I could get up and walk out anytime."

Hannah laughed again. "Lenny, Lenny, Lenny."

Leonard closed his eyes. He wasn't strong enough to fight muggers. He could smell Hannah's perfume from under the door.

"Fine," he muttered. "I'm your hostage."

Inside the apartment Hannah really was naked, straddling the black panther. She really was deriving pleasure from the animal between her legs. But what thrilled her even more, what had both her groin and her mind tingling, was the animal she had trapped outside.

"I want to relay some information," she told him. "I want to ask some questions."

Leonard's erection had faded. Now he had to go to the bathroom.

"First of all, I'd like you to know an interesting fact. My father, Gerhard Glorybrook, killed both of these animals, the harpy and the panther, on big-game hunting trips."

"Fascinating," sighed Leonard.

"Not really. The fascinating part is this. In both cases he wasn't hunting that particular animal when he killed it. He was lion-hunting in Africa when he killed the panther, and he was crocodile-hunting in the Amazon when he bagged the harpy."

It occurred to Leonard that perhaps Hannah was building a riddle for him, and that if he solved it, he could have her. "Am I supposed to ask why your father changed prey?"

Hannah clapped her hands again. "Good deduction, Lenny."

Leonard's ass was sore, but his groin was once again hopeful.

"The thing is, Lenny, my father, Gerhard Glorybrook, didn't change prey at all. He was in the process of tracking the lions and the crocs when the panther and the harpy, respectively, attacked him. What do you think of that?"

Leonard searched for insight. "So he killed the panther and the harpy in self-defense?"

"Exactly," shouted Hannah.

Leonard jumped to his feet. "Is that significant? Is that the moral of the story?"

"Yes," cried Hannah.

Leonard smiled, breathless. "So will you open the door?"

"Hell, no." Hannah cleared her throat. "We're just starting to converse."

Leonard cursed under his breath. He dropped himself back to the floor.

"Lenny?"

Leonard didn't answer. He considered urinating on Hannah's door.

"Lenny? Hello? Is there a naked lawyer in the house?"

"What," said Leonard evenly.

"I'd like to pose a question."

Leonard heard the panther move closer to the door.

"Me and my nakedness are only two feet away now, Lenny."

"I have to go to the bathroom," said Leonard.

"Well, hold it, buster. Here's my question. Do you know what line of business my father's in?"

Leonard stared at the lamps on the walls. He wondered if, rather than snuffing the lamps, he could spread their oil down the hall and start an inferno. Naked husbands and wives would teem out of their apartments and Leonard wouldn't be alone.

"Would you care to hazard a guess?"

Leonard sighed. "He's a butcher. He sells panther meat."

Hannah laughed. "Sarcasm. Breezy sarcasm. I knew Alison must have a reason for letting you fuck her."

Leonard caught his breath.

"Oh, yes, Lenny. I know about your little romps. I also know that Ms. Shippers is in love with you, and that you could care less about her."

The door one apartment down from Hannah's opened. A man wearing blue jeans stepped out.

"Yah," squeaked Leonard. He cupped one hand over his groin, the other over his birthmark. His face pulsed.

The man yawned, looked up and down the hall. When he noticed Leonard, he laughed.

"Not again." The man shook his head.

Leonard stayed on the ground, but renewed his pounding on the door. "Hannah, for God's sake, let me in. There's a guy out here."

"Uncle Walter?" called Hannah.

The man winked at Leonard. "Hi, honey," he yelled.

"Lenny, it's my uncle Walter," explained Hannah. "He lives next door."

"Jesus Christ," said Leonard.

"Later," yawned Walter. He hitched his jeans, went back inside, shut his door.

Leonard closed his eyes. "Hannah, please let me in. I'm sorry if I did something to make you dislike me, but please let me in. I'll get my clothes and leave."

"Walter's a hot-dog salesman," said Hannah. "He got me this place for wicked cheap."

Leonard kept his eyes closed. He understood now that he wasn't going to be shown mercy. He wondered if Hannah treated all men this way, or if she fixed her wrath only on scar-faced ogres. Watching the red pepper sparks behind his eyes, Leonard tried to ignore the womanly scent coming to him from under the door.

"Hannah, what'd your uncle mean by 'Not again'?"

"Let's get back to my father. I'll give you three guesses as to what he does for a living. If you guess right, you can come in and fuck me."

"Yeah, right."

"I mean it. Cross my tits and hope to die."

Leonard's blood sang. "Really?"

"Sure. You'll never get it, though."

Leonard crossed his legs like a guru, thought hard.

"He's a lawyer," guessed Leonard.

"God, no. My father's no pussy."

"Excuse me?"

Hannah coughed. "It's chilly in here from my air-conditioning. My nipples are firming up. Can you imagine how firm they're getting, Lenny?"

From Walter Glorybrook's apartment came a female giggle. Leonard glared around, his thoughts of arson returning.

"Anyway," said Hannah, "where was I?"

Leonard folded his arms. “Lawyers were pussies.”

“Well, you’re a pussy, anyway.”

“Is that right.”

“You’re supposed to be all dauntless in court, but you spy on me like a schoolboy.”

“I do not.”

Hannah snorted. “I feel your eyes, Lenny. Following me, ripping off my outfits.”

Leonard scowled. In the movies men did the impossible. They battered down locked doors with their shoulders.

“You’re a pussy, Lenny. You don’t have the balls to talk to me, so you’re humping poor Alison.”

Leonard thought of Alison’s toenails, which she’d painted to please him. He winced.

“Maybe Alison’s enjoying it.”

“Why don’t you ever talk to me? Do you think I’m a dumb blonde?”

“No.”

“I got a fourteen fifty on the SATs. Seven fifty on the verbal.”

Leonard sighed. In the morning, with any luck, he’d be helping Joanna Krickmire maneuver her husband into roughly the same position that he was in now.

“Congrats,” said Leonard.

“My theory is, you’re insecure about your scar.”

Leonard’s shoulders stiffened. “It’s not a scar. It’s a birthmark.”

“You look like Frankenstein’s monster,” said Hannah, “and you feel lousy about it.”

Leonard was shocked. What with political correctness he hadn’t received a direct insult about his birthmark since high school.

"Ms. Glorybrook," he began, "I take bitter offense to—"

"Oh, shut up. Why not cash in on your freakhood? You know, play the misunderstood monster. Women love that shit. Let's try it out, Lenny."

Leonard thought of Hannah's tits, her hips, her knees gripping the panther. He adjusted himself so his penis wasn't touching the floor.

"Let's try what out?"

"We're in a bar. I'm the hottest chick in the place. You've just walked up to me. I'll begin." Hannah made a startled sound. "Ooooh, what happened to your face?" Her voice was laced with drama now, extra girlish.

Leonard's hand flew to his temple. "I have a birthmark."

"No." Hannah sounded furious. "Clever, Lenny. If you want to score a woman, you have to talk clever. You have to say just the right things. And quit covering your forehead."

Leonard turned his head, stared at the door. Hannah's scent was strong in his nostrils. He told himself that it was nothing magic. But she'd somehow known—she'd sensed—what he was doing.

"Ooooh," repeated Hannah, "what happened to your face?"

Leonard's mind whirled. "Motorcycle accident."

"Ooooh," crooned Hannah. "Where'd it happen?"

"Pittsburgh."

"Boring," said Hannah, her voice lapsing to normal.

"Ireland."

"Oooooh."

"The roads are narrow there. Lots of blind curves." Leonard had his eyes closed. "I was driving along the coast, near the cliffs, when a touring van broadsided me."

"How terrible." Hannah sounded intrigued.

Leonard roamed the black behind his eyes. The lying was erotic.

"A child in the van was killed," fantasized Leonard.

"Oh, no."

"A little boy named Seamus. He wasn't wearing a seat belt."

"Oh, God."

"They have less strict seat-belt laws overseas."

"Boring," said normal Hannah. "Circumstantial."

"I attended the funeral for the boy. In Kilkenny."

"How sweet of you."

"The family welcomed me. They knew I wasn't responsible. Seamus's kid sister sang a dirge."

"Poor little Seamus."

Leonard opened his eyes. He'd run out of words.

"See, Lenny?" said Hannah. "It's easy."

Leonard bit his lip. "You think I'm being cruel to Alison?"

"Yep. But she's bound to realize what a beast you are."

"Oh, I'm a beast?"

"Sure. But don't worry about it, Lenny." Hannah's voice had dropped an octave. "That's sex. Beastly, cruel, and necessary."

Leonard had an erection again. He turned and knelt close to the door.

"Is that what *this* is?" he whispered. "Sex?"

"I told you," Hannah said coyly. "Only if you guess what my father does."

Leonard's mind darkened. He was frustrated, sick of banter. He thought of Gollum and Rumpelstiltskin, of guessing games with grave stakes.

"Weapons," he threw out. "Your father sells weapons. For hunting."

"Nope." Hannah drew in a breath. She sounded suddenly excited. "Well, wait. Wait a minute. In a figurative sense he does."

Leonard thumped the door, his heart drumming.

"Let me in," he hissed. "I win."

"Uh-uh." Hannah's voice was thrilled but firm. "You only have one guess left. You have to say exactly what my father makes and sells. You have to get it just right."

Leonard's cock ached. "You'll keep your promise if I do?"

There was silence. The fooling was over.

"Yes," whispered Hannah. "I'll keep it. But you'll never get it."

Leonard stood and paced. He didn't want contention. He wanted to know what Hannah was thinking, whether she was anxious, how attracted to him she really was. He was stripped, in need, and tonight was about beating strange, terrible odds. He stared at the door.

"You'll really have me?" he said.

Hannah giggled. "Monster, monster, at my door."

Leonard stalked back and forth. His lust was immense, his wagging penis ridiculous. He thought of Hannah's girlhood, of pink icings and jealousies, wondering what her father could have been doing to sustain her through all that, to rear her into what she was now. Leonard stroked his face, felt the night crushing in around him, coming to a head.

"Come on, buster," said Hannah. "Guess. What's he sell?"

Leonard Bunce stopped before the door. There was flair coming at him in Hannah's voice, flair and vicious daring. But there was something else coming at Leonard, and for the first time that night he tuned everything else out and honed in on this thing: Hannah's smell. It was more than a smell, though. It was a musk, an assault on the senses. It had been leaking out around Leonard all night, surrounding him like vaporized honey, or warm limbs, or sweet breath. Leonard realized that this scent was something that was with Hannah always, something that she put on, and radiated, and gave like an inheritance to the world around her. Leonard stood still and breathed in this sweetness that, offered or not, was coming to him. He understood that the musk, the element around him, was worldly, costly. He let it fill him until he forgot his office, his apartment, Cherrywood's Lounge, Central Park, all the sad haunts where he refused to end up tonight. His birthmark tingled like a sixth sense, a dormant gift that was finally waking. He filled his lungs, triumphantly.

"Perfume," he said.

Telling It All to Otis

At the end of a century, in the city of New York, there lived a young man named James Branch. He was slender and quiet, with sleepy blue eyes and straight teeth, and he lived in the Preemption apartment building. James worked on Wall Street, as an accountant for Harrow East, a financial juggernaut stock company. At Harrow East and elsewhere during the day, James spoke to almost nobody. At night, though, James talked to Otis, the elevator in the Preemption. He didn't talk to any elevator operator or any elevator passengers. He talked to the elevator itself.

Ever since he'd been little, being silent around others had made sense to James. An only child, he'd grown up in northern

Minnesota, in a small town called Morris, where his daily options had been hockey or homework. Ruthlessly shy and in possession of a severe stutter, James had chosen his bedroom and his books over the company of his peers. Throughout his childhood he had a succession of private speech tutors—all men, all American—who failed to unlock James's thickly crippled tongue. Each tutor lasted around six months and was then sent away. James was content to see them go. In high school, while other Morris boys studied beer and sex and fishing, James sat cross-legged on the floor of his bedroom, rocking back and forth, mastering calculus and memorizing tax laws so he could help his father with write-offs.

James's parents lived in a drafty, ramshackle mansion that had once been the country home of a rich Chicago industrialist. By the time the Branches owned it, the mansion was nearly condemnable, with dubious floorboards and poor insulation, but James's father adored the place, and when he put candles in the windows at Christmastime, the mansion became stately and grand. As for James, he cared little for Christmas or any festivity. What he loved was the mansion's old but functioning dumbwaiter, which ran from the attic to the cellar, with stops in several rooms, including James's. Large enough to hold a grown man and operable from the inside, the dumbwaiter served as James's childhood fort, his cubbyhole for naps, and his stash for racy books. In adolescence, when his stutter put an ever-growing distance between him and any friends, James used the dumbwaiter like a monastic cell. He took a lantern inside with him, pulleyed his way to the attic, and stayed in the dumbwaiter for hours. By lantern light, he pored over his calculus books, loving the numbers that, unlike people or his tongue, could be relied on never to play cruel tricks on him. Sometimes James merely closed his eyes and rocked back and forth, smelling the wood of the dumbwaiter's walls, telling himself he was happy.

Beginning when he was fourteen, James was obliged, three evenings a week, to meet with a young woman named Anamaria. She was a speech pathologist, hired by James's parents for her alleged rapport with introverts and for her classically Latin good looks. Mr. and Mrs. Branch hoped, in one swoop, to cure their son of his addled tongue, his seclusion from girls, and his obsession with the rickety dumbwaiter.

To an extent the Branches' plan worked. Though Venezuelan by heritage, Anamaria spoke clear, lovely English. Unlike James's male tutors, who'd conducted James's lessons at the kitchen table or in the living room, Anamaria ushered herself into James's bedroom and shut the door. She sat cross-legged on the floor while, several yards away, James perched cross-legged in the open door of the dumbwaiter. As Anamaria rounded words out in her mouth or curled them off her tongue, James heard traces of her girlhood, the labor and frustrations she'd endured in learning English. In time James came to trust the sounds that issued from Anamaria's lips. He emerged from his dumbwaiter and sat on the floor of his bedroom opposite her, his knees touching hers. He concentrated, and breathed the way she wanted him to breathe, and he came to mimic her English so perfectly that he even picked up her foibles: the Spanish lilt of her vowels, the flair of her consonants.

Not surprisingly, James fell in love with Anamaria. She wore open-collar white blouses, and a crucifix necklace, and when she leaned forward, James could smell a light, private heat coming from her charcoal-colored hair. If he spoke just right and pleased her, Anamaria would smile and lay her palm against his cheek and say, "Yes, Señor James. Yes."

To his parents' chagrin James did not begin speaking more

in public. In fact, he spoke less, nodding answers to his teachers, muttering a syllable or two to relatives. By his junior year in high school—his third year with Anamaria—his stutter was all but conquered, but nobody would have known it. James noted the looks of pity on the faces of Morris adults, but he didn't care. His speech was a secret, an art, an intimate gift he wanted to share only with Anamaria. James was handsome, and there were girls in his school who would gladly have consorted with his quiet blue eyes. But they were simple girls, James thought, girls with nervous giggles and Midwest accents and concerns about their weight. Anamaria was different. She was a woman. She had wonderfully full hips, a nonchalance about her body, and a dark, reverent mood in her glances and in her speech that made James wish to travel with her, to cities far away from Minnesota, where he and Anamaria could pursue a breathless, impossible romance.

Alone in his room at night, many hours after Anamaria had finished tutoring him and left the house, James would rise from bed and crawl into the dumbwaiter, close its door, and suspend himself between floors of the house. In this utter isolation James would sit cross-legged, hug his arms around himself, rock back and forth, and imagine Anamaria sitting before him. Then James opened his mouth, and with a fluency no one ever suspected of him, he poured out aloud to Anamaria the secret longings of his heart. He whispered jokes to her, too, or bits of gossip from school, or else he thanked her for curing his stutter. Mostly, though, James explained to his phantom beloved how dear she was to him, how the cast of her voice and the curve of her shoulder made him feel like he could scale a cliff or swim in molten lava.

"Or I could just get a job," James whispered. "I'm good with numbers. I could make money for you and buy you whatever you want. You could have flannel nightgowns and Reese's peanut butter cups, or else diamonds, or beer and tamales."

At the height of these confessions James told Anamaria how he wanted to cling to her, naked, and roll across the peaks of the Himalayas—which James's history teacher, Mr. Fenwick, called the rooftop of the world—and fill her with himself and be filled by her and be so utterly happy and exhausted that neither of them would ever have to speak again.

The week before James's eighteenth birthday tragedy struck him. Anamaria announced one afternoon that she was moving back to Venezuela. A long-lost boyfriend, Ramón, had emerged from her past and was calling for her hand in marriage, and Anamaria was going home to him. She loved this Ramón. In a happy flush she told James of her excitement at becoming a bride. She told him about love, passionate, soulful love, and about how when it flared up hot between you and another person, you had to follow it and obey it. Inspired by her words, and desperate to keep her in Morris, James confessed to Anamaria his own love for her. Breathing right and fighting off his stutter, he told her about the Himalayas, and the things that were flaring up inside him. Anamaria's face fell. She laid her palm against James's cheek, patted it, kissed his forehead once, hard.

"Oh, Señor James," she said. "Someday it will happen for you too."

After that day James Branch hid inside his mind for seven years. He attended the Pratt School of Business in Manhattan, graduating summa cum laude in accounting and international economics. Harrow East recruited him straight out of Pratt and paid him lordly sums to keep their money safe from Uncle Sam. By twenty-five James was a recluse of the kind that only New York City can sustain. For breakfast each morning he got coffee and corn muffins from a bodega outside the Harrow East building. He worked alone in a cubicle each day, keeping his head down, skipping lunch. Every evening, he took a cab to Flat Michael's, a spartan restaurant in the East Village.

To get home to the Preemption, James took the subway. Out the train window he watched secret places rushing by, dark concrete hovels, and portals leading nowhere. As for his fellow passengers, James guessed at the sport and the strength in their bones if their arms brushed against his. What he liked best, though, was these people's indifference to him, their ignorance of his existence. The men on the train were on their way home from commanding the earth: they wore olive-colored suits and grim expressions. The one exception to them and their brooding silence was a street musician named Morality John, a lanky, black-eyed wraith who rode the same lines as James and sang for money. James gave Morality John a five-dollar bill at least once a week.

Meanwhile, the women on the train wore black clothing all year round, colored scarves, and boots. They were book editors, James decided, women who monitored character. James liked to study these women and imagine against their earlobes the pair of lovely opal earrings that he carried in his pocket the way some people carry rosaries. A strange jeweler had once given these earrings to James, and when he held them in his hand, James recalled Cinderella's slippers or King Arthur drawing Excalibur from the anvil. In other words, James knew that there was only one woman for whom the opals were meant, and from his shy, quiet heart he watched for her.

At home, in the Preemption, James shared an apartment with Patrick Rigg, a hotshot Harrow East stock trader.

They'd met at the cocktail party that had welcomed them both to the company, and they'd both happened to be apartment hunting at the time. James agreed to have a housemate in order to save rent money—the Preemption was ancient, famous, and expensive—and because Patrick, who was obsessed with women, left James entirely alone. It was because of Patrick Rigg, however, that James first began talking to Otis the elevator.

It happened this way. Toward the end of his time at Pratt, when he had a single dorm room, James had once again taken up his old nocturnal habit of rising from sleep, sitting on the floor, and rocking back and forth. Perhaps it was the stress of exams, or the looming threat of having to earn wages in Manhattan, but James found that he needed the comfort of his old ritual, the fixed reliability of it. The difference was that, while James still wanted to speak out the secrets of his heart, no phantom Anamaria appeared—or rather he wouldn't let her appear—for him to confide in. Also, there was no dumbwaiter to transport him into a warm, dark abeyance, to suspend him between the cracks of everyday life. James tried talking to God, but felt corny and embarrassed. In the end he muttered half-heartedly to himself, severely disappointed with the audience.

All this changed once James got an apartment with Patrick Rigg. For Patrick kept bizarre hours and had even weirder nighttime habits than James. He'd slip into the apartment at eleven o'clock with a smashingly dressed woman on his arm, scuttle her into his bedroom, and shut the door. James eavesdropped sometimes, listened for sex groans or conversation. But he heard nothing, and Patrick's door always remained closed. An hour or so later the same woman emerged from Patrick's room wearing sweatpants, a T-shirt, and a look of either great confusion or peace. She left, and then, around midnight, the apartment filled with shady characters: bouncers in muscle shirts, lanky, grinning men with Ziploc bags of hashish, and tall, stunningly dolled-up women. They were associates of Patrick's, or else his minions, and they stayed for hours, drinking gin and whiskey, whispering in corners. James could never make sense of them. The men were a crew of eccentrics, who did drugs and spoke languages. The women were beautiful to the last, but eerily so. They had dimples or moles or freckles like normal human beings, but they watched Patrick so intently or held their bodies so close to him that James wondered if his roommate wasn't a pimp or a hero. He'd planned one morning to question Patrick about his personal affairs, but on that very morning the door to Patrick's room was open just a crack, and through it James saw Patrick crouching naked before his dormer window, polishing a handgun and loading it with bullets. This was enough to make James consider moving out. Somehow he never did, though, perhaps because Patrick was faultlessly cordial with him. On many nights Patrick even invited James to come out and join the dark circus of his parties.

James, however, stayed in his room and slept. When the urge came over him to rise and rock on the floor and talk to himself, he often found that he couldn't. The action on the other side of the wall was rarely loud, but James could feel its presence. The malice of the men—their little chuckles—and the smell of the women came to James through his door and spoiled his quiet. So James fell into the habit that came to define his nights.

It started very simply on a Wednesday. James awoke in his bed around midnight, ready to rock and address the darkness. He heard the clatter of glasses and laughter through his wall, though, and decided to leave the Preemption and go for a walk.

He dressed, slipped out of his room, past the party, and into the hall outside his apartment. He got into the Preemption elevator, intending to ride it down to the lobby and stride off into the city. He put his hand on the lever and was about to push it down to the letter *L*, but he paused. Perhaps because it was late and quiet or perhaps because he was alone, James stood staring at the elevator's interior, not moving. He'd been living in the Preemption for barely a month at the time, and he'd never been alone enough or calm enough to bother looking at the elevator closely.

It was a wonderful elevator, with dim, solemn lighting. It had a square maroon carpet with just the right amount of pile beneath your feet. It had brass trimmings, and fine mahogany walls, and the floor-selection lever looked like the throttle of an elegant schooner. When you pulled this lever and chose your destination, the elevator sighed softly, once, and set you gliding seamlessly up toward the roof or down toward the earth. Beside the lever was a brass key fitted into the elevator's wall. The key couldn't be removed, even by the most stubborn child's hands, but it could be clicked to the right or the left. If it was clicked to the right, as it usually was, the elevator ran smoothly. But if you clicked the key to the left, the elevator hushed its action and came to an easy, immediate halt, without any grinding or alarms.

Everything about the elevator connoted an ancient craftsmanship and grace, the qualities of another age. Now that he considered it, James recalled that his fellow residents never spoke to each other in the elevator. They seemed to hold their tongues not out of embarrassment or estrangement—James knew several of them to be friends or siblings—but due to some unconscious respect they were paying the Preemption or the elevator itself.

In fact, the Preemption's elevator deserved respect. It was the oldest working Otis elevator in Manhattan. Installed in 1890, it had never needed replacing. The gears and powers that drove it had been engineered for perpetuity, and the only person in the building who even knew how to access the elevator's inner workings was Sender, the Preemption's doorman. Perhaps Johann Rook, the current owner of the Preemption, also knew the elevator's secrets, but Johann Rook was an absentee landlord. He was an avuncular German doctor who, it was believed, spent his time chiefly in Paris, Ghana, and the rain forests of Brazil. A Preemption resident was lucky to set eyes on Dr. Rook even once in his or her lifetime, and all that James Branch knew of his landlord was from the portrait that hung in the Preemption's lobby. The portrait showed a severe-looking gentleman with shock white hair standing partially in shadow, wearing a black tuxedo.

In any case, it had been Elias Rook—Johann's ancestor and the original owner of the Preemption—who'd overseen the installment of the elevator, and, as James stared at the chamber in which he stood suspended, he nodded at the man's fine choices. There were no mirrors or benches in the elevator. The air had a vague fragrance of wood, but it was a warm, constructive smell, like the inside of a carpenter's shop. Also, there were no stains or black fossils of gum in the carpet. There was nothing in the carpet at all except one brass placard, centered in front of the doors, which bore the name Otis.

James stared at this placard. He thought of his childhood afternoons and evenings, when he'd boxed himself off from the world in his dumbwaiter. Standing there at midnight, gazing at the floor placard and recalling the knotted wood walls of his childhood hiding place, James Branch had a strange, sudden vision. He imagined—or his mind imagined for him—the workman who'd built the elevator in which he stood. The man was tall, strong, and silent. He was a man from another century, but he had a patient face and wore a blue workshirt and dark blue trousers. The man also had deep brown eyes and brown hair, and his sleeves rolled up on his biceps. With no evidence to the contrary, and on a whim that was somehow comforting, James decided that this man's name was Otis.

What James did next was even more whimsical, or perhaps, by objective standards, simply crazy. He pulled the lever, and lowered the elevator until it was halfway between his floor—the seventh—and the one below. He clicked the brass key to the left, and the elevator stopped. Then, inspired by the seclusion, James sat cross-legged in the middle of the carpet, closed his eyes, and began to rock and speak.

"Hello, Otis," he said quietly. "I'm James Branch. I'm from Morris, Minnesota, and I had Eggs for dinner at Flat Michael's."

James waited. He wasn't insane enough to expect a response from the darkness. He was just waiting to see what he himself would say next.

"I do the books for Harrow East," he explained. "I work there with a guy named Patrick Rigg. He's my roommate too. Sometimes I need to get away from him. That's why I'm here, Otis." James rocked and whispered. "There's this guy on my train, Otis. He's a street singer. You know, a vagrant with a guitar. He calls himself Morality John. He's always staring at me when he plays his songs. They're pretty good songs, though, and I think they're originals." James rocked and thought. "Morality John's creepy, but I give him money."

It went on like that for an hour. If it had been the middle of the day or early in the evening, more people would have been summoning the elevator and James's privacy might have dissolved. But somehow either the late hour or some sixth sense on their parts kept Preemption residents away. At twelve-thirty one young woman named Hannah Glorybrook did burst into the lobby with an eager suitor who hoped to share her bed. But Sender the doorman, who always seemed to know what was afoot in the Preemption, pointed the couple away from the elevator and told them to take the stairs.

"Otis," said James, "I'm glad to have made your acquaintance. I live right on the seventh floor. I'm sure I'll come talk to you again sometime."

James opened his eyes, blinked. Around him was wood and brass, and the warm impression his body was making on the carpet. James blushed, stood, and turned the brass key to the right. He brought himself back to the seventh floor, slipped into his apartment. A woman named Donna stood on the coffee table in the living room. She wore a velvet vest and slacks, and she was singing a Billie Holiday song for Patrick and the other men. James hurried past her, into his bedroom, got under his covers. He was grinning and panting a little, like a boy who'd disobeyed a rule. He'd forgotten to take off his shoes and his jeans, and he fell asleep that way.

So James Branch had a new confidant: Otis the elevator. Every night, at midnight, James sneaked into the elevator, suspended himself between the sixth and seventh floors, opened his mouth, and testified. He talked about his sinus problems, about the New York Knicks, about how much he liked visiting the Cloisters, about the bone-crushing loneliness inside him.

"There was this woman on my train today, Otis," said James one night. "She wore a polka-dot dress. She was forty years old, at least. This dress she had on, it was like something out of a comic book. It was bright red with giant white circles on it, like a girl's dress, like Little Orphan Annie." James kept his eyes closed, remembering. "This woman was beautiful, Otis. I mean, everything else about her except the dress was very adult, her coat and her shoes, and there were wrinkles on her face, and she looked so sad. She had these dark, burnt-out-looking eyes, but she wasn't a whore or a junkie. I'm sure of it. The thing is, I don't think I would've noticed how beautiful she was if she hadn't been wearing that silly dress. In fact"—James rocked back and forth—"in fact, Otis, I don't even know if she would've *been* so beautiful and sad if she hadn't been wearing that dress. You know?" James paused. "Isn't that weird?"

That's how it went. Sometimes James was on the elevator, with the brass key turned left, for just ten minutes. Other nights he was there a full hour. James talked to Otis about his parents, about his frustrations at Harrow East, about "Never Love Another," a song that Morality John sang on the trains, a song that seemed to have been written for him and Anamaria. James spoke candidly and soberly to Otis, the way women speak to diaries. Often, as he sat and spoke, he took from his pocket the pair of opal earrings that were always on his person. He rubbed these opals between his thumb and forefinger as if they were rabbit's feet or some other talisman of fortune. Whether all this was helping him or not didn't concern James. He simply obeyed the impulse to speak to Otis every night the way some people drink alcohol or seek out chocolate or slice sharp metal across their wrists.

James's habit took shape over the course of a year, from a November to a November. He guarded the fact and location of his nightly confessions the way a superhero guards his lair.

Sender the doorman shot James curious glances, but he held his tongue and, without discussing it with James, told Preemption residents that the elevator was off-limits nightly between midnight and one A.M. Meanwhile, James's boss, Phillip, noticed a new, fierce introspection in the eyes of his already ascetic accountant. But Phillip found James a strange guy anyway and avoided conversation with him. Even Patrick Rigg knew as little about where James sneaked off to every night as James knew about what transpired between Patrick and the women who frequented his bedroom. All in all, nothing threatened James's ritual or the insular room of his thinking until December 21, 1999.

On that night Patrick Rigg was kicking off what he called the Millennial Solstice Debauchery Spree. This was to be a ten-night-long bacchanal celebration headquartered in Patrick and James's apartment. Patrick, who was uncommonly wealthy, had also rented out his favorite Manhattan haunts for certain nights of the Spree. For one hundred of Patrick's associates there would be a dinner served on the twenty-third at Duranigan's Restaurant on Madison Avenue, a cocktail and storytelling night on the twenty-sixth at Cherrywood's Lounge, an evening at the Lucas Theater on the twenty-ninth, and a New Year's Eve Rave at Minotaur's Nightclub. Every night that one of these functions wasn't under way, the door of the Preemption would be open to any of Patrick's thuggish chums or femmes fatales who wished to mingle in Patrick and James's apartment. Through whispers or perhaps telepathy Patrick had promised these men and women ten days of the finest company, champagnes, and carnal delights the city had to offer.

At eleven P.M. on the twenty-first, Patrick emerged from his bedroom and sat James down in their kitchen.

"You want a beer?" asked Patrick.

"Not really," said James.

"Have one anyway."

Patrick pulled a cool bottle from the fridge, gave it to his housemate. Patrick was drinking what he always drank, an old-fashioned with Old Grand-dad whiskey and two spoonfuls of sugar. He also wore a finely tailored black suit, and he grinned, James thought, the way a hyena might.

"Here's the deal, Branch," said Patrick. "There's going to be some serious festivities around here, starting tonight."

"Okay," said James.

Patrick scowled. He didn't like to be interrupted. "I want you to be part of the action."

James nodded noncommittally.

"I want you to stop brooding. I want you to talk to some chicks and drink some alcohol."

James sipped his beer.

Patrick handed James four tickets, each slightly larger than a business card. The tickets were identical to one another, pure black, with the letters *Spree* written on one side in silver sheen cursive.

"For Duranigan's, Cherrywood's, the Lucas, and Minotaur's," said Patrick.

"Hmm." James pocketed the tickets.

"Those things are hot property, my friend."

"Okay. Um, thanks."

Patrick patted James's shoulder like a guidance counselor. "For the next fortnight you're in my corps. All right? You know how long a fortnight is, Branchman?"

"A fortnight is two weeks," sighed James.

Patrick laughed his tinny, eerie laugh. "That is correct," he said.

James heard a thump and a creak in Patrick's bedroom. The creak sounded like the boxspring of a bed.

"What's that?" asked James.

"That is nothing," said Patrick.

The guests arrived at midnight. It was only a Tuesday, and not even Christmas yet, but spirits were high. Like Patrick most of the men had packed themselves into suits, and they swept into the apartment bearing bottles of Old Grand-dad for their host. James sat on the couch, nursing the same beer he'd held for an hour, watching the cast of the next two weeks take shape. There was Henry Shaker, who worked at FAO Schwarz and who had one giant, united eyebrow. Wrapped in a white scarf that he refused to remove was Tony DiPreschetto, the surprisingly down-to-earth cellist, and with him was Jeremy Jax, a crabby actor. Two Iranian gentlemen sat beside James on the couch. They ate Toblerone chocolate and wouldn't reveal their names.

James noticed that none of Patrick's male friends ever had dates, except for a man named Checkers, who was part of Checkers and Donna, a notorious couple. Loads of single women came, though. A young nanny from Munich named Eva came, and so did Crispin, a bartender with a sharp, beakish nose. Marcy Conner, a sloe-eyed, uncommonly tall Preemption resident, drank champagne straight from a bottle. A serene Jewish girl, Sarah Wolf, posted herself beside the fish tank, and the lovely Hannah Glorybrook dropped in. Just by standing still Hannah made all the other women jealous, except for Liza McMannus, who had splendidly black skin and who, at twenty-eight, had already sold three screenplays to Paramount Pictures.

Besides Checkers and Donna the only other couple in the room consisted of young Nicole Bonner—a teenager who lived in the Preemption penthouse—and the much older man on her arm. A locally known rock singer named Freida showed up smoking a clove cigarette. She wore a red-and-white-striped candy-cane tube-suit and black boots and she told the Iranian gentlemen, when they approached her, to kindly fuck off. The real hit of the night, however, was Walter Glorybrook. He was a burly hot-dog vendor who lived on the sixth floor, and he brought to the party his trained pet ferret, Eisenhower. Both Walter and Eisenhower were incurable show-offs, and Walter took great delight in letting the ferret lap eggnog from a shot glass and scamper around the rock singer's ankles.

"Call off your beast," shrieked Freida, but Walter wouldn't, and everyone laughed. Sinatra crooned from the stereo.

"Let's play something," said Nicole. "Charades."

"Or Mindfuck," said Hannah.

"Scrabble?" said Marcy Conner. Marcy wrote for *Powergirl* magazine and loved words dearly.

"Let's get plastered," said Henry.

"Let's get schnockered," said Tony.

Eva wrinkled her forehead. "Let's get *what*?"

Nicole snapped her fingers. "Twister," she suggested.

The Iranians raised their glasses, winked at Freida.

James Branch sat among the loud, bright-minded guests. He didn't want to insult Patrick's wishes by leaving, but he felt distinctly out of place, especially when Crispin the bartender and Walter Glorybrook began arm-wrestling on the coffee table. James felt even more befuddled when Sarah Wolf, who'd appeared to be shy and pleasant, swallowed three of Patrick's goldfish on a dare. Not long after that Crispin and Walter switched from arm wrestling to a heated debate about cryogenics, and James stood to go. He squeezed between bodies in his kitchen. A drunk girl seized his biceps.

"Where's the Jacuzzi?" she yelled over the music.

James pointed at nowhere, got past the girl. He headed down the crowded hall toward the foyer, toward Otis. In his way, though, gathered around the door to Patrick's bedroom, were Hannah Glorybrook, Freida, and the German au pair. They were grinning and cackling, and Hannah held the wriggling ferret, Eisenhower, in her hands. When Freida opened Patrick's door a crack, Hannah shoved the animal inside.

"Hey," said James.

The women whirled around. Freida clicked the door shut.

"What're you doing?" said James.

Hannah showed James her teeth. "Nothing," she said sweetly.

Something behind Patrick's door squealed.

"Patrick doesn't like people messing with his room," said James.

Freida folded her arms on her chest. She was tall, and her hair curled over one eye like a sickle.

"And who are you?" she demanded.

"Patrick's housemate," said James.

The women backed off at that. They melted away into the party, still cackling.

James bit his lip and studied the closed door. He could hear Patrick's laughter in the distance, but for all James knew, ferrets could chew a bedroom to pieces inside of sixty seconds. So, for the first time ever, James slipped into Patrick's room and closed the door behind him.

"Eisenhower?" whispered James. There was no light on, no switch on the wall. "Eisenhower?"

James heard the ferret chirp.

"Come on, Eisenhower." James slapped his thigh. "Come here."

"Patrick?" said a voice. "Patrick, is that you?"

James froze. The voice was human, female. It was in the room with him.

"Hello?" The voice sounded nervous.

"I'm not Patrick," James told the darkness. "I'm James. James Branch. Patrick's housemate."

"Oh." The voice cleared its throat. "Well, then, Patrick's housemate, could you please get this rodent off my stomach?"

James took three steps further. His eyes adjusted to the darkness, and there was enough moonlight from the window for him to see what lay on Patrick's bed. It was a naked young woman. She was spread-eagled on her back on top of the covers, with her ankles and wrists bound tightly with black neckties to the four bedposts. She had honey-colored hair, cut razor short, like a cadet's. Her body had curves that pleased men and angered women, and flitting back and forth across her nude torso was Eisenhower the ferret.

"Whoa." James looked at the floor. His face burned. "Hello—I'm sorry to—um. I should go."

"Please don't," said the young woman. "I'm so bored."

James glanced up, unable to resist.

"It's okay. You can look at me, I don't care, I've been here like this for hours. Just get this freaking ferret off me."

James drew in a breath. He had virtually no experience with naked women. He'd only ever had one real girlfriend, a fellow Pratt student named Eleanor, with whom he'd slept a shy handful of times. Eleanor, however, never stood or lay naked before James. She always wore an elaborate, drapey nightgown during sex. The nightgown was purple and billowy, like the robe of a high priestess, and James somehow got it in his head that women, during their high-school years, were issued such gowns to be used in their future lovemakings.

"Come on, Eisenhower." James swallowed hard, moved to Patrick's bedside, reached down carefully. "Come on, Eisenhower, let's go." The ferret screeched, tried to scurry, but James grabbed it. His fingers grazed the edge of a naked rib cage, but otherwise he didn't touch the young woman. He held the ferret up for her to see, as if she'd given birth to it.

The young woman rolled her eyes. "Little bastard. Honestly, who names a ferret Eisenhower?"

"Walter Glorybrook," said James. "Apartment six-F."

"It was a rhetorical question."

"Oh." James tried not to fixate on the splendid thighs before him. He was still blushing.

The young woman sighed. "Toss him outside. But come back and talk to me."

"All—all right."

James got rid of Eisenhower. He made sure the door was closed, then turned back to the bed. He picked up a blue flannel blanket off the floor, spread it over the naked stranger. It covered her from her toes to her neck.

"You don't have to do that," she said. "I'm past being modest."

James started loosening the necktie on the girl's left wrist.

"You'd better not untie me. It might piss him off. My name's Rally."

James dropped his hands. He stood blinking down at the young woman. "You mean, it might piss Patrick off?"

Rally sighed again. "Why don't you pull up a chair?"

James scanned the darkness around him. He peered out the window at the moonlight on the Hudson, looked over his shoulder at the door. Then, calling on all the bravado he possessed, he did what Rally had suggested. He pulled up a chair. He sat down.

"This, um," said James. "This is very strange."

"Tell me about it."

"Are you Patrick's girlfriend?"

"I don't know what I am."

James surveyed Rally's wrists and ankles. "Are you sure I shouldn't untie you?"

"Yes."

"Are you being . . . punished?"

Rally shrugged. Neither of them spoke for a few moments.

"I'm not very good at talking to women," explained James.

"Don't worry. Right now, you could recite the alphabet and I'd be fascinated."

James shook his head. He took in Patrick's room, which contained nothing spectacular except for the stripped, bound woman. On the floor near the bed lay a black brassiere and other lacy trappings.

"This is weird," said James.

"You sound Spanish." Rally smiled at James for the first time. "Are you Spanish?"

"No. I, um. . . ." James rubbed his neck. "I was tutored by a Venezuelan woman in high school. She helped me get over a stutter, and I sort of picked up her accent."

"Really? How'd you used to sound? You know, when you stuttered?"

James blushed. The blanket was thin, and he could still make out Rally's hips and nipples.

"Come on, tell me."

"All right." James spoke a few lines as his old self.

"Wow. You had it bad, all right."

"Yes."

"But now you're totally cured, huh?"

"I guess so."

"And I'm totally naked." Rally glanced to her left and her right. "I thought Patrick's room was off-limits. What'd you come in here for, anyway, James Branch?"

"Eisenhower. Some girls set him free in here. I, um, thought he might . . . chew stuff up."

"What girls?"

"Hannah and Eva are two of them. And a girl dressed like a candy cane."

"Morons," sniffed Rally.

Another lull happened. James thought of Eleanor, who'd always wanted to get dressed and play gin rummy immediately after sex.

"So, what do you do, James?"

James didn't answer. His groin had already swelled and deflated once. He stared out the window, focused on the river.

"Listen," he said, "I think I should untie you. Aren't you . . . uncomfortable?"

"No," snapped Rally. "And me being tied up is none of your business."

"Sorry."

Rally had her head turned so it was resting on the mattress, facing James.

"That's all right," she said. "Apparently, it's none of my business either. He never tells me why he does it."

"This isn't the first time?"

"Nosy, nosy."

James surprised himself by almost laughing. He caught the laugh in his throat.

"Do you want me to go away?" he asked.

"I want you to talk to me. Tell me what you do."

James looked at Rally. She had high, rounded cheekbones and a finely drawn chin. He couldn't make out the color of her eyes, but he sensed there was power in them, a hard focus that matched the cut of her cheeks. James also guessed, without knowing how, that the young woman wasn't accustomed to wearing her hair short. Her face, though pretty, looked startled, as if it were as naked as her body and unused to full exposure.

"Hello? Earth to James?"

James blinked. "Yes. Sorry. Um. I'm an accountant, for Harrow East."

"A numbers man." Rally nodded. "So you live *and* work with Patrick. You must know all about him."

"I know nothing about him."

"But you party with him. You're partying with him tonight."

"Sort of. I was actually . . . on my way out." James wore a floppy flannel shirt and jeans. Inside them he flexed his forearm and calf muscles, imagining how it might feel to have these muscles constrained, bound with rope, like Rally's were. His glance drifted again over the length of the shrouded woman.

Rally followed his eyes. "Don't I have a good body?"

James ducked his head. "Sorry."

"Don't I, though?"

James nodded, still looking down.

"Patrick makes me stare at it. He makes me stand stripped in front of his mirror there and stare at my body."

James kept very still. He'd never heard a woman speak like this. He couldn't understand why she hadn't dismissed him.

"He wants me to understand that I'm sexy, I guess. So fine, I'm sexy. Right?"

James inspected his cuticles. "I should probably get going."

"Wait a minute. So, if I'm sexy, and he keeps me all naked and helpless in here while he's out there flirting, is that like some mambo turn-on?"

"I don't—"

"Is that a guy thing?"

James looked at the young woman's feet sticking out from under the blanket. They were slim, petite. "I don't know. I've never . . . tied someone up."

"Could you imagine it, though?" Rally fidgeted her shoulders, propped her head on a pillow. She peered at James as if they were study mates, as if they had a paper due. "Could you imagine trying it and having it totally rock your libido? You know, your sex drive?"

"This is really very weird," said James softly.

"Oh, cut that out."

"But—look, I don't even know you."

Rally rolled her eyes. "I'm Rally McWilliams, I'm thirty-one, I'm a travel writer, I hang out at Minotaur's. Okay?"

"A travel writer?" James sat up a little straighter. "Really?"

"Oh, brother," sighed Rally.

"I'm sorry, I just . . ." James trailed off. He thought of Venezuela, of foods he imagined Anamaria cooking for her husband. He looked fully into the young woman's eyes.

"That just sounds like a good life," he said.

Rally opened her mouth, as if to vent a grievance, but she stopped. She noticed, finally, the fact of the slender young man beside her, the lazy cropping of his hair, the slouch of his jeans. He was sitting very quietly, with his hands almost folded in his lap, and, in the moonlight, the expression on his face was one of a rare, charming distress. Rally tilted her head, took a closer look at her attendant.

"Have we met before?" said Rally.

"I don't think so."

"You're cute around the eyes. You look sort of drowsy. You know?"

"Well," said James. "Um. Thank you."

Rally laughed. "I'm freaking you right out, huh?"

"I'm just . . . not very good at talking to women."

"You said that already."

"Sorry."

They looked at each other, full on. Through Patrick's window, which was slightly open, came the sound of distant carolers or drunkards, singing of Christmastime in the city. A dusting of snow lay on Patrick's window eave.

"Hey," said Rally, "how old are you?"

"Twenty-six."

"Why were you so interested in my writing? Are you a big traveler, James Branch?"

Under his jeans James felt sweat on his kneecaps. He didn't know why he was sweating, except that the young woman's haircut was stark and lovely against the pillow.

"I used to want to be," said James.

"Yeah? Where'd you want to go? Maybe I've been there."

"Probably not."

"Maybe, though."

"The Himalayas," said James.

Rally smiled. "The rooftop of the world."

James's lower jaw dropped a fraction of an inch. He was about to recover, to address Rally's smile, when the bedroom door opened.

"Whoa." James jumped to his feet.

A body staggered through the door. In a block of light from the hallway the interloper turned a groggy pirouette. It was Crispin the bartender.

"Wheresa toilet?" she demanded. "Thissit?"

She started unbuckling her belt. Rally giggled, and James hurried over, got Crispin by the armpits. He tugged her into the hall, closed Patrick's door behind him.

"Hey, fella." Crispin leaned heavily on James, still fiddling with her belt.

"Keep your pants on," suggested James.

"Wheresa toilet, fella?"

James dragged the girl down the hall to the bathroom door.

"What's this?" It was Patrick, suddenly at James's side.

Crispin stood up, wearing a dignified expression, her pants at her knees.

"I muss evacuate bladder," she told Patrick.

Crispin fell into the bathroom. Patrick sniggered.

"She was lost," panted James, "wandering around."

Patrick smiled thinly. "You having fun?"

James peeked over Patrick's shoulder, into the kitchen, where Henry Shaker laughed into a cell phone, and Checkers and Donna were mashed against each other. James also glanced at the left breast pocket of Patrick's coat, which—James was pretty sure—was where Patrick carried his gun.

"I—" said James. "Sure. Yes. I am." His face was flushed, pulsing.

Henry guffawed into the phone, waved Patrick over. "Rigg. Come hear this."

Patrick gave James a queer look, then patted his cheek. "Good man," he said.

Patrick moved toward Henry, but cast a glance back at

James. With his housemate looking on, James didn't dare return to Rally. Instead, his breath still quickened, he quit the apartment, hurried into the hallway and then the elevator. He pulled the lever, turned the key, and arranged himself on the floor.

"Otis," he whispered, "you aren't going to believe this."

James Branch had never been a ladies' man. His parents hadn't modeled much in the way of romance for their only child. They never kissed or embraced in front of James, they never went out for dinners or movies, and James had never heard anything resembling heavy breathing coming from their bedroom. The only time James ever had a baby-sitter was one Saturday when his parents overnighted in a Minneapolis hospital to have his mother's appendix removed. James's father never slid James a porno magazine—nor would he ever have owned one—and he never pulled James aside to discuss the physical merits of Bo Derek, Kathleen Turner, Princess Di. James's mother never counseled James about the perils of sex, or its allure and dominance of American culture. She wore plain dresses, cooked pot roasts, followed football stats. All of the sexual breezes and storms of James's youth had their epicenters in Anamaria, the unattainable ideal with whom James had never practiced the fumblings of real romance, where the other person's breath could be stale or the menu could be in French.

James had had only two real experiments with the opposite sex. The first was as a college sophomore. Frustrated by his lingering pangs for Anamaria, James had gone out alone to a bar one night, gotten drunk on three sloe gins, and ended up in an alley, pinned against a Dumpster, kissing a heavyset sorority girl named Clarice. The kissing lasted about five minutes, during which time Clarice grunted repeatedly, clawed at James's trousers, and instructed him to stick his tongue in her ear. After James repeatedly refused to obey this instruction, Clarice invoked the name of Jesus Christ, slapped James across the face, and stormed away.

After Clarice there'd been only Eleanor, who occupied two months of James's senior year with her purple capes and her rummy. Neither Clarice nor Eleanor had sparked any joy, hope, or dread in James's heart. He never fought with them or for them, never danced with them, never learned to waste time with them or to kiss the tips of their eyelashes or to leave certain things unsaid.

So when Rally McWilliams came along, James was unprepared.

He saw her again two nights later. It was the third evening of the Spree, and Patrick's coterie was expected at Duranigan's Restaurant at nine o'clock. James would ordinarily have begged off, but he wanted a chance to see Rally in clothing, so he kept his suit on after work. He killed some time in Rockefeller Center, watching tourists and ice dancers. At the corner of Fifth Avenue and Fifty-first he found Morality John playing his guitar for a small crowd. The vagrant man sang in a dark, tender voice, looking straight at James.

"Somehow, all is falling into place," sang Morality John, *"and love is yet awaiting me."*

James made it to Duranigan's by quarter till the hour. The restaurant was magic for the holidays. The first-floor lobby was an arboretum of holly, white and red roses, and a simply dressed, towering pine tree. Two celestial beings, twenty feet tall and shaved from ice, stood in a marble pool, their wings reaching higher than their halos. A ruby-red carpet had been laid on the staircase that spiraled to the second floor, which Patrick had reserved entirely for his party. At the head of these stairs was a closed oaken door and before it stood a tall, bony, olive-skinned woman, whose charge it was to collect the black-and-silver Spree tickets. The woman bore a haughty Mediterranean air, and she wore a black-and-silver dress that matched the ticket colors exactly.

"Yes," she said when James handed her his ticket, and, without smiling, she opened the door.

When James passed inside, he almost reeled. Before him was the most gratuitous and lovely array of etiquette he'd ever seen in one room. The floor was a square rink of the same ruby carpet that led up the lobby stairs. In a corner, at the end of the room farthest from James, was an enormous hearth with a fire high and alive across its base. In this hearth the largest animal James had ever seen indoors turned roasting on a spit. James couldn't tell by the splay of its legs or the gold of its hide, but he guessed that the creature was some giant, imported pig. Turning the pig on the spit was a man in a white chef's uniform. He wore one large black glove on the hand that was turning the spit, and he appeared to be whispering threats to the pig, forbidding the meat to char or dry out. The spit handle itself, a brass wheel that jutted out from the hearthstones, had a circumference of more than four feet and looked like the winding mechanism of some wonderful doomsday clock.

In another corner sat Tony DiPreschetto, playing his cello, wearing a black tuxedo and his perennial white scarf. Two wine carts, complete with sommeliers, were situated at either end of the room, stocked with every great year of every great wine. Across the floor itself five tables with twenty settings each—ten settings to a side—were arranged in long, elegant dashes. Everything on the tables looked to be either silver, crystal, or edible, except for the lighted, vanilla-colored candles, and even they, to James's staggered mind, could have been twisted, flammable sticks of taffy or marzipan.

Finally, of course, there were the guests. The men, except for Checkers and James himself, wore classic black tuxedos. James couldn't recall Patrick having mentioned a black tie requirement, and the ticket had said nothing at all, but these dozens of males, with some collective urban instinct, had known to choose gentlemen's dress. Walter Glorybrook, minus his ferret, looked stout and correct at the bar. He was drinking gimlets with Henry Shaker, who appeared to have trimmed his eyebrow. Also at the bar, alone, was the sloe-eyed Marcy Conner, gripping a champagne bottle by its neck and hating how single she was. The Iranians were not in attendance, but there were identical twins from Juneau—Inuit girls named Kettle and Fife—whose father was a musical iconoclast. They stood close to the cellist, listening.

"Hey, there."

James turned around. It was Nicole Bonner, and her older guy, and Liza McMannus.

"This is Douglas Kerchek," said Nicole.

James shook hands. Douglas wore a plain, rumpled tuxedo and a bewildered expression, as if he were confused by the girl on his arm. Looking at him made James feel better.

"Isn't this beautiful?" Liza smiled around at the room.

"It's Rivendell," said Douglas quietly.

"No," said Nicole, "it's just Patrick."

At the bar James drank a highball. He scanned the crowd,

dismayed as much by the wrappings of the women as by the army of tuxedos. For tonight, Patrick's female guests had gone beyond the call of mere formality. Their dresses, almost all in shades of black and silver, fell perfectly from their shoulders or luxuriated over their hips. Eva Baumgarten was in furs, Hannah Glorybrook wore satin, and Sarah Wolf kept laying her white-gloved hand against her cheek, hoping someone would notice. There were handfuls of other women on hand, some wicked, some nervous and kind, but all of them exquisitely outfitted. James got the sense that every woman's clothing, after severe thought and expense, had been tailored precisely to her body and her temperament. There was something too prepared, James thought, too carefully glorious about these girls, about the whole room, and he wondered if he was somehow in danger.

Then James saw Rally. She was standing beside the hearth, chatting up the chef. She wore a dress the color of a deep red wine, and it came just barely to her knees. Her earrings were fine, simple drops of silver, but her closely cropped hair, against the firelight, looked even more to James like that of a cadet or an army private. He fantasized for a moment that she was in fact a militaristic woman, that she spent her days enduring some top-secret, vital, very physical training, and that tonight she was away on a lucky, rare leave. The cello played a bass note, and as James stared at Rally, he remembered the arcs of her body, the privileged view that he'd had. He thought, not for the first time, of the opals in his suit-coat pocket, of the light they might catch against Rally's skin. Then James finished his highball and, already blushing, moved to the hearth.

"Um," said James. "Hello."

Rally turned from the chef. She touched her hand to James's arm.

"If it isn't James Branch," she said.

James nodded dumbly. Rally watched him, smiling, while he prayed for something to say. Finally he jutted his thumb at the hearth.

"What is that animal?" he blurted.

The chef scowled darkly. "It's a boar."

"Well," said James. "Yes. I thought so."

"It's a boar," emphasized the chef, "and so are you, if you have to ask."

"Oh. Very good." James rocked on his heels, suffering. "Ha, ha," he said.

Rally giggled, wrinkled her nose.

Kill me now, thought James. But Rally took him by the elbow, led him away from the hearth.

"No tuxedo, James Branch?"

James's blush hadn't faded. "I guess not," he said.

"Aren't you the brave one."

Rally led James to a wine cart where no one else was standing.

"You look like you need a drink."

James accepted a glass of Frascati. He peered at Rally's wrists, looked for marks of binding.

"So," said Rally. "You haven't been to a lot of Patrick's shindigs."

James straightened his back. "I stick out that much?"

"Sticking out among Patrick's boys is a good thing." Rally yawned, turned it into a smile. "You're different," she said.

James said nothing. At the door Freida and Crispin were entering, arm in arm. Walter and Henry Shaker left the bar and bore down on these women.

"Ha—have you actually been to the Himalayas?" James asked.

Rally snapped her fingers. "The Cloisters. That's where I've seen you before. I saw you once at the Cloisters."

James shook his head. "I would remember you."

"I had long hair. We were looking at a tapestry. Of a unicorn."

James couldn't think about the Cloisters. He was wondering what would happen if he took Rally's arm and sank his teeth into it, or kissed it from her wrist to her shoulder.

Rally sipped her wine. It made her lips glisten.

"You're thinking about the other night, aren't you, James Branch? You're thinking about how I looked."

"I'm thinking about how you look right now," said James.

Rally raised her eyebrows. She'd been about to speak, about to say something smart and coquettish. Instead, she checked out James's shoulders, which were wider than she'd guessed in the dark of Patrick's bedroom. Her glance settled on James's eyes, on the kind blue wash of them, on the deliberation behind them. Rally drew in a breath.

"How's the wine?"

Rally and James both jumped. Their host was beside them, smiling, a hand on each of their shoulders.

"Patrick," breathed Rally. "Hey."

Patrick stood tall and lordly in his tuxedo. He kissed Rally on the cheek. Then he kissed James on the cheek, and stood grinning back and forth between his roommate and the woman.

"You look radiant," he told Rally. "Scintillating. Scrumptious."

Rally pulled away. "Patrick."

"Doesn't she, though, Branch? Doesn't she look good enough to eat?"

"Patrick," scolded Rally.

"Well, doesn't she?" demanded Patrick.

James had backed up against the wine cart.

"I—" he said. "I . . . suppose."

Patrick thumped James on the shoulder. "Branch here is a little shy around the womenfolk."

Rally finished her wine. "Some womenfolk find that very attractive."

"I'll bet they do. I'll bet they do." Patrick was finished laughing now. He was still grinning his hyena grin. "Rally's a travel writer, Branchman."

James cleared his throat. "I—"

"He knows what I do," cut in Rally. "James was just asking me about the Himalayas. I was saying that I've never been there, but that I'd love to go."

"Well." Patrick bobbed his head. "It sounds as if James and Rally were having a bona fide conversation. Is that what you were having, Branch?"

"I suppose," said James.

"You hear that, Rallygirl? He supposes."

"I hear him fine," whispered Rally.

"*Well.*" Patrick extended his hand, took Rally's elbow between his thumb and forefinger. James thought he saw Rally flinch.

"Ms. McWilliams," said Patrick, "you've finished your wine. Can I escort you to the bar?"

Rally sighed. "Patrick—"

"I'd like to have a private word with you, Ms. McWilliams."

"Ow—all *right*, Patrick. All right."

Patrick turned his head to James. "I'm very glad that you've come," he said evenly. Then he steered Rally off toward the bar, leaving James alone.

"I don't know, Otis," whispered James. "It's weird. Patrick gets all these men and women together. The men are handsome and the women are beautiful, but if one guy talks to one girl for too long, Patrick steps in, like a chaperone. Except that he's not a chaperone, he's a—"

James held his tongue. He didn't know what his housemate was, didn't have a word for it. He only knew that whatever power or quality Patrick exuded made him nervous. So he switched topics.

"She looked wonderful, Otis. She had on this burgundy dress, and silver earrings, and her hair looked all golden and bristly. I wanted to run my hand through it." James rocked, kept his eyes closed. "We weren't seated at the same table. She sat next to Patrick, and I got stuck between Liza McMannus and some guy from Harrow East."

James furrowed his brow. "I don't think Patrick's in love with her, Otis. That's the thing. I don't think he's in love with any of them."

It was one in the morning. There was a ticking in the walls that came on and off intermittently, and James liked to hear it. He imagined it was the Preemption digesting all that he said.

"For dinner we had roasted boar and some weird kind of port wine. It was like a medieval feast, except that Sarah Wolf wouldn't eat any boar, because she's kosher, and Liza kept asking for vegetables, because she's a vegan. I don't think they had vegans in the Middle Ages, Otis."

James kept rocking. He breathed in and out, smelling the trace of mahogany that he liked. It was warmer in the elevator than normal, and cozy after the bracing wind outside.

"I don't think Rally is short for anything," said James. "I think she's just Rally, and that's her real name."

James thought of the way Patrick had gripped Rally's

elbow, the way Rally had winced and gone off with him. James didn't get to be alone with her or even speak to her again for the rest of the night. He'd planned on trying to corner her after dinner, but when he came out of the lavatory around midnight, she was gone.

"I hope she's just Rally," whispered James.

To get to the Spree story night at Cherrywood's, Patrick insisted that he and James share a cab downtown. It was the evening after Christmas, and James stared out the cab's window at the snow-covered sidewalks, which were quieter than they'd been in weeks. The eye of the storm, thought James. New Year's will be a madhouse.

James wore a tuxedo, not wanting to repeat his underdressed, eyesore status from Duranigan's. Patrick wore a black overcoat, a black blazer, a black T-shirt, and chinos.

"Here's the thing, Branchman." Facing James, Patrick sat with his back to the cab door, as if he were in a limo. "We need to discuss something. A young woman."

James caught his breath. He knows, thought James.

"We need to discuss this chick, Freida."

"Freida? Candy-cane Freida? With the weird hair?" James swooped his fingers over his eye, demonstrating.

Patrick whinnied and nodded.

"What about her?"

"She's totally into you." Patrick had his arms folded. His eyes were green cuts of attention.

James frowned. "She's—she's never said two words to me."

"Listen, Branchman. Freida's the lead singer in an all-female band. How much do you know about lead singers in all-female bands?"

"Nothing."

"Well, I would describe them as highly fuckable individuals."

James licked his lips. He was confused.

"What?" he said.

"You know, lead singer chicks are all sensitive and empathetic deep down, because they're the songwriters for the band, usually. But they're also the front women, so they have to be brassy and sexy too. Add it all up, and you get a highly fuckable individual named Freida Wheeler who wants you to drop the hammer on her."

James blinked at Patrick. "The hammer?"

"The hammer. The mojo. She wants you in bed."

The cab stopped at a traffic light near Lincoln Center. Out the window, just ten feet away, stood Morality John, playing his guitar. The window was open a crack and James could hear through it.

"It's getting harder," sang Morality John, *"making lovers out of strangers."*

The light changed, and the cab drove on.

"Patrick," said James, "what are you talking about?"

Patrick smiled. "Don't ask questions, Branch. Don't look a gift horse in the mouth. Let's just say I had a little conversation with Freida recently, and she spilled the info. The goods." Patrick snickered.

James gazed at his housemate, at his slick, wolfish grin. Something seemed contrived in Patrick's voice tonight, as if he were a TV showman, speaking with warm, sincere insolence to a contestant.

"Just wait and see, Branchman," said Patrick. "She'll come right up and talk to you. Just wait and see."

When James and Patrick arrived, Cherrywood's was already

filled with the Spree elite. By now acquaintances had been struck, running jokes established, and secrets revealed. Everyone knew that Hannah Glorybrook walked to work barefoot in the summer, that Crispin had once taken a bath in a tub filled with vodka, that Liza McMannus, when she was seventeen, had slept with Orlando Fisk, the Hollywood muscleman. Laughter reigned, and Walter Glorybrook and Henry Shaker were inseparable chums, and everybody except James wore casual clothes.

Cherrywood's had a tradition of live storytelling, and on a small wooden stage between two bookcases stood an upholstered chair with a small microphone attached to it. What Patrick wanted was for his guests to take the microphone one at a time and tell the room a story. It had to be either very sweet or very terrible, Patrick said, and those who couldn't dream something up were required to say what they considered the worst or most wonderful thing that happened in the twentieth century. All in all, it was the kind of game that fails in most crowds, leaving the host embarrassed. But Patrick Rigg was not a man to be disappointed. He moved among his guests, and when he patted a man's shoulder or whispered in a woman's ear, that person fixed his hair or smoothed her dress, then took the stage and spoke.

Checkers went first.

"The most wonderful thing," he said, "that happened in the twentieth century is my woman, Donna Reichard. Period."

The crowd applauded, the women sighed, and Donna blushed. Next onstage were Kettle and Fife. They squished into the chair together, held hands, and sang a long, eerie song in their native tongue. After that Douglas Kerchek said the name of his favorite book, and Jeremy Jax told a joke that, to Jeremy's surprise and almost tearful delight, got laughs.

Throughout all these performances James sat at the bar,

nursing a Coca-Cola to settle his stomach. He was embarrassed to be in a tuxedo, and afraid to be called to the stage, to be forced to speak. He also couldn't see Rally anywhere. Making him most nervous of all, though, was Freida Wheeler, who, as Patrick promised, had sought James out as soon as he'd entered the room. She stood next to James now, very close to him, leaning back against the bar, flaring her chest out. Half of her face was hidden behind her sickle of hair, but her one visible eye, which disdained most men, was staring exclusively at James.

"So," she chatted, "you know how people say the sun gives you vitamin E?"

"Um," said James, "no."

"Seriously. Apparently, according to scientists and whomever, just standing outside in sunlight fills your skin with vitamin E. It fortifies the human epidermis."

James surveyed the room. He was trying not to look at Freida, because her eye was intense and because her shirt revealed a creamy slice of her belly.

"Oh," he said.

"Listen, buddy. I'm very intelligent. I read a great deal."

"Okay." James tried focusing on the stage, where the two Iranians were arguing into the microphone.

Freida took James's chin in her hand, steered it toward herself. "What I'm saying is, how much sense does that make? The sun being able to fill us up with vitamins? I mean, vitamins coming from food, no problem. You eat a steak, you get vitamins. You take a pill, you get vitamins."

"I understand," said James desperately.

"Vitamins come out of objects in your stomach and pass to your bloodstream. No problem. But sunlight? I'm sorry." Freida tossed back her sickle. "Unless there's some, like, photosynthesis that goes on in our skin. Which would be freaky. Do you need a drink?"

"Yes, please," said James. He still couldn't see Rally anywhere.

Freida ordered two whiskeys. Patrick Rigg took the stage, the microphone.

"My parents met on a blind date," said Patrick. "They were set up by my father's fraternity brother, Emilio Snodgrass."

Patrick's voice boomed. The guests turned toward it, and the room fell silent.

"According to my mom, my dad was a nervous jerk the first time they went out." Patrick grinned. "He hardly said two words to her, and he took her to see *Night of the Living Dead*, which completely creeped her out. Also, my dad was in love with a different woman, a beautiful blond girl, who was involved with another man." Patrick glanced at James. "My dad even discussed this blond girl with my mom, right there on their first date. But my mom, who has dark hair, by the way, she stuck it out. She watched the zombies, and listened to my dad's whining, and at the end of the night, when my dad brought her home, my mom gave him a kiss that made him forget all about that blonde."

The dark-haired women in Cherrywood's whooped.

"My parents got married three months later." Patrick raised his glass. "And so. A toast to Emilio Snodgrass."

Everyone laughed and clinked glasses, except James, who stared at his drink. He felt sure that he'd just heard a fable. He felt sure that any couple named Snodgrass would not name their son Emilio.

Freida bumped James with her hip. "Cute story."

James watched the women in the lounge. He watched how, no matter where they stood or with whichever men they were flirting, their eyes checked on Patrick every little while. They were sly little checks, but they were there.

"Hey," said Freida, "let's get out of here."

James came to attention. "What?"

Freida leaned close. "You look scared," she whispered, "like maybe you don't want to talk in front of all these people."

James breathed in and out. It was true, he was scared. He had nothing to say to the crowd, and Freida was wearing a sexy perfume that James seemed to remember smelling when he stood beside Rally at Duranigan's. But Rally wasn't beside him tonight, and James had little experience turning women away, and Freida was pushing her hip insistently into James's thigh.

"If we bolt now," she whispered, "we can skip our turns onstage."

James scanned the crowd one last time.

Be here, he begged. But Rally wasn't there, and Freida tugged James out the door. She hustled him into a cab, escorted him to the Village, fed him beers at Chumley's. Two hours later she had James in her apartment, a den with pink shag carpets, black walls, and strobe lights. She gave him more beer, then sat him on her bed, grabbed her guitar, and sang him a song called "Fuck the Buffalo." When she finished, Freida kissed James wildly on the mouth.

"Wait a minute," protested James. He was dizzy with beer, but he moved away from Freida on the bed.

"What's the matter?" whispered Freida. She trailed her fingers down James's arm.

"I—" James breathed carefully, fought down his stutter, which came back sometimes when he drank.

"I want to know what's going on," he said.

Freida nibbled James's ear. "Me and you, that's what."

James pulled free again. The air pulsed with strobe light.

"I—I mean it. Why do you like me, all of a sudden?"

"Do I need a reason?"

"*Why?*" James stood up.

Freida curled her legs beneath her on the bed. She shrugged.

"It's the millennium," she said. "You're cute."

James's legs were trembling. He felt trapped.

"Do you know Rally McWilliams?" he blurted.

Freida patted the bed. "Come on," she said. "Get in. I'll fortify your epidermis."

James swallowed. He stared at Freida's chest, at her black stretch pants, at the inviting leer on her face. This was supposed to be easy. He was horny, and Freida was lovely, but his being there had been orchestrated. James was unwilling to pass Freida off as a slut, but, as crazy as it sounded, Patrick had somehow convinced this girl to seduce him. James was sure of it.

"I have to go," he stammered.

Freida ran her hands down her figure. "Are you nuts? Look at me."

James grabbed his coat. He needed Otis.

"I'm sorry," he said.

"You can't be serious. Hey. Buddy? Hey!"

James was out the door and gone.

That night, in the elevator, James didn't do a lot of talking. He rocked and rocked, with his eyes closed, and he thought of nothing. He sat, and breathed, and felt the way his limbs and muscles came together to make him who he was. After a while three peaceful images swam into his mind. The first was of his mother, lying on the couch in the living room, reading the sports section. The second was of Kettle and Fife, sharing their seat at Cherrywood's, singing their Inuit song. After finishing they'd explained that it was a creation song, a tribal myth about how the world came to be. James thought he'd seen Kettle wipe moisture from her eye as she spoke about this myth.

The last peaceful thing that James thought of was the shape of Rally's skull. There was a funny, sloping lump to it just behind her ear, he remembered, an extra grade of bone that wouldn't have been visible when she'd had her hair long. The lump was symmetrically present on both sides of her head, so James knew it wasn't something cancerous or harmful. It was just her.

James searched for Rally at the remaining Spree events. On the nights when his and Patrick's apartment filled with guests, James surveyed the hairstyles in the room, hoping for Rally's clipped, honey-colored head. He talked toys with Henry Shaker, got to know Douglas Kerchek, even endured Freida's hawkish flirting. During the group's outing to *Fizzle,* the Lucas Theater's millennial revue, James laughed and applauded with Patrick's cronies. Each night James reported to Otis his lack of a Rally sighting.

"She might be away, Otis," pondered James. "She might be off on some end-of-the-century assignment in Europe or Asia."

What James wouldn't articulate to Otis, or even to himself, was his deeper suspicion, his fear that Patrick had banned Rally from the Spree, simply because she'd socialized with James. James knew that his housemate had handfuls of women in his thrall, but it unnerved him that Patrick might hold enough sway over these girls to puppet them about, ceasing one's access to James entirely, forcing another to throw herself at him. What exactly, James wondered, did Patrick offer these women that gave him authority over them? And what pleasure did Patrick get in return? James pictured Freida bound naked to Patrick's bedposts the way he'd found Rally. He pictured Liza McMannus that way, and Eva, and Crispin, and Sarah Wolf and Hannah Glorybrook, all of whom he'd seen slip out of Patrick's bedroom on various nights over the last year. James had first written all of this traffic off as hedonism, plain and simple, but now, during the Spree, he thought otherwise. James watched the way Patrick spoke intimately in a corner with Crispin, the way he held hands with Eva at the *Fizzle* performance. It was clear that Patrick followed some loopy, chivalric personal code, that he cared intensely for and wanted to protect each woman he befriended.

But James didn't want to think about or get to know all of Patrick's women. He only wanted Rally, and it was the first time his adult heart had ever lurched so hard toward one woman. So he needed to see her, to speak to her, to find out if the clutch in his stomach would ever stand down while she was beside him. What frightened James was the thought, the diabolical possibility, that Patrick had sniffed all of this out, that he would push a random, sexy distraction like Freida at James just to keep him from pursuing something wonderful, maybe even honorable, with Rally.

"Is he jealous, Otis?" said James.

The darkness said nothing.

"He must be jealous," whispered James.

There was a new order in James's blood. He rocked inside Otis, and caught himself holding his breath. He realized that he'd rather be impaled on the Chrysler Building spire than think about Rally ever returning to her naked, bound place in Patrick's bedroom.

Jesus, thought James. Am I in love?

New Year's Eve answered the question. James showed up, black ticket in hand, at Minotaur's Nightclub in the meat-packing district. He'd never been to a rave before, and he'd never been to Minotaur's, but he remembered Rally saying she hung out there, so he risked it. He wasn't prepared for the club's dark indulgences, its maze of cubby rooms, its bars with steel counters and bright blue lights behind the bottles. In one room stood an authentic iron maiden, its door thrown open, while in another room the furniture set of a 1950s American kitchen—stove, refrigerator, table, and chairs—had been nailed upside-down to the ceiling. In the Forum, Minotaur's cavernous main hall, Freida Wheeler and her band, The Great Unwashed, cavorted onstage, thumping their instruments, moaning lyrics. Kettle and Fife and Hannah Glorybrook were goths on the dance floor. They all three wore black cloak dresses with plunging necklines and they sported thick black eye-shadow and silver cross studs in their tongues.

Presiding over the Forum was Half Stack, Minotaur's renowned DJ and bouncer, who'd once locked the drunken, disorderly manager of the New York Mets in the iron maiden for an hour. Half Stack was angry at being supplanted by a band for the night, and pissed at the club's owner for allowing Patrick's private party on a Friday, not to mention a millennial New Year's Eve. Friday was normally ska night at Minotaur's, the night when Half Stack's most loyal tramp followers filled the club, and the only thing assuaging the DJ's wrath was the sight of Liza McMannus in her electric-pink miniskirt.

James puzzled his way from room to room. The club was underground, and it extended for a whole city block, and James never entered the same nook twice. In one corner James found Tony DiPreschetto on one knee, proposing to a woman James had never seen before. Not far from them Marcy Conner leaned against the iron maiden, stroking her lonely forearms. In another room were Jeremy Jax and Lucas Theater owner Michael Hye, toasting each other with petal glasses of a fluorescent yellow liqueur.

"In the new millennium," said Jeremy, "I shall bed a virgin prostitute."

"I," giggled Michael, "will swindle the Chinese mafia."

"I will cochair Mensa."

Michael burped. "I will disinvent candy."

In still another alcove sat a man with a pug face and a woman with hair to her waist. They were holding hands, and when they saw James, the pug-faced man said, "Join our vigil."

James wandered on through Minotaur's, lost but unafraid. Many of the chambers had walls but no ceilings, and the lights and noise coming from on high showed always the direction in which lay the Forum, the center of the labyrinth. So James meandered, hearing conversations, watching high-heeled strangers, till he came to a room that was empty except for a man sitting on the floor in the shadows, playing a guitar. It was the room with the kitchen on the ceiling.

"*You'd better do something about it,*" sang the guitarist, "*'cause I don't want to live without it.*"

James peered into the shadows. He knew the voice.

"You're John," he said. "You're Morality John."

The singer finished his song. James could see only teeth and a chin. He'd never spoken to this man before, but he felt bold.

"What's that song called?" asked James.

" 'I Can't Wait Another Day,' " said the teeth.

"I've heard you play it before. I hear you on the trains."

"I know." The man in the shadows hadn't moved. "I know who you are."

James glanced at the ceiling, at the frozen home there.

"How'd you get in here? Did Patrick invite you?"

"That's not what you want to know," said the teeth.

James caught his breath.

"You want to know what you're going to do," said Morality John.

James looked to his left and his right, made sure they were alone. "What I'm going to do about what?"

Morality John only smiled.

James stepped closer. He didn't dare move near enough to see the guitarist's face—that seemed against the rules tonight—but he felt like a commoner come to Delphi.

"Is it her?" whispered James. "Is it her and me that you . . . sing your songs about?"

In the distance the guitars of The Great Unwashed quit in midchord. There was a crash and a holler. James looked to the doorway. The noises came from the direction of the Forum. There were yells, and the tramping of boots.

"What's happening?" James wondered out loud.

"Go see," said Morality John.

James tapped his pockets. He moved toward the door, stopped, looked back. Morality John laid a finger over his lips, pointed toward the Forum.

"Go see," he said.

By the time James got there, skinheads were flooding the dance floor. There were over one hundred of them, kids with nose rings and muscles, girls without eyebrows, guys James's age with tattoos and bald skulls and steel-toed boots. It was a coup: Half Stack stood grinning beside the stage, at the club's fire-exit door, which he'd thrown open to admit his exiled punk brethren, who were still pouring in. Kettle and Fife and Hannah whooped and welcomed the newcomers, but Eva Baumgarten, a claustrophobe, frowned. Freida and The Great Unwashed stood uncertainly onstage, their instruments limp at their sides, while Patrick Rigg leaned viciously over a bar counter, arguing with Minotaur's owner. Patrick gestured at the uninvited punks. The owner shrugged and held up his palms and Patrick kicked the bar counter, shattering a pane of glass. Meanwhile, Half Stack bounded into the DJ booth and fired up the BossTones. The dance floor became a stompfest of pounding Doc Martens and flying elbows. Sarah Wolf, who only knew the tango, ran for cover. James stood on the edge of the mosh pit, watching the melee. It was eleven-thirty.

"They've stormed the Bastille," said Douglas Kerchek, at James's side.

James nodded, then froze. Twenty feet away from him, in a denim skirt, brown leather boots, and a white cowgirl blouse with blue sequins, was Rally. She was whirling and laughing in the mosh pit, and by the way she shoved the men around her and got shoved back, it was clear to James that she was one of their kind, that she'd surged in on the interloping skinhead tide. This depressed James, made Rally seem even more alien and unreachable. But seconds later, in midtwist, Rally saw James. She shouted, charged through the crowd, half tackled him with a hug.

"You're *here,*" she squealed.

James held her away from him, but didn't let go of her forearms. Rally had amaretto on her breath but didn't seem drunk.

"I—I'm here," confirmed James.

"Happy New Year," panted Rally. "Dance with me."

"Oh. Um. I'm not really a—"

"You're dancing with me." Rally tugged James into the madness. She flung him away from her, laughed as he pinballed among the bodies, trounced him happily on the shoulders when he stumbled back to her. James lurched around as best he could, tried to match the zeal of the girls and guys around him, tried to stay near Rally. The music drove on at a heart-attack pace, until just before midnight, when a pleasant piano melody kicked in. As if on cue the skinheads bowed to one another, like debutantes and escorts, and coupled off. Rally found James, curtsied before him, took his hands in hers.

"Whoa," said James.

"It's Dolly Parton," explained Rally. "It's 'Here You Come Again.' I'll lead."

James fumbled his feet, blushed. The music was sweet. Rally's sequins were absurd.

This is crazy, thought James.

"Half Stack plays this every Friday at midnight," said Rally. "It's a Minotaur's tradition."

James followed Rally's feet. She waltzed him in circles. All around them were couples—men with men, men with women, women with women—turning elegant arcs. Their more savage movements, for now, were gone. Several of them sang along. They were dressed in torn leather and had viciously pierced bodies, but they winked at James, as if at a new recruit.

"This is crazy," whispered James.

Rally had her cheek against James's cheek. She steered him over the floor.

"It's tradition," she said.

James danced on. He didn't ask Rally where she'd been lately, didn't ask her about Patrick. He danced and smelled Rally's hair. There was sweat on her cheek. The twin lumps behind her ears were inches away.

"I can't stop thinking about you," whispered James.

"It's almost midnight," said Rally. "Happy New Year."

"Did you hear me? I—I can't stop thinking about you."

Rally dipped James, held the dip, met his eyes.

"Then kiss me, silly. The song's almost over."

So James did it. Arched back, with her face looming over his own, James kissed Rally. It was a good kiss—not a great one—with some touching of their tongues, and a hard click of their front teeth. When it ended, Rally stood James on his feet. The dance was over, and James blushed, waiting to find out how he'd done.

"Have you . . . been thinking about me too?" he said.

Rally took James's hand.

"I'm hungry," she said. "Let's go for slices."

Rally tugged James toward the fire exit. He looked at her cowgirl clothing, watched her skirt press to her thighs. He'd once seen her naked, but this, somehow, was sexier.

"Wait," insisted James. "Have you?"

"Out, out, out." Rally hustled James through the door. "We need pizza pie. We need slices."

They were in an alley, with snow on the ground, and a plot of stars overhead. James thought of his coat, still inside Minotaur's, in the coatroom. The fire door clicked shut, locking them out.

"Jesus," he said, "it's freezing."

"I'm starved," said Rally.

They stood looking at each other. Steam rose from their arms.

"I'll bet you're a pepperoni man," said Rally.

"I'm crazy about you," said James.

Rally canted her hips, crossed her arms. "You don't even know me."

I said it, thought James. I'm standing here. I said it.

"I'm a pepperoni man," he told her.

Rally threw her arms around him for kiss number two.

It can happen like that, sometimes. The city can tilt its hand, let two people fall for each other as completely as James and Rally did. That night they not only went for pizza, they took a cab ride around the island. In honor of the New Year the cabbie offered them squares of acid, but they refused. They sat in the backseat, content with each other's tongues, kissing softly, saying little. By three in the morning they were at Rally's SoHo apartment, in her bed, slowly getting to know each other's bodies. They petted, teased, smiled, held off on consummation. They whispered and made each other orgasm. Rally sang James a song she remembered from when she was a girl. At sunrise they stood outside her window on the fire escape, wrapped in blankets, watching the light.

A halcyon week followed, during which James and Rally barely parted. James took five days off work, and Rally cleared the week of distractions. They tussled in Rally's bed for whole afternoons. They took the train to Coney Island and walked on crunchy winter sand. James treated Rally to Flat Michael's, where she'd never been, and Rally introduced James to the incomparable hamburgers of the Corner Bistro. They held hands at the Angelika, saw two plays, experimented with lingerie, slept until ten. They were in love, and after midnight on Thursday, their sixth night together, James sat on the floor of Rally's bathroom, weeping his happiness. Rally was asleep in her bed, and James stayed in the bathroom with the lights off for half an hour. He missed Otis, missed the part of himself that observed without sentiment the passing facts of his life, but the new current inside him was entire, ineluctable. The smell of Rally's skin was a fix in his lungs, and her voice was what he had to hear. Morris, Minnesota, and Anamaria, and his own history of quietude, vanished with the precision of a nuclear strike, and all James saw were Rally's arms and thighs and throat. When he walked with her through SoHo, holding her hand, he checked the eyes of people passing them, to see whether he and Rally were still physical entities or whether their happiness had rendered them invisible. James and Rally disagreed only about what films to see, about what streets they should walk down, about where in the world they would travel together first.

"New Zealand," said James.

Rally kissed his calves. They were in bed, naked.

"The Isle of Skye," she said.

"The Serengeti."

Rally knelt between his legs. She moved her lips up his thighs. "The Isle of Skye."

James lay back, closed his eyes.

"Tokyo," he whispered.

"Hmmm. Are you really in a position to argue?"

"No," gasped James.

They avoided James's apartment for the whole week. James dropped by there a few times to pick up clothes, but he always did so late on weekday mornings, when Patrick was at work. James wasn't exactly afraid of seeing his housemate, but neither he nor Rally wanted to deal with Patrick yet. They didn't know how he'd respond to their togetherness, and they didn't want to articulate to Patrick or anyone what they were to each other. As a result they neither knew nor cared how the Spree had wrapped up its blitzkrieg. They figured Walter and Henry would stay buddies, and they hoped Nicole Bonner would marry Douglas Kerchek, but other than that, they let the last ten days drop. To Rally's delight she realized that Patrick had no idea where she lived. She'd only ever been to his Preemption apartment, never he to hers. So she and James were left to each other. Manhattan, the world, all time, seemed spread out like a honeymoon.

They ice-skated in Rockefeller Center. They went to the Cloisters, stood at the spot where they now knew they'd first met. They drank coffee, chewed pastry. They talked of the snow, the death penalty, but of nothing so much as each other. James found himself compelled to tell Rally what she looked like, as if the mirrors she'd looked in all her life hadn't been truthful.

"You're beautiful," he told her.

"No," countered Rally.

James kissed her behind the ear. "You're beautiful."

To get revenge Rally told James that he was her tiger.

"I'm what?"

They were naked in Rally's bed again. It was a Saturday evening. Rally sat up, reached to a shelf, pulled down a book. "This is my favorite poem," she said. " 'Disillusionment of Ten O'clock.' It's by Wallace Stevens. Listen. 'The houses are haunted by white nightgowns—' "

"Lie back down." James tugged her elbow.

"No, listen. 'The houses are haunted by white nightgowns. None are green, or purple with green rings, or green with yellow rings, or yellow with blue rings.' "

"You're not even wearing a nightgown," teased James.

Rally poked him. "Listen, baby. Please. I want you to."

"All right."

" '. . . or yellow with blue rings. None of them are strange, with socks of lace and beaded ceintures. People are not going to dream of baboons and periwinkles. Only, here and there, an old sailor, drunk and asleep in his boots, catches tigers in red weather.' There. That's it."

Rally tossed the book, snuggled down beside James.

James breathed her in. He folded his arms behind his head.

"So I'm the tiger," he said.

"And I'm the drunk. The sailor." Rally sucked on James's neck, then stopped.

They lay with their heads on the same pillow, looking at each other.

"I used to think Patrick was my tiger," whispered Rally.

"Oh." James's stomach roiled.

"Don't be mad, baby. I'm telling you because that's why I let him do weird things to me. Tie me up and stuff. I thought he was all unique."

"Oh."

"But I don't think that anymore." She put her finger on his chest, pressed hard. "It's you. You're the one."

James closed his eyes. He wanted to fistfight Patrick Rigg, to sprint the Verrazano-Narrows, to stay right where he was, in this bed, always. He thought of Otis.

"Is that what you want me to be?" he said. "Weird?"

Rally kissed him. "No, baby."

James looked at her. He wanted to tell her about Otis, but his heart said wait. Save it, his heart said, for an emergency.

It was a Saturday night, the second of the new year. Patrick Rigg paced in his apartment. He'd simmered for a week, tried to ignore James's absence. He knew James was with Rally. At Minotaur's they'd been dancing together, protected by a sea of punks, and then they'd been gone.

Patrick had tried to busy himself with work, to fill his evenings with his other women. He'd lured Crispin and Kettle into his bed one night, wheedled the two of them into feats most men only pray for. But in his heart, for seven days, grew a black, factual weed: Rally had chosen James. The sentence filled Patrick's mind like a chant. Rally had chosen James. Rally had chosen James. Rally McWilliams, his sexiest, most stubborn and self-obsessed moll, had thrown herself at quiet, corny James.

So what? thought Patrick, still pacing. You've got handfuls of women. Let the bitch go.

But he couldn't. Patrick's soul was a fragile house of cards, and the cards were the women of his life, stacked upon each other, every one in her place. He spent all his money on his women, fondled them, manipulated them. They were all he had. He had a dead mother and a dead brother, the memory of whom haunted Patrick daily. His Manhattan acquaintances drew near him only for his parties and his dark philanthropies. So Patrick counted on his women, on their bodies and their society, the way James counted on Otis. The removal of certain peripheral distractions like Freida wouldn't have fazed Patrick, but having another man claim certain women of his, especially Rally, tightened Patrick's breathing. It made him feel as if he were collapsing in upon himself, losing backbone, integrity, as if the horrors and loneliness of the universe, with which Patrick had struck a delicate truce, were breaking his terms and attacking. Besides, Rally was the only one of Patrick's women who'd met his unspoken, impossible demands. Standing before his mirror, lying bound to his bed, she'd fallen in love with herself—become enamored of her own body and soul—and, because of that, she'd grown infinitely more gorgeous and necessary to Patrick.

I made her, thought Patrick darkly. I made her what she is. And no dopey-eyed accountant is going to take her away.

Patrick grabbed his coat. Gritting his teeth, he stormed out of the Preemption, unable to shake the twitching in his legs, the wrath in his lungs, the memory of his hands on Rally's naked stomach.

This is crazy, thought Patrick. He stalked down Broadway, tramping the grates above the Seventy-second Street subway. Below him, under the grate, were shapes, voices, the sound of a guitar.

This is crazy, thought Patrick again. But his fury was a ticker tape in his mind, and the only way to pull its plug was to use the weapon in his left breast pocket.

"I'll always hope to change things someday," sang a voice from below.

Patrick stopped, stared underground. Beneath the grate was a tall, dark figure holding an instrument.

"Is it me?" yelled Patrick. He stomped on the metal.

"I was wrong," sang the man, *"and you'll belong."*

Patrick kept stomping, glaring down. "Are you singing about me?"

The figure faded in the shadows.

Patrick walked on. He headed south, toward Wall Street, toward St. Benedict's, the church he sneaked into every weekday evening to hear a priest talk. The church was half the length of the island away, but Patrick had delirium and adrenaline in him tonight. He strode with intent, with a singleness of purpose, rarely turning his head to either side. His exhalations hurried from his mouth like phantoms, and people on the sidewalk, seeing his glare, moved aside.

I need the priest, thought Patrick. Rally chose James, and I need the priest.

Patrick wasn't religious. He wasn't after traditional sacraments. What he wanted was the one thing besides women that could stop him cold: the voice of Thomas Merchant. Father Merchant, the pastor of St. Benedict's, gave sermons that somehow galvanized Patrick's heart, sermons that, like a slap, could knock light into the space behind Patrick's eyes. Tonight, Patrick felt he needed that light. He felt that without it, he'd pull his SIG and squeeze the trigger and somebody would go down.

So Patrick marched down the island, all the way to Wall Street. It took him two hours, but he made it to St. Benedict's. He pushed through the doors, found the priest in the confessional, slid into the stall built for sinners. Alone, in the dark, he began to speak.

In Black

Thomas Merchant was born with a good, clear heart, but little else. He was not handsome, articulate, or muscular. He spent his boyhood in the west of Ireland, in the seaside town of Spiddal. His father built boats and his mother was a mother, but both of his parents died from a strange, virulent skin disease when Thomas was only seven. He was then sent to New York City, to Harlem, where he was raised by his three aunts, Mabel, Margaret, and Mary Jude Merchant. These three women were six-foot-tall triplet sisters, and they were thought to be fairy creatures by Harlem's children. From their girlhood to their deathbeds the Merchant sisters had jet-black hair that fell to their waists and identical, piercing green eyes. Their heads never went gray, they never married, and they never held jobs. They lived together on the edge of a vacant lot in what had once been a furniture warehouse. They were wealthy, and rumor went that they'd sailed from Galway in 1959 with two sacks full of gold coins. The sacks were supposedly hidden in the warehouse, and Mabel Merchant, the quietest sister and the eldest by two minutes, was supposedly the one who drew coins from the sacks. The warehouse stood on 125th Street, the main artery of Harlem, but even the hardest thieves stayed away from the place and the hope of its gold, for fear of the Merchant fairies.

Into this corner of Manhattan came Thomas Merchant, a simple boy from a fishing village across the ocean. Following the death of his parents Thomas uttered not a single word for the length of one year. He sat in the vaulted chambers of the warehouse, staring at broken looms, pianos, and wardrobes, the wooden behemoths of another age, abandoned now to darkness and cobwebs. He inhaled and found good the musty airs of these chambers. On the top floor of the warehouse was the apartment where Thomas's aunts lived. It was a warm, cheerful series of rooms, clean and full of sunshine. In these rooms the Merchant sisters cared for Thomas every evening. They fed him hot lamb stew and washed his hair. They read him stories and sang him to sleep. But they never nagged Thomas about his silence, and during the day they let him wander the warehouse and stare at whatever he wished. They were Irish, and they understood mourning in all of its incarnations. They knew what perversions of character could arise if a child's reckoning of the world was harried and tampered with too often by adults. As a result they didn't enroll Thomas in a school, and on the day that Mr. Gammer, the social worker who managed Thomas's immigration, ventured out to the warehouse, the three sisters descended arms akimbo upon the door.

"Good afternoon," said Mr. Gammer. "May I please see Thomas?"

"You may not," said Mary Jude. She was the sternest sister, the one who approved least of men.

"Well . . ." Mr. Gammer wore a tie that looked like a fish. "What has Thomas been up to?"

"He's been searching his soul," said Mabel.

"And playing a little piano," smiled Margaret Merchant. Margaret was the friendly sister, the one most enjoying her life on earth.

"He's been teaching himself," added Margaret.

"Piano." Mr. Gammer nodded approvingly, wrote something on his clipboard. "And has Thomas been mixing with other neighborhood children?"

"Good-bye," said Mary Jude.

Thomas watched and heard this conversation from his hiding place behind a Scottish sideboard. He also hid there and watched when Jack Lance, the butcher's son, delivered parcels of lamb and cuts of steak wrapped in white paper, or on Sundays when Brenda McMannus, the black, fifteen-year-old paper girl, came bearing *The New York Times*. Thomas watched Jack press bricks of lamb into Aunt Mabel's hands, the price of the meat scrawled in blue ink on the white paper. He admired the way Brenda McMannus carved parts in her hair, the way halter tops hung from her shoulders, the way she held the bound newspaper between one wrist and one hip while she chatted with Aunt Margaret. When Thomas focused on these rituals, these small, reliable physical events, everything else in his mind faded to black. He forgot the yellow pustules that had mottled his mother's arms, the close and stifling air of his packed transatlantic plane flight. Mostly Thomas found that if he could sink himself into a moment and trust it and feature against the black velvet curtain of his mind the one thing his eyes were beholding, then his loneliness dissolved, and he was at peace.

Thomas's aunts noticed his single-mindedness, his alarmingly clear, constant gaze. They discussed it when Thomas wasn't around.

"He'll be an inventor," predicted Margaret.

Mary Jude snorted. "He'll scare the hell out of people is what he'll do."

"He'll be a priest," said Mabel.

At age eight Thomas began speaking again, little by little. He went to high school, played basketball, suffered puberty, enrolled at Columbia. He dated and grappled with girls, one of whom, Jocelyn Rich, rattled his heart when he was nineteen. Sustaining him through all these trials was the hermetic, honing instinct of Thomas's mind, the ability he'd always had—on the seaside rocks of Spiddal, in his aunts' cavernous warehouse—to rule out of his concentration everything but the object or company at hand. It was this instinct that made much of the world either sad to Thomas or evidently off-limits. For he found at a young age that very few things could endure his scrutiny. Nature could do it—trees and grass and the Hudson River could take being stared at, and Thomas spent countless happy hours of his youth sitting in Riverside Park, witnessing the breezes there, breathing in the flowers and the snows. Creatures, however, were another matter. Animals, except for the occasional, slavishly friendly dog, were as skittish as squirrels, and anxious to avoid contact with Thomas. People were no different. In high school Thomas had never minded sitting on the bench during basketball games, admiring his teammates as they leapt and streaked down the court, their arms and legs as smooth as pistons. To Thomas's horror this staring habit prompted Coach Laverty to pull Thomas aside one day and inquire whether Thomas was a freaking queerbag homo. In similar fashion the first night that Thomas removed Jocelyn Rich's bra, he gazed at her naked chest so long and so quietly that Jocelyn pulled the blanket up over herself.

"Come on," she told Thomas. "Let's go. Grab me."

Thomas was startled by her words. He was in the presence of something lovely, namely Jocelyn, and he wanted to stay there with the loveliness, not rush to another moment.

"I'm looking at you," he whispered.

Jocelyn scowled. "Well, don't."

Thomas tried to pull the blanket back off his date, but Jocelyn held it to her neck.

"Let me see you," said Thomas.

Jocelyn rolled her eyes. "They're breasts, Thomas. They're just sacks of fat and milk ducts."

Thomas felt like he'd been slapped. Nothing to him was just anything.

"I'm only a girl," said Jocelyn curtly. "I'm not something to worship."

"I wasn't worshiping you," said Thomas. "I was looking at you."

"Well, stop it."

Thomas tried to smile. "You smell nice," he said. "Sort of . . . warm."

"Thomas," sighed Jocelyn, "are we going to screw or what?"

For Thomas it was like that with almost everybody. Not that every woman asked him to screw her, but it seemed to Thomas, especially at college, that human beings charged around at far too vicious a pace, expecting to be assessed or used or summed up very quickly. Students argued about Plato and Alfred Hitchcock, as if, after a couple of books or movies, they'd become metaphysically privy to these men's hearts and minds. Thomas didn't blame his peers for this habit, or label it as pretension. He just didn't understand it. It seemed to Thomas that he belonged to some alien race, from some other planet, where the creatures sat around looking deeply into one another's eyes, sometimes for centuries, before they dared utter a word to each other.

In fact, during his junior year at Columbia, Thomas took an acting class where the teacher made the students do just that. They had to pair off and sit cross-legged opposite each other, staring quietly into one another's eyes for five minutes. Speaking or looking away from your partner was forbidden. Thomas was paired up with a girl named Elvetta Vandemeer, a senior who'd recently been cast as Juliet for a campus Shakespeare production, and who'd had lunch at the cafeteria with Thomas once or twice. Elvetta had a black fence of bangs across her forehead and midnight-blue eyes, and the first thing Thomas saw when he looked into those eyes was Elvetta's pride, the pleasure she took in believing herself a tragic, stunning Juliet. But after about a minute, when the other couples in the room were starting to snigger, Thomas's vision pierced the Juliet in Elvetta's eyes and got a glimpse of what lay beyond.

Elvetta took a sharp breath. "What?" she whispered nervously. "Thomas, what?"

Thomas didn't speak or blink. He was lost suddenly in the young woman before him, the blue galaxies of her fears, the vastness of her heart. Everything else went black and Thomas stared into Elvetta, into stories that either she was imagining or he was, stories where Elvetta was tied to a rock, being devoured by a sea monster, stories where Thomas and Elvetta were naked together and she lay in his lap and he counted every hair on her head.

"Stop it," hissed Elvetta. She didn't want to lose, to look away. "Stop it, Thomas."

Thomas gazed on, at another story behind Elvetta's eyes, a story where she was holding a man by the throat.

Elvetta slapped Thomas's face. "Stop it!"

Thomas blinked, woke from his reverie. He was back in class, seated on a hardwood stage, his cheek stinging. He rubbed his cheek, while Elvetta glared at him.

"Why did you do that?" asked Thomas.

The teacher hurried over, breathless with hope.

"Yes, why?" said the teacher.

Elvetta blushed. The whole class gathered around.

"Thomas was . . . being rude," said Elvetta. She stood, left the class, and never spoke to Thomas again.

Thomas was stunned. He was stunned even further when Elvetta quit the Shakespeare production the day after this acting exercise.

"Why are people afraid of me?" Thomas asked his aunts. He still lived at the warehouse during his college days. It was only ten blocks from school.

"Because you aren't afraid of anything," said Mary Jude.

Thomas thought about this. He was drinking coffee with his aunts, playing a card game they called Sluice, a game only he and his aunts knew the rules to. It was February, and the tree branches outside the window were sleeved in ice. Thomas was twenty. Mabel was smoking a briar pipe.

"I'm not a hero," muttered Thomas.

"I never said you were a hero." Mary Jude snapped up a card. "I said you weren't afraid of anything."

"And you play the piano wonderfully," added Margaret.

The three sisters nodded simultaneously. They agreed on very little, except for Thomas, and the peculiarities of his nature. Every evening, Thomas came back to the warehouse apartment and collapsed on the couch, his mind frazzled and spent from the input that Manhattan threw at him, the bodies, the walls, the trash, the food. If an object that he stared at seemed peaceful or whole in its nature, like a tree or a watchful baby, then Thomas drew strength from focusing on that object. But more often he felt, through a sort of draining visual empathy, the terrors that gripped Manhattan's denizens. He read haste and greed in graffiti and in the propped-up ceilings of bodegas. At clubs he gazed at women in slick black dresses, wishing he could fall prey to their magic, sensing instead that they had sad, splintered hearts. At a party once, when he shook the hand of a young man, Thomas felt a conviction in his fingertips that the man would beat his girlfriend that very night.

In the end Thomas had few friends, because he didn't know how to joke about women or sports or tragedy. It took a back rub from his aunt Mabel—the sister with the strongest hands—and cups of her brandied coffee and several rounds of Sluice before he could fashion into words the strange truths that had assailed him that day.

"I saw a woman in the park today," said Thomas one night.

The Merchant sisters exchanged glances.

Margaret touched Thomas's wrist gently. "What was she doing, Thomas?"

"She was sitting on a bench." Thomas gazed at his cards, threw one on the table. "She was tearing at the cuticles on her thumbs. Tearing and tearing."

Mary Jude plucked up the card Thomas had cast away. She laid down what she held.

"Sluice," she said.

"Shoot," whispered Mabel.

"This woman was bleeding," said Thomas.

Margaret poured Thomas more coffee. The heat vent in the corner ticked.

"How long did you watch her?" asked Margaret.

"A long time."

Mary Jude pulled her hair back, clipped it. She faced her nephew, her widow's peak a black dagger point on her forehead. "That woman isn't your affair, Thomas."

"Mary," warned Margaret, "let him talk."

Thomas looked at the floor. "She was making herself bleed. She was weeping."

Mary Jude frowned. She wanted to break her nephew of his obsession with fellow feeling, his penchant for compassion. She wanted him to want whiskey, and girls, and joy.

"Forget that woman, Thomas," growled Mary Jude.

Thomas smiled sadly at his aunts.

"I can't," he said.

Two years later Thomas was in a seminary in Pennsylvania. He'd been baptized a Catholic, and though his aunts had never taken him to church, the warehouse had fostered Thomas's instinct for contemplation. He'd stared so long and intensely at the furniture of the world—at chairs and people and the sky through the warehouse ceiling—that his mind had asked for more. Thomas explained this as best he could to his confessor and novice master, Father Reese, as they sat in Father Reese's office.

"You mean," said Father Reese, "that you've discovered Christ at the root of creation?"

Thomas shook his head. "I mean God's the only thing that can stand me thinking about Him all the time."

"That sounds prideful," said the priest.

Thomas shrugged. He was twenty-three years old.

Father Reese, a portly man and an avid golfer, leaned back in his chair. When he raised his eyebrows, his forehead dented.

"What about women?" asked Father Reese. "Can you stand thinking about them?"

Thomas looked into the priest's eyes. He thought he saw gluttony there, a love of red meat, a keenness for pleasure.

"I've been in love," sighed Thomas. "I've been with women."

The priest smiled. "And?"

"They don't know enough about their own beauty for me to be in awe of them." Thomas scratched at a pimple on the back of his neck. The priest's office smelled like cigarettes.

"Is that right," said Father Reese.

"None of us knows enough about his own beauty," said Thomas.

Punk, thought the priest. Snot-nosed punk.

"And who's going to teach us about our beauty, Thomas? You, by becoming a priest?"

Thomas gazed deeper into the man before him, gazed past the long putts and the London broils, until he saw jealousy in Father Reese's eyes.

"No," said Thomas. "I'm not a hero. I just see things."

"You see things." Father Reese had large feet. He wiggled his large toes inside his large shoes. "Have you heard the line from Scripture, *No one shall see the face of God and live?*"

Thomas sighed again. He hated semantics. In fact on most days, Thomas hated talking, period.

"I'm not trying to see God's face," said Thomas quietly. "I'm trying to see His mind."

Father Reese snorted. Good luck, kid, he thought.

Thomas graduated seminary when he was twenty-six. He got his master's in divinity, then did an intern stint at a Brooklyn parish. When he was thirty-two he applied for and received the sole pastoral position at St. Benedict's on Wall Street. St. Benedict's was a dark, moody cave of a church, with a red carpet down the center aisle and great stands of white candles back by the doors. Priests traditionally groaned when assigned to St. Benedict's, but Thomas liked the place for its silent stone walls, and its sparse patronage. Most of his Wall Street neighbors were busy making money and running the world, so Thomas was left with an audience of aging Irishwomen clutching rosaries. This suited Thomas absolutely. He was a mystic, not a missionary, and he preferred a subtle, monkish obedience to and contemplation of the Divine over any heroic work in conversions. Every day at St. Benedict's was like a quiet, solemn Christmas, and Thomas, at the daily five o'clock Mass, gave sermons on discernment and grace, rather than abortion or politics. When he delivered these sermons, Thomas stared from the altar over the heads of his parishioners to the clean white candles gleaming at the far end of the church. They were a reliable focus point, the candles were, and if enough of them were burning, they gave off a light, pleasing incense. Thomas found that if he stared at these candles intently enough, and took in their scent, good words came out of him.

Thomas's three aunts took the subway down from Harlem once or twice a week to hear their nephew preach and to wink at him slyly from the pews. Thomas still joined them for Sunday lamb dinners at the warehouse, while on weeknights in the rectory basement he ran the small St. Benedict's soup kitchen, which served the first fifty mouths that came in off the street. Thomas's favorite homeless person was a mute woman named Esther. Esther looked to be in her late fifties, and she was missing one front tooth. She was thin, tiny, and given to smiling. She wore a bedraggled pink ribbon in her hair each day, she never missed Thomas's Mass, and she nibbled ham sandwiches quietly by his side every weeknight between seven and nine o'clock.

So this was Thomas's life. He passed a decade and a half in delightful peace at St. Benedict's, reading, praying, feeding the hungry, smiling at Esther. He baptized an occasional baby and said his share of funerals, but mostly he stared at his candles and delivered his sermons and was quietly, reverently happy.

The change came when Thomas was forty-seven. It began on a cool Monday evening in late September. Thomas was delivering his sermon—the one about the vineyard workers that the master hires late in the day—when he noticed a man standing in back by the candles. At least, it seemed to be a man. Beyond the candles was darkness, and Thomas could just make out the hunched shoulders and lowered chin of what looked to be a tall man in a black overcoat. The man stood stock-still, like a hunter or a bodyguard, and he seemed to be listening intently. Thomas also noticed a sharp stench of something oily in the air, but attached no importance to it at the time. The moment that Thomas finished his sermon, the church doors whispered and the man was gone.

The next day, after lunch, Thomas sat at the rectory kitchen table, staring at the salt and pepper shakers. The Bible lay open before him. This was where Thomas sat and stared daily as he composed his evening sermon. Today, however, Thomas's focus was broken. The man from the night before, the figure in black, stood in the hallway of Thomas's mind, a distant but definite figure. Thomas wondered what the man could have wanted, lurking in the shadows like that, leaving before the real ceremony had taken place. Perhaps the man had been homeless and hungry. Perhaps he was a Wall Street trader who'd lost a fortune and needed redemption. Or maybe, Thomas thought, a lover of architecture, come to admire the St. Benedict's ceiling. Finally, Thomas shook the man from his thoughts, fixed his mind on the Bible.

That very night, though, the man appeared again. He slipped inside the church just before the gospel, and stood in the shadows. Thomas paused in his preaching, got a bead on the man's proportions. The stranger was over six feet tall, and again wearing the black overcoat. From the cut of the man's torso and the quick way he'd entered the church, Thomas figured him to be young, perhaps in his early thirties. More disturbing, though, was the acrid, burnt smell that seemed to have come into the church with the man, a smell that overpowered the fragrance of the candles. Thomas had a lifetime of experience gazing into the heart of things: he could predict the weather with a knack that alarmed even him, and, on his hospital visits, he knew at a glance how many hours left on earth this or that cancer patient had. But now, as Thomas stood before the altar, he'd never been so jolted by the smell, the aura, of another human being. The stench was clearly emanating from the man in black.

"And—and Christ will reach you where you live," stammered Thomas, trying to return to his sermon. "He'll work with whatever circumstances you find yourself in. . . ."

Thomas paused again, tried to breathe only through his mouth. The smell was noxious, unrelenting. It was a bitter, dark smell, not like garbage or dung or an unwashed person, but like acid-soaked wood that had been torched and charred and was polluting the air around it. Thomas stared at his parishioners. Esther sat in the front pew, smiling at him. Esther, Thomas thought, Esther who plugs her nose at the smell of tuna fish or even burned toast. She seemed to smell nothing tonight, and when Thomas checked other faces in his small crowd, they were at peace too.

Thomas was amazed. He fought his way through his sermon, and when he'd finished, the man in black vanished once again. When the doors of St. Benedict's clicked shut, Thomas took a gulp of air, and coughed.

"Guuh? Gunh?" From her pew Esther grunted and frowned up at the priest. She knew something was wrong.

Thomas breathed in and out. The bitter stench was gone. There were only the candles.

"I'm fine." The priest wiped his forehead, cleared his throat. "I'm fine."

It began happening nightly. The man in black and his terrible odor would arrive just before the gospel and leave just after the sermon. The man stood always in darkness, and Thomas realized after a few nights that his parishioners were oblivious to the man's presence. Despite the putrid air the faithful in the pews never turned up their noses or tried to spy out the source of the poison. After the first few Masses the man in black attended, Thomas asked Esther and his aunts casually whether they'd smelled anything funky in the air.

"You know," he chatted, "like a burnt smell? Like maybe the vents are failing?"

The women shook their heads no, but Mabel Merchant

studied her nephew carefully. She was the sister most sensitive to intrigue and shady goings-on. Every year, around Easter, Thomas found one pure gold coin in the collection plate and knew without asking that his aunt Mabel had slipped him some treasure. He knew now, meeting her eyes, that she sensed a mystery afoot, but when he held his tongue, Mabel nodded softly and turned away. Thomas wanted to confide in his aunt, but he was honestly frightened. How could a man radiate a filthy, bitter essence that only a priest could smell? Why would the man materialize only for the gospel and for Thomas's sermon and then melt away again?

Thomas pondered all of this in his heart as he sat in his kitchen and stared at his salt and pepper shakers. He began to wonder very practically whether a demon hadn't taken up house in his church. Or maybe it's an angel, Thomas hoped. Maybe it's Gabriel or Michael and they just smell nasty to mortals and no one knows it. Whatever the visitor in black was, though, Thomas knew that it was no ordinary man. He knew only—through the gifted empathy that had become almost a muscle—that the visitor was male, and deeply troubled, and capable of an immense concentration of mind. For, as the man in black stood in the shadows and Thomas delivered his sermons, the priest felt power drain out of himself toward the man. Normally, Thomas hoped his words might be a fuel of sorts for his parishioners, a boost to their humors, an option of grace and kindness. But, for Thomas, facing the man in black was like rapture, or a duel to the death. The man seemed to be listening to Thomas with a palpable greed, a forward incline of the head, a voracious ear for truth. Thomas grew physically conscious of the words leaving his mouth, of their becoming a vapor that the man in black sucked into his lungs and took away from St. Benedict's. Each night, when the man left, Thomas all but collapsed on the altar. He closed his eyes, felt sweat on his forehead. His fingers shook on the chalice.

"Are you sick?" asked Margaret Merchant.

"Have you puked?" said Mary Jude.

Esther made grunting sounds, clung to Thomas's arm.

Margaret touched her nephew's cheek. "What's gotten into you?"

Thomas set his jaw, answered no one. He almost did feel sick and nauseous. He began preparing his sermons with the man in black in mind. They were severe, loud, apocalyptic sermons that the stranger seemed to call out of him, as if Thomas's decades of watchfulness and gentleness had been one extended gathering of strength for the battle that had now arrived.

"There is no favoritism with God," Thomas preached. "All moments are equal in the eyes of the Lord." The priest stared past the candles at his single, shadowy target. "If God has filled your life with joy, or chosen to show you His dark side, it's of no consequence to your actions, either way. Saint Paul instructs us to pray that we don't become articulate in evil matters. But if we do grow familiar with evil, and we understand it, we're no less obligated to speak against it. To live beyond it."

When Thomas spoke this way, his parishioners fidgeted. Esther worried her pink ribbon around on her thumb, and several regulars stopped showing up. Nobody seemed to want to hear about evil, but Thomas couldn't help himself. The smell of the man in black was drastic and otherworldly, and judging by the fine cut of the man's overcoat, it had nothing to do with poor personal hygiene. It had to do with evil, Thomas thought. As he stood on his altar and spoke to the figure beyond the candles, Thomas's knees quivered slightly beneath his robes. Somehow, he knew that the man's bitter smell was the scent of a rank and blistered soul. Beneath the man's coat and kempt appearance lay some monstrous violence, some hatred or grudge or some aberrant sexual appetite. Perhaps the man wasn't even aware of his own fetidness. But, for reasons he himself couldn't fathom, Thomas would have bet the bank that the man was carrying a gun.

"We're worried about you," said the Merchant triplets. They had Thomas at the warehouse for Sunday lamb and Sluice, but he picked at his food and played his cards wrong.

"You've lost weight, Thomas," said Margaret.

"Yeah," growled Mary Jude, "and your sermons are getting psycho."

Mabel raised her hand. Her sisters went quiet.

"Thomas," said Mabel. "What is the matter?"

Thomas stared out the window at the October moon.

"There's someone I have to help," he said.

"Who?" said the sisters.

Thomas shook his head. "I have to do it alone. I'm the only one who can . . . speak to him."

Mary Jude slapped the table. "Him who, dammit?"

Thomas met his aunt Mabel's eyes.

"*Him,*" whispered Thomas.

The confrontation happened months later, on a Saturday night, in the dead of winter. Thomas was in the two-doored, closeted room at the rear of St. Benedict's, hearing Confessions. In his chamber of the closet Thomas sat on a small stool, listening through a grille to the sins of his kneeling parishioners. It was early in January of the new millennium, and the invisible voices through the grille pondered how they should repent, what resolutions they might pursue. Thomas generally closed his eyes when he heard Confessions. He enjoyed the oaken smell and the darkness, but he was embarrassed by the physical intimacy of the closet. It often seemed to Thomas that the person inches away from him through the wall was naked, in the changing room of some very important clothing store or else in the solitary-confinement box of a prison. Thomas could hear every sigh and every sob with a proximity that, despite his office, made him feel uncomfortably voyeuristic. His strongest natural faculty, his vision, was denied him, and Thomas had to reach across the darkness with other, faultier senses. So, even on a good evening, Thomas disliked hearing Confessions. But it was with pure dread one night that Thomas heard the click of the door in the chamber opposite his. This dread prickled over his skin, stirring goose bumps, for coming through the grille now was a familiar, scalded smell.

"You know who this is?" said a low voice.

Thomas shuddered, crossed himself, covered his nose with a handkerchief. "Yes."

"How do you know?"

Thomas's mind raced. He'd thought there'd been a pact between him and the figure in black, an unspoken agreement that whatever this creature wanted from Thomas, it would get it by keeping its quiet distance beyond the candles and listening to Thomas's sermons.

"I just know," said Thomas.

The stranger sniffled fiercely. "You're wondering why I've come to you now. After all this time."

Thomas's heart pounded. He sensed, correctly, that the pews outside the closet were empty. It was nine o'clock, and the hearing of Confessions had technically ended. But there would be no sending this creature away. Thomas drew a breath, opened his eyes to the dark wall between him and the stranger.

"Yes," said Thomas, "I'm wondering."

There was a rustling, then a silence. The stranger had settled in.

"I've come to tell you," said the voice, "that human lives are absurd."

"I see," said Thomas.

The hidden stranger laughed. "I doubt that you do. But, even so, human lives are absurd, and I'm going to end one."

Thomas kept his handkerchief to his nose. "You're going to end a human life?"

"Yes."

"Your own?"

"No." The stranger seemed to yawn. "I'm going to kill another man."

Like an athlete Thomas cleared his mind. He ignored the stench around him, prayed a prayer for himself and the stranger. *Lord Jesus, help us* is what Thomas prayed.

"Say more," said Thomas.

"The man's name is James Branch," said the stranger. "He's my roommate. I'm going to shoot him dead."

"Why?"

In the quiet Thomas could almost taste the man's sneer.

"There is no why, Father. There's only absurdity. People die. That's all."

"I'm afraid that sounds terribly convenient for someone who's considering murder."

"Go to hell, Father."

Thomas sat in silence, waited. He thought of things in his

life that he'd stared at and marveled over. He thought of Jocelyn Rich's abdomen, of dead flowers, of the hands of beggars.

"What could you possibly know about absurdity, Father?"

"A little, I suppose."

"Really. Well, I know a great deal about it. A great deal."

Thomas kept his mind a blank slate. He forced his thoughts away from suspicions that the unnamed man was armed.

"My brother was killed when he was a boy, Father. He was killed at an amusement park by a man dressed as a cartoon character. A giant Guppy fish."

Thomas waited. The dank, bitter stench of the stranger had seeped completely through the grille now, filling the confessional like an outhouse.

"You can go ahead and laugh, Father. I know it's funny."

"I don't feel like laughing. I'm sorry about your brother."

"Yeah, I'll bet you are."

Thomas was getting a feel for the stranger's voice. It was a young man, after all, a powerful, cynical young man who needed to speak his piece.

"Tell me about James Branch," said Thomas.

"I'll tell you what I feel like," snapped the stranger.

"All right."

Moments passed. The darkness was a limbo.

"I'll tell you about my women."

"All right."

"I have tons of them. They're like a harem. I'm rich and I take these women out to dinner and they come over to my apartment every night and strip and I tie them up and they do whatever I say."

"Sounds like a rare setup."

"Shut up, Father Merchant."

Thomas was surprised to hear himself named. It sounded like a conscription notice being read out.

"These women," muttered the young man. He sounded disgusted, compelled. "These women can make me . . . they can make it hurt less inside me. Sometimes."

Thomas thought of men and women in Manhattan. He thought of them in restaurants, waiting for coffee, or tensely, wordlessly sharing elevators with each other, or kissing one another in Battery Park, or arguing in their beds. Then, in a flash, Thomas saw his way into the young stranger's mind. He understood.

"This James," guessed Thomas. "This James Branch. He's taken one of your women. Fallen in love with her."

The figure through the grille said nothing.

"And she's fallen in love with him," said Thomas. "And she's your favorite."

Thomas heard breath seething out of the man.

"There's no point in having favorite people, Father. God only takes them away."

"Not always. And if He does, He was just lending them to you anyway."

"Quiet, priest." The stranger stirred in his cage. "Don't get all wise with me. There's absurdity out there and you know it."

Thomas closed his eyes again. "Then why have you come?" he asked gently.

The visitor was quiet for a long moment.

"You're right about the girl," he said finally.

Thomas's mind was a black satin bedsheet now. Spread across it was a naked young woman with hair the color of honey.

"So why kill your friend?" asked Thomas.

"I never said he was my friend. He's my housemate."

"Even so."

"I can't let . . . He's trying to . . ."

The stench in the closet intensified. Thomas wondered for the first time whether there might be a base, supernatural odor, a redolence, that happened when one human soul tried to control another.

"Can't your housemate have this one woman?" asked the priest. "You say you have a harem. Aren't they enough?"

"In my life," hissed the other, "nothing is enough."

Thomas breathed only through his mouth. He was hunched forward now, his face close to the grille, his eyes still shut. "Are you carrying a gun?"

"Yes."

"Is that why you never come to Communion?"

"Yes."

"You believe that the things that you do and the things that you think are so awful that God could never approve of you?"

The stranger's teeth made contact with each other. "Yes," he said.

Thomas wiped his brow. His head throbbed with the weight of another man's life. Thomas's past, his aunts' rearing of him, the clarity of his own heart, had come to a sudden point. There was only one thing left to talk about.

"Listen," said the priest, "you can't kill another human being. It's against the law of God and you know it or you wouldn't have come. But there's something else you don't know."

"What's that?"

"God does approve of you."

The stranger sucked air in, released it. "How do you know? How in hell could you know?"

"Because God gave you a special gift. A smell."

"A smell?"

"Don't laugh," urged Thomas. "I'm serious. Every night, when you come through the doors, this church fills up with a smell like something burning. It's bitter and awful, and nobody smells it except me. But it's not the candles or anything else that makes that smell. It's you."

The darkness didn't move.

"You're crazy," whispered the stranger.

Thomas nodded, agreeing with the ridiculousness of his own words. But the fear of the Lord is the beginning of wisdom, he thought, and it's time to scare the hell out of this guy.

"I can smell you now," said Thomas quietly. "It's disgusting. It's almost unbearable."

"You priest." The young man was on his feet in the closet. For the first time there was panic in his voice. "You crazy goddamned priest."

Thomas stood too. He faced what he couldn't see. He opened his eyes. "You should be grateful. This smell of yours is a gift, a warning sign. God gave it to you because He loves you, but He knows you're tempted to use your gun."

"Shut up," sputtered the young man. He jiggled the door of his chamber.

"Now that you know you smell," said Thomas, "you're not going to let yourself hurt anybody."

Both men were out of the confessional now. The figure in black fled toward the church doors.

"You think you're weird and hopeless," called the priest, "but you're not."

"Fuck off," yelled the young man. He blundered his way out onto Wall Street, disappeared.

Thomas Merchant drew a clean lungful of air. He hurried to the rectory, wanting the phone and his coat. There hadn't been any contrition or absolution, but Thomas buttoned himself into a parka. After all these years he was ready to leave his hermitage, the cave of his mind, ready to take action, ready to follow into the streets the awful grace that had been loosed upon the city.

The Green Balloon

James Branch was nervous. It was the second Saturday in January, and he was out with Rally McWilliams, his new love, for dinner at Flat Michael's. They sat at a corner table and ate Chicken prepared with garlic, rosemary, and some unknown wine. When they finished eating, they drank coffee. Their waiter was a little man named Juan, who, delighted with their bliss, bowed to them and fetched their requests.

James was nervous tonight because he wanted two things. He wanted to tell Rally his strange, secret habit of talking to the Otis elevator in the Preemption apartment building, where he lived. And he wanted to give her a pair of opal earrings that had long been in his possession and even now were in his pocket.

"What?" said Rally. Both she and James wore blue jeans, and under the table Rally had her ankle resting against James's calf.

"Nothing," said James.

Three tables away were a band of skinheads, sharing a plate of Squid. James recognized them as regulars, and Rally knew them from Minotaur's Nightclub, but the lovers and the punks only nodded at each other. Their nights were going perfectly. They needed no one but themselves.

"Come on," teased Rally. "You're thinking about something juicy. What is it?"

James sipped his coffee. "Nothing," he lied.

What James was thinking about, as he gazed at Rally, was happiness. Inspired by love or caffeine, his mind tonight was on the fine and illicit pleasures of the planet, on their merits and dispersement. Some people cut daisies, thought James. Some visit Wales, or choose cocaine, or dig latrines for the poor and the weak. James fingered the opals in his pocket. He'd acquired them in a mystical place, and now, as he watched a blood vessel pulse in Rally's neck, he understood that these gems might be bearing him forth toward someplace just as rare, the kind of country you could reach only if you lay in the dark with a woman and gave in to the quickening colors behind your eyelids.

"Tell me," begged Rally.

"I will," promised James.

Outside the restaurant the air was bracing. James breathed it in, held Rally's hand, made sure of the moon. They walked a few blocks, then took the subway to the Preemption apartment building. James was bursting to tell Rally about Otis and to give her the earrings, but he wanted to clear the air first with Patrick, his housemate and Rally's former boyfriend. James wanted to end any bad blood with Patrick, to make his and Rally's new couplehood official. So, saying he'd explain later, he asked Rally to take the seven flights of stairs with him instead of the elevator, and they climbed to his apartment. James held Rally's hand and led her through the door, and his heart hammered. But Patrick wasn't home.

"It's only ten," said Rally. "He's probably at Duranigan's with a woman."

"Duranigan's?"

"That's where he always takes us. Them." Rally squeezed James's arm. "I meant them, baby."

James looked at the floor.

Rally whispered in his ear. "I love you," she said. "Remember?"

James nodded. Rally kissed his temple.

"Well," she said, "should we wait?"

James glanced toward Patrick's bedroom. He shrugged. "He's usually back by eleven. It'd only be an hour."

So James and Rally waited. They sat on the couch, and tried to watch TV, but James couldn't concentrate. He also wouldn't take off his shoes, which made Rally nervous, and then she couldn't concentrate either. Finally, James turned off the set, and they sat there, holding hands in silence. With nothing else to do, James pressed the messages button on the answering machine. There were several bright greetings from friends, and then there was this:

"Hello. My name is Father Thomas Merchant. I'm a priest. It's a Saturday night at nine-thirty. I have an urgent message for a James Branch."

James sat up.

"Father who?" said Rally.

"Shhh," said James.

"—your number from the operator. The message is this. Get out of your apartment right now, please. Your roommate, a parishioner of mine, has just left me and he's in a very . . . agitated state. He may be heading home, and you may be in danger. He mentioned your name specifically. He is armed."

"Holy shit," whispered Rally.

"—reach me at St. Benedict's Parish on Wall Street, whatever the hour. I suggest we meet at once. Your friend needs help. In fact, I might—"

The machine beeped. The priest's voice ended.

"Patrick's Catholic?" said Rally.

James stood up, grabbed her hand. "Let's get out of here."

They slid on their coats, and hurried out into the hall. They started for the stairwell, but Rally yelped in surprise. Standing before them, twenty yards away, blocking the entrance to the stairs, was Patrick Rigg.

"Hey, you two," said Patrick.

He stood in a black suit, facing them, his hands open at his sides. He looked as if he'd been standing there some while, and he looked dangerously set, like an athlete at a starting line, about to lurch into action. Halfway between him and the lovers was the closed door of Otis, the elevator.

"H—hey," said James.

Rally moved half a step behind James.

"I haven't seen you guys," said Patrick. "Not since New Year's."

James could hear his housemate's breathing. It sounded loud, labored.

Patrick cleared his throat. "I gather things are going well for you two."

"We're in love," blurted Rally. "We . . . came to tell you."

Patrick drew himself to his full height. "You hear that, Branchman? Rallygirl says you're in love."

"I hear her fine," whispered James.

"*Well.*" Patrick scratched his jaw. "People fall in and out of love all the time, I guess."

"I mean it, Patrick." Rally's voice was solid now. "I can't see you anymore. I'm with James."

"There's no hard feelings," said James. "We just . . . you know. Um. We wanted to tell you. To be clear."

"We're on our way out, Patrick," said Rally.

Patrick sighed. Smoothly, as if following instructions, he drew a gun out of his coat pocket and pointed it at James.

"Oh, Jesus," said Rally.

The hall was empty except for the three of them. James moved himself in front of Rally.

"Maybe you should stay still, Branchman." Patrick trained his eyes and his weapon on James.

"Oh God," said Rally.

In his gut James felt hungry or empty. He'd never been in the presence of a drawn gun—especially not one directed at him—and he stared at it with horror and dizzy respect. Patrick's fingers were locked around the SIG so tightly that his knuckles might have been cogs in the gunstock. It reminded James, as he swallowed air, of a health teacher he'd had in grammar school, a wiry man who'd often repeated the sentence *The human body is a machine*.

"Patrick," said James. "Listen—"

"Maybe you should stay quiet too," insisted Patrick.

James rubbed his hands together. He thought of the opals in his pocket, of what he hoped they meant. He watched Patrick's gun.

"Patrick," James said quietly. "You . . . Um. You have, like, one hundred girlfriends. And they all adore you."

Patrick closed his eyes, once, hard, then opened them. "Rally. Would you mind coming over here by me a minute?"

Rally was crying. Her fingernails, short and sharp, dug into James's biceps.

"I'm not going anywhere with you, you psycho," sniffled Rally.

James backed up two paces, moving Rally with him.

"Stop it," said Patrick. "Don't move."

James stopped. "She's upset," he explained. "Um, you're not a psycho."

Patrick's chin, James thought, was quivering.

"James," said Patrick, "did I ever tell you that I had an older brother?"

"No, Patrick."

"Well, I did. His name was Francis. He got killed at an amusement park."

"Jesus. I—I'm sorry, Patrick."

Patrick scowled. He still hadn't taken a step forward or back.

"Patrick, please," begged Rally.

"Isn't that amusing, Branchman? Isn't it amusing that Francis died at an amusement park?"

James remembered something he'd read. He'd read that when people got shot, they messed their pants.

"It doesn't sound amusing, Patrick," he said.

"Well, it was. It's a long story, but if you read it in the paper, it would've made you laugh."

"All right," agreed James.

"What do you mean, all right? There wasn't anything all right about it." Patrick clicked off the safety on his SIG.

"Help!" shouted Rally. "Help."

"Shut up," said Patrick fiercely. "Shut up and get over here by me right now."

Rally whimpered. She buried her face in James's shoulder.

"Make her come over here, dammit."

James's eyes flashed at Patrick. "No," he hissed.

The elevator door opened. A priest stepped off. He looked to his right at Patrick, to his left at James and Rally.

"Whoa," said James.

Patrick's eyes swelled. He took a step backward. "Father Merchant?"

The priest wore a red parka, with gray Eskimo-style lining around the hood. It was a cheap parka, the kind a child would've worn tobogganing in the 1970s. Under it the man wore a black shirt, a stiff white clerical collar.

"Put that gun away," said the priest. He pushed his hood back off his head, stepped into Patrick's line of fire.

"You followed me?" said Patrick.

"I looked up your roommate's address," said Thomas, "and your doorman gave me the apartment number. Put that gun away."

"I'm James," said James from behind the priest. "James Branch. I'm the one you telephoned, Father."

"I'm Rally," said Rally.

The priest said nothing. He was facing only Patrick, boring all the force of his mind and his countenance into his one desperate parishioner. If James and Rally could've seen the priest's face, they would've witnessed two fine blue eyes, but beneath those an expression of revulsion, a hint that the man was smelling something nasty.

"Give me that gun," said Thomas Merchant. "Leave these people alone."

Patrick's hand quaked on the gunstock, but the SIG was pointed at the priest, who stood just ten yards from Patrick.

"She has to be with me," said Patrick.

"Nonsense. Nobody has to be with anybody." The priest

unzipped his parka, revealed his collar. "Now, give me that gun. You've got no business pointing it at people you care about."

Patrick's eyes rimmed with tears. "I don't care about them."

"Uhm-hm. Give me that gun." The priest held out his palm.

"You—you can't talk to me like that." Patrick's fingers clutched the SIG. "No one talks to me like that."

"Father," began James.

"Give me the gun," said the priest.

With his free, left hand Patrick petted the gun barrel.

"It's mine," he stammered.

The priest stamped his foot. "Give it here, I said. Let this nonsense end."

"I can't." Patrick sobbed loudly.

"Let it go," ordered the priest. He took a step toward Patrick.

"Don't. I can't. I can't." The gun wavered back and forth.

The blood drained from Thomas Merchant's face. He took in the pitiful man before him, the dark, expensive clothes, the shaky arms, the lost, snuffling, bewildered expression. Patrick's index finger quivered on the trigger, and the priest sensed terribly what he'd sensed in the sob of confessing voices, in the bombast of wartime headlines, in the deepest heart of Scripture: the time for words had ended. A gun was drawn, a foul human will was acting, and there were young lives present. For the sake of those lives, for the sake of charity, Thomas did the one thing he could think of to keep all of Patrick's violence focused on himself. He aimed a mocking sneer at the armed young man.

"You utter fool," the priest taunted.

"Stop it," begged Patrick.

"Father," warned James.

The man in the silly red parka laughed. He made himself do it. "Good God, boy," he scoffed, "do you have any idea how *ridiculous* you look?"

The gun fired almost by itself. Rally screamed, and Patrick jumped back in surprise, as blood streaked from the priest's temple. Thomas Merchant collapsed in a heap.

"Oh my God," screamed Rally. "Oh my God, you shot him."

"Patrick," whispered James.

They watched the fallen, bleeding man.

Patrick staggered forward, his eyes fat with horror. "Oh, Jesus."

"You shot him," screamed Rally. "You killed him."

Patrick dribbled to his knees. He reached out with his left hand, pressed a thumb to the priest's bootheel, pulled the thumb back as if scalded. Thomas Merchant's head lay on the floor, blood matting the hair.

"Oh, Jesus." Patrick's breath came in gulps. His entire body shivered. His right hand brought the SIG to his own temple.

"No," hollered James. He dived over the priest's body toward his housemate, but Patrick had already fired.

The nurses at St. Luke's Hospital got used to James quickly. Perhaps they could see, or even smell, the traces of passion on him, the love affair that awaited him outside the hospital walls. For James came always alone to St. Luke's. Whatever their reason, the nurses smiled on the young man with the sleepy eyes who sat beside Patrick Rigg's bed every day.

The priest had survived. The bullet had gone through the edge of his temple. It did enter his skull, just nipping his brain. If James and Rally hadn't been there to bandage his head and call an ambulance, Thomas Merchant might have bled to death in the Preemption hallway. As it was, just two days after the incident the priest was out of his hospital bed and gingerly on his feet. He wasn't allowed to leave the hospital yet, but he padded up and down the hallways, visiting the ill and dying, a thick blue dressing wrapped around his skull. The only permanent damage to his person, if it could be called such, was a new, slight, but constant watering of his eyes that his doctors said might be with him for life. It had been caused, they said, by the bullet bruising his brain just so, leaving scar tissue that was impossible to remove and that tweaked certain nerves. So Thomas Merchant, previously a man of uncannily clear vision, would spend his days now with a handkerchief in hand, working to keep his world from blurring.

Meanwhile, Patrick Rigg was paralyzed, in a coma. The paralysis went down his entire right side, from his eye to his toes. His suicidal bullet had struck the meat of his frontal lobe. The bullet had been successfully removed in surgery, and Patrick's chances for recovery from coma and subsequent survival were fair. The doctors held little hope, though, that his paralysis would clear.

As for James, he took another two weeks off from Harrow East to sit with his wrecked housemate. Traumatized from the shooting, and afraid to be near Patrick despite his condition, Rally waited in SoHo for news from her lover. James called her from St. Luke's, whispered plans for their future.

"We'll get some spumoni," he said, "in Palermo."

Rally was cranky. She didn't like Palermo.

"Eelburgers," said James. "In Shanghai."

"Why do you have to stay with him?" snapped Rally. "He wanted to kill us."

"I'm his housemate," said James. "I'm all he has. He's got a dad somewhere, but the dad's unreachable."

"He shot a *priest*."

"The priest is okay."

"Tell me you love me."

"I do."

Rally didn't sound convinced. "Who's my tiger?"

"I am."

Rally paused on the line. "This is real, right?" She sounded frightened. "I mean, no matter what happens to Patrick, you and me are . . . This is real?"

"Tell me you love me," said James.

Rally did.

James sat with Patrick for fourteen days and most of the nights too. When he stayed at night, the nurses made him sleep on a cot in the hall across from Patrick's room. It was against the rules, but the nurses liked James and wouldn't kick him out.

Day by day James watched Patrick get skinnier. He watched nurses bathe Patrick, watched them stretch the limbs on Patrick's left side. James tried sitting motionless for ten minutes, to see what being paralyzed was like. He wondered if people in comas could think, or pray. He ate vending-machine sandwiches, and thought of Rally. One night, after peeking at Patrick's chart and seeing that he'd lost twenty pounds, James spoke with Patrick's doctor and asked for a prognosis. The doctor, a small Haitian man, did not say good things. James called Rally.

"Please come," he said. "Please come here tonight. I have to talk to you."

So Rally came. She met James in the ground-floor cafeteria, the closest she felt she could get to Patrick. James sat with her at a table with a white plastic top. They drank fruit juice.

"Patrick's losing weight fast," said James. He had blue skin beneath his eyes from poor sleeping.

Rally nodded softly. She'd gotten dressed up for James, to remind him of her. She wore a black dress and black heels.

"Your eyes look all bruised," she told him.

"I think he's dying," said James.

Rally sighed. "Is that what you need to talk to me about?"

James looked around the cafeteria. There were four bald children sitting around a table nearby, and a twisted, drooling man in a wheelchair beside a water fountain. Also, at a table by itself, abandoned by human company, was a green balloon. The balloon had just enough chemistry or magic left inside it to hover above the tabletop.

"Everybody's dying," said James.

Rally touched James's knee. "James. Honey, what *is* it?"

All at once James was unafraid. "I have to tell you something about myself," he said. "It's very important."

"All right."

"It's something that I do."

"All right."

James watched the cancerous children. He knew there were ravenous, invincible forces at work in their bodies, in their blood. He knew, too, that Rally was probably expecting him to confess something felonious, something perverse or difficult. But the children were playing a card game together, and for all James knew, they were siblings, content with their fate. Also, moved by an air draft or its own volition, the green balloon was floating slowly above and past these children now, like a reconnaissance blimp. On top of it all Rally was holding James's hand.

"I talk to my elevator," said James.

"Excuse me?"

"I talk to the Otis elevator in my building. I do it every night for almost an hour. I shut myself in the elevator and stop it between floors. I sit cross-legged and rock back and forth and I talk to Otis the elevator about everything under the sun."

"You—" Rally leaned closer. "You do what?"

James looked at Rally. There was tender shock in her eyes, and bewilderment, and a willingness to hear the rest. James smiled simply and shrugged and kissed Rally once on the lips. Hoping she'd always look as sturdy and fragile as she did just then, he pulled the pair of opal earrings from his pocket and pressed them into Rally's palm.

"Also," said James, "these are for you."

Rally looked down at her gift. She breathed in sharply. Any confusion, any questions she had for James, could wait.

"Oh, sweetheart," she said.

James spent three more days and nights keeping vigil at Patrick's hospital room. During the days he read some of his favorite books aloud to Patrick, but he avoided conversation now with the Haitian doctor and he tried not to note the shrinking skin on Patrick's bones. Each night he fell asleep on his cot, sure that his housemate would perish before morning.

On the third of these nights, however, James raised his head groggily from his cot. It was two A.M., and the hall around him was dark and lonely. What had woken James was a persistent chanting sound that he thought had been part of a dream. When he looked up, though, and peered fuzzily into Patrick's room, he thought he saw three figures dressed in white bending over his housemate in the dark. They seemed to have their hands on Patrick, on his head and his right leg, and James wondered if they were the chanters. One of the figures looked like Sender the doorman. One of them looked like Thomas Merchant. The third was a white-haired man that James didn't recognize for sure, but he could have sworn it was John Castle, the underground stranger who'd once given him something precious. When this man turned his gaze toward the hall cot, James, gripped by a mighty fatigue, fell back to his pillow.

The morning after this apparition a green-eyed nurse shook James awake.

"Your friend," she said. "He's conscious."

Yawning, stunned, James went to Patrick's bedside. Thomas Merchant was in the room, too, standing at the foot of the bed, his face calm, his eyes crying automatically. The nurse left.

Patrick's eyes were open, but gauzy. His cheeks held less pallor than they had the day before.

"Hey, Patrick." James sat beside the bed.

Patrick's eyes traveled, found James.

"James," he said weakly.

"Your right eye," said James. "It's open. It works."

Patrick nodded. With tremendous effort he lifted his right knee slightly.

James stared at the knee. He touched it gently. "You're cured?"

Patrick set his knee back down. "Not all of me," he croaked.

"Your friend's right arm is still paralyzed," said Thomas Merchant. "And the four smaller toes on his right foot."

"But they could heal, too, Patrick," said James.

"No, son." The priest's voice was firm. "Those injuries are permanent."

James turned to the cleric. He studied the man's bearing, his tears of indeterminate emotion.

"How do you know?" said James.

"Never mind about that," said the priest.

"Branchman. James."

James looked to the bed. The bandages on Patrick's head were twice as thick as those on the priest's head. James wondered if Patrick would have to see shrinks now. He wondered if Patrick would have to go away.

"Yes, Patrick," said James.

Patrick coughed. His eyes had the scratchy red look of infection or sorrow.

"I'm glad you're here," whispered Patrick.

James patted Patrick's leg.

"I'm so sorry, James."

James didn't know what to do. He sat there. He patted Patrick's leg again. From the hallway he heard morning sounds, carts being wheeled and sheets being snapped, as if Patrick weren't in a hospital at all, but a glorious, well-staffed hotel. James thought of Rally's breakfast breath, of Dolly Parton, of the bald young cardsharps waking up. He rocked back and forth a little on his chair.

"I'm . . . saying it to both of you," whispered Patrick. "I'm sorry."

James sighed. "How about, instead of talking right now, you just stay still and get better?"

Patrick glanced down at himself. He stared at his limp right arm. He closed his eyes, began to laugh feebly.

"I really fucked myself up, didn't I, Branchman?"

James looked to the priest to see if he was going to take over. He figured there were official words of comfort, words he didn't know. But Father Merchant waited for James to speak.

"Patrick," said James. "I—um. Maybe you should, um, just be quiet right now. Just rest and heal up."

"I don't want to be quiet," croaked Patrick. "I just came out of a coma."

"I know," said James.

"How long was I . . . you know. How long was I out?"

"Two weeks," said the priest.

"A fortnight," said James.

Patrick reached out with his left hand, his good hand now. He closed his fingers around James's thumb. It took him a long time to do it.

"Do you know what that's like?" Patrick's face was strict with fear. He looked appalled. "Do you know what it's like, going that long without talking? Being awake inside, but not talking?"

James bowed his head in assent. He let Patrick keep holding on to him.

"I do," said James.